Up To No Good

The plastic of the phone was cold against my cheek.

'Is someone there with you?' asked Geoff.

I could feel the tension crackling in the silence.

'And what are you doing?'

'I'm here with Kit,' I told Geoff. There was no point lying. 'I'm blindfolded, naked, and tied to the bed.'

I felt as if my only function was as a conduit between Kit and Geoff. To get both men hot and hard. This, and with the way the bonds were pulling my legs wide apart, turned me into an excited, helpless object. The feeling of being completely out of control was immensely liberating. I began to use words that were anonymous and pornographic. There was no way back now.

By the same author:

Sleazy Rider

Up To No Good
Karen S Smith

BL

This book is a work of fiction.
In real life, make sure you practise safe, sane and consensual sex.

First Published by Black Lace 2001

2 4 6 8 10 9 7 5 3 1

Copyright © Karen S Smith 2001

Karen S Smith has asserted her right under the Copyright, Designs and Patents
Act 1988 to be identified as the author of this work

This edition first published in Great Britain in 2009 by
Black Lace
Virgin Books
Random House, 20 Vauxhall Bridge Road,
London SW1V 2SA

www.blacklace.com
www.virginbooks.com
www.rbooks.co.uk

Addresses for companies within The Random House Group Limited can be found
at: www.randomhouse.co.uk/offices.htm

The Random House Group Limited Reg. No. 954009

A CIP catalogue record for this book is available from the British Library

ISBN 9780352345288

The Random House Group Limited supports The Forest Stewardship Council [FSC],
the leading international forest certification organisation. All our titles that are
printed on Greenpeace-approved FSC-certified paper carry the FSC logo.
Our paper procurement policy can be found at www.rbooks.co.uk/environment

Printed and bound in Great Britain by CPI Bookmarque Ltd, Croydon CR0 4TD

Contents

Chapter One
The First Wedding

I was alone in the vestry. Just through the open door I could hear the full church breathing; my relatives, my friends, my soon-to-be husband, all waiting for me. 'Let them wait a moment,' I thought. I looked down at my body, giftwrapped in white lace. I ran my hands over my breasts, pushed up and together by the tight, boned bodice, imagining my new husband running his hands over them tonight, undoing the tiny pearl buttons, unwrapping my breasts and taking the nipples in his mouth.

A polite cough made me turn: the vicar, come to see what was keeping me. He was blushing slightly, embarrassed at catching me touching myself so brazenly in his church. 'Are you ready?' he asked in a husky whisper. He was young: big, brown, serious eyes fixed on mine, big hands fiddling with the trimmings on his robe. I turned right round to face him, my hands still on my breasts. He was looking at me intently, with fascination, almost with fear. I held his gaze, testing him, seeing how far I could stretch this silence. In the church, I heard a small child begin to wail.

'Nearly,' I replied. 'There's just one thing – perhaps you could help me with it?'

'Of course – what is it?' he asked.

I just had time to whisper 'This' before my mouth was on his, my fingers in the curls at the back of his head pulling him into me. For a split second shock held him rigid, and then his animal instincts took over and his tongue plunged into my mouth as fiercely as mine had entered his.

Even through his robes I could feel his erection, big and hot. 'He's been stiff since he first came in and saw me,' I thought. His hands were on my breasts, my buttocks, squeezing me to him. It was as if he wanted to devour me, swallow me, pull bits off me like fresh bread and stuff them into his mouth.

I wanted to get my hand inside his clothes, to touch that prick I could feel pushing against my belly, but I couldn't find the hem of the cloth, so I put my hand over it and squeezed it through the layers, hard and quickly. A little moan, like a cry of surrender, escaped from his mouth that was still pressed against mine. He seemed momentarily to lose control of his limbs and, as his hands loosened, I slid down to my knees in front of him, my train spreading out into a pool of white lace.

Now I could get under his skirts. I unzipped his fly and finally had my hand on his cock. It was almost burning hot, swollen taut with desire. I was trying to get my head through the priestly layers and put this beautiful prick in my mouth, but my reverend friend had other ideas: nearly falling on top of me in his urgency, he dropped to his knees and pushed me backwards on to the stone floor.

It was my turn to have my skirts thrown aside. He was so desperate to get his cock inside me that he didn't even stop to take my knickers down; he pulled them to one side and entered me in a single stroke.

2

Excited as I was, and slippery with arousal, I gasped at the force with which he penetrated me. With one hand he held my head back, fingers twisted in my hair, and kissed me as if his tongue were fucking me as well as his cock. The other hand gripped my shoulder, bracing me against his thrusts. My bare thighs above the white stockings rubbed against the cold paving stones.

He fucked me hard and deep and fast. The end of his prick hit the neck of my womb with every thrust, and his body banged against my clit. The pleasure was nearly pain, so big was his cock and so merciless his ploughing. I felt that nothing could stop him now till he had come.

I looked up and saw, behind him, rows of hymn books lined up on the shelves. I thought of the congregation sitting, patiently waiting for us to join them. As I stuck my middle finger into his arse, I imagined my bridegroom coming to look for us and seeing us here, me on my back on the floor, my white dress spread out in the dirt, and the vicar fucking me like an animal. He pressed his face into my breast to smother the cry he gave as he came, his whole body shaking as his thrusting gave way to uncontrollable spasms. Biting on a handful of his vestments to stifle my voice, I was overtaken by my own orgasm, waves which shook me from inside to out, as I pictured my bridegroom's face: shock and disgust mingled with arousal at the sight of me being fucked on the floor.

'Emma?' The familiar voice startled me. 'Wake up, we're nearly there.' My sister's amused eyes were looking at me in the rear-view mirror, and my brother-in-law shifted irritably as I removed my head from his shoulder.

'Sorry,' I mumbled, 'have I been asleep long?'

'Nearly an hour. We got held up on the motorway, so we're going straight to the church.'

My relatives knew that the only way to ensure my attendance at family weddings was to drive me there and drive me home again, with the advantage for me that I never had to endure one sober.

In truth, my feelings about weddings were ambivalent. On the one hand there was the excruciating round of polite conversation with people you saw only at weddings and funerals, and with whom you had nothing in common except, at best, a surname. On the other hand, as my dream had just reminded me so vividly, there was something perversely sexy about a wedding. Maybe it's the virginal bride waiting to be ravished by her groom; maybe it's the one central fact of a wedding – that it's official sanction for two people to fuck each other senseless – being the one thing you must never ever mention directly. Whatever it is, it wasn't the first time I'd had a hot dream on my way to a cousin's wedding.

As my sister slowed the car, looking for somewhere to park in the narrow lane that led to the village church, I tried to uncrumple my cream silk suit. Kevin, her husband, was brushing the shoulder of his jacket where I had been resting my head. He looked uncomfortable. I smirked inwardly, wondering how much I had betrayed the sleazy nature of my dream. Kevin was nice, but – well, he was nice, that was just it. Sometimes my sister, who was two years younger than me, seemed ten years older.

We were indeed late. The bride, our cousin, was already waiting outside the porch as we hurried up the churchyard path under the blossoming lime trees. We flashed apologetic smiles at her and slipped into the dark church. Entering first, I stood for a moment as my eyes adjusted to the gloom after the spring sunshine. The heads of the congregation had turned, expecting the bride: suddenly I was aware of being the centre of attention for quite the wrong reason. I felt my cheeks grow hot as I threw myself into the nearest pew, just as the organ struck up the bridal march.

'What a relief,' a deep voice murmured on my left. 'For a moment there, I thought you were about to get married to my old friend Robin.'

Stung, I whipped my head round to meet an amused pair of light-brown eyes. 'What do you mean, what a relief?' I whispered back. 'Your old friend Robin could do a damn sight worse than me!'

'Ssh, don't be so quick to take offence.' The speaker laid a calming hand on my knee. 'I meant what a relief not to spend the rest of my life trying not to fancy my best friend's wife.'

I was lost for words. As my cousin Sarah came past in a flutter of ivory satin, I was able to hide my confusion and shrug that cool hand off my knee by standing with everyone else. The hand slipped off reluctantly, I thought, as my neighbour also stood and turned his eyes towards the altar.

He was tall. I am no midget, standing five foot eight in my socks, but his shoulder was level with my cheek. He had long, slim, brown hands with square finger-tips. Still looking forward to the front of the church, he opened his hymn book, holding it low and to his right so I could read it too. Seeing it, I remembered my dream and felt a kick inside. Before I could think, I took hold of the book with my left hand, so my fingers were touching his. He did not move them away.

'We are gathered here in the sight of God to witness the marriage of Robin and Sarah . . .' Not me. I had forgotten any reason for being here apart from to touch those fingers. Those three square centimetres of my flesh which were electrified by contact with him

5

were the only ones that mattered. I knew it was the same for him, this tall, tanned stranger. I could tell from the way he was holding the book perfectly still, as if to give me no possible excuse for letting my fingers slip away from his.

The first hymn began. 'Come down, O love divine . . .' His singing voice was as deep as his whisper: my shoulder was touching his arm and I could feel it vibrating in his chest. My voice is high, clear, untrained, like a choirboy's. 'O comforter, draw near, within my heart appear,' I sang, 'and kindle it, thy holy flame bestowing.' I swear he could read my mind – not missing a note, he moved his hand so it was gripping mine between his and the book.

At the end of the hymn, the congregation sat for the sermon. I think it was about God wanting us to love each other. Or something. To tell you the truth, I didn't hear a word of it. My tall basso profundo had kept a tight hold on my hand and I was fast turning to liquid. Those fingers were moving exquisitely slowly on mine, the tiniest changes of pressure setting off currents of electricity that made instant connections with my throat, my nipples, my clit. We were both looking at the vicar with such attention that he must have thought he had a couple of new converts. I didn't dare look into those caramel eyes again: I felt sure the whole church would burn down if the circuit were completed.

We stood, we sang, we sat, we listened, we joined in the responses. All the while that hand stayed on mine, scarcely moving, torturing me. He was making love to my whole body but only touching the back of one hand. By the time the happy couple, now joined together as man and wife, passed us on their way out of the church, I felt helpless with arousal. If he had picked me up, laid me down on the pew and fucked me in front of everybody, I would have offered no resistance.

We followed everyone else out into the sunlight. At the door, we stared stupidly as the young usher put his hand out. 'The hymn book?' he said. 'Or did you want to keep it as a souvenir?' I dropped my hand as my companion gave up the book, our cover gone. Like slow dancers when the music ends and the lights come on, we stumbled awkwardly out, no longer touching but held together by that invisible current.

We stepped on to the grass and took our first good look at each other. He was slim and suntanned and had dark hair clipped short at the back and flopping freely in front. He put his hands in the pockets of a chocolate-coloured linen suit and stared frankly at me. 'Very nice indeed,' he murmured.

'You're not a complete dud yourself,' I retorted, wishing I felt as in control as I was trying to appear.

He raised one eyebrow (a trick I've practised for years with no success). 'Very kind of you to say so.'

He seemed about to say something else, but the best man appeared at his side and, with a hand on his arm, began moving him away. 'Kit, we need you at the house,' he told him firmly, adding as they walked away 'You don't change, do you?' Kit (at least I knew his name) looked back over his shoulder as he was led away, eyebrows raised ruefully.

Congratulations, photographs and repetitive enquiries from aunts and uncles as to my career and marital status all rolled past me as I stood in a daze. I blamed the car journey, but I knew that the real distraction was the memory of that hand – Kit's hand – on mine. Eventually we made our way over to the house, where the reception was being held in a marquee in the garden, and I laid my hand on the first comforting glass of champagne.

I glimpsed Kit at a distance. As one of the groom's

friends, he had duties to perform, pouring wine, showing aged relatives to seats. A few times I caught him looking across at me so intently that the hairs on my neck stood up. Was it my imagination, or did he try to work his way over to me a couple of times, only to be intercepted by the best man, smoothly appearing from nowhere? Was it I who was being protected from Kit, I wondered, or vice versa?

At last we were invited to take our seats for the wedding breakfast. I was between the young usher and one of Sarah's old schoolfriends. I looked around for Kit but couldn't see him anywhere. 'Oh well,' I thought, 'there's no point in worrying about it. It's not as if I'm ever going to see him again after today.'

I turned to talk to the usher, only to find Kit pulling him firmly to his feet. 'I need you to go and sit next to your Uncle Bernard,' he was telling him, brooking no argument. 'He needs someone to look after him.' And he sat next to me in the newly vacant seat. My insides lurched. I had my hands flat on the table to steady myself. 'No point in being in charge of the seating plan if you can't abuse your position,' he said cheerfully, reaching for a glass. 'Now, where were we?'

I've never known anyone flirt so shamelessly in a public place as Kit did over that meal. It wasn't the clichéd stuff of eating suggestively or letting our hands touch as I passed the salt. In fact, we scarcely touched at all; it was all in his eyes and how he spoke to me. He could make 'How was your journey?' sound like 'How would you like me to fuck you?' It was torture.

As the meal gave way to a stir of activity around the edges of the marquee, people beginning to clear away the food and set up for the dance band, I could see the best man hovering at a distance, giving Kit pointed 'get-over-here-now' looks. 'I think your furniture-moving talents are required,' I told him.

Kit looked over his shoulder and caught the best man's eye. As he did it, though, he dropped his hand under the table and touched me, one light finger drawn down the top of my thigh to where, even through my skirt, he could feel my stocking began. As if nothing had happened, he looked back at me and answered, 'You're right.' I wanted to grab him right there and kiss him, and I knew he could read that in my eyes, but he stood up and walked off to the little stage.

I managed to find a little group of younger relatives and their friends hovering by the drinks table, and as the band set up we drank and made each other laugh. The music started – a swing band, Sarah's choice – and the happy couple led us on to the dance floor. They could do real swing dancing. Even though she still wore her long dress, Sarah's new husband threw her around, over his shoulder, flicking her into spins and twirls at his arm's length. No wonder she'd chosen this kind of band! The piano player and the string bass were hammering out an energetic beat, and a small brass section were enjoying themselves, moving in unison as they played. The girl singer was crooning and growling in a very seductive way, looking stunning in a sequinned dress that must have been painted on and allowed to dry.

Luckily, even those of us who couldn't string two proper steps together could dance to this stuff, and soon we were all flinging ourselves about with enthusiasm. What with the exertion and my overexcited state, I was soon building up a sweat: I could feel it trickling down the small of my back. I spun round and nearly careered into Kit. He caught me neatly with his left arm, using my own momentum to pull me into him, not hard but firmly. His right hand took mine and we were dancing close together, not missing a beat of the music. His other hand was in the small of my back, holding me loosely enough so my hips could move with the music, but close enough to feel that he was as excited as I was.

He was a good dancer; he knew a few more of the right steps than I did, but his whole body moved easily in time with the band, and he led me with such natural authority that all I had to do was let my thighs follow his, and my feet found the place of their own accord. My head was tilted back, so I could keep looking into his eyes, and our faces were a couple of inches apart. If he'd bent his head even slightly, we would have been kissing.

Again, the touch of those hands promised so much without even moving over my skin. 'I know what you want,' they said. 'When the time comes, your pleasure will take you beyond your control and into mine.' I was willing him to move the hand on my back, down to my buttocks, or round my side to the swell of my breasts. I was practically squirming, as much as I could while continuing to dance. The saxophone was squealing out a passionate solo. All the while, Kit's eyes were holding mine, daring me to look away.

The number finished with a burst of sound and the band segued smoothly into a slower number. Some people left the floor to get more drinks. We stayed, taking advantage of the change of pace to dance really close. I was deliberately rubbing my belly against the front of his trousers, where I could feel an erection so hard and hot I almost thought he was about to come right there on the dance floor. He was using his thumb in the small of my back, delicately finding the exact spot which made my knees go weak.

'Emma.' It was Kevin, his timing as bad as usual. 'How much longer do you want to stay?'

'How about forever, to start with?' I wanted to reply, but I held my tongue. Kevin had opted to stay

10

sober and drive back, so he was clearly bored already and ready to get home to one of his gardening books. You'd never think, to look at him, that he was still in his twenties.

'It's just that we've got a long drive ahead, so I'd like to set out soon. Twenty minutes all right?'

I nodded helplessly. I could probably have stretched it to half an hour, but what was the point? Either way, I would soon be in the back of Kevin's car, speeding back to my sister's house, and away from this man that I wanted to strip naked and lick all over.

As Kevin picked his way back through the dancers, Kit looked at my stricken face. 'Aren't you staying overnight?' he asked.

I shook my head in despair. 'My sister's driving me home tonight,' I answered. 'I've got another twenty minutes.'

He didn't say a word, and he didn't let go of my hand. He just turned and walked quickly off the dance floor, pulling me after him. We went straight out of the marquee, and he turned immediately right, away from the lights in the garden and into the darkness. I couldn't see a thing. We narrowly missed several guy-ropes and a flowerbed. Kit stopped in the shadow of a small tree, moved me so my back was against the trunk, and kissed me at last.

He had his hands either side of my face, holding it like a bowl he was drinking out of. His lips were full and soft, and he covered my whole mouth with his while his tongue entered my wide-open lips and rubbed itself over mine. I was melting. I was holding on to his arms so as not to fall over. He licked my teeth and my lips, unhurried, leisurely. His mouth was so warm and wet. He kissed my chin and neck, and little stabs of pleasure travelled down to between my legs. Without fuss, he pulled down the top of the body I was wearing, cupped my breasts in his two

11

hands, and licked them where they were pushed out above my lace bra.

I had my fingers in his hair now. He smelt clean, like baby shampoo. From the marquee, only a couple of yards away, I could hear the band, a soulful saxophone playing the introduction to 'Summertime'. He hooked his thumbs in the top of my bra cups and pulled them down so my nipples were exposed. Delicately, he ran his tongue around each of them, before taking one between his teeth and nipping it gently. I was so wet, I could feel the lace body getting soaked between my legs. As he sucked sharply on one nipple, Kit put his hand on the front of my skirt and squeezed my clit through the fabric with finger and thumb. I gave a little moan.

'Summertime . . .' the singer's voice floated out from the tent, '. . . and the living is easy.' Kit's long, slim fingers were rubbing me through my skirt; smooth, unhurried strokes that made my legs tremble. I was hanging on to his shoulders for support. He was looking into my eyes now, passing his other hand slowly over my nipples, just the palm catching them as it moved slowly to and fro. I moved my head forward and my mouth found his and kissed him hungrily.

He pulled my skirt up, pushing me gently back so I was pressed against the tree. The body fastened with poppers between my legs, and he pulled them open with one urgent hand. I felt the cool night breeze in my pubic hair and on my damp sex. His thumb flicked my clit lightly from side to side as he slid three fingers into me. I was so wet now that my juices were running down his hand. His eyes were still on mine as he continued to kiss me. He slid his hand in and out of me, pulling his fingers out to the very edge of my cunt and then pushing them in till his knuckles were stretching me open. With his other hand, he unbuttoned his fly and released the erection I'd been rubbing against on the dancefloor.

It was long, delicately curved, with a big head. In the darkness, I could just make out a drop of moisture glistening at the tip. I stretched out my hand and took hold of it, pulling it towards me. Now it was Kit's turn to groan as I moved my grip gently up and down. He took my lip between his teeth and bit me, not hard, just to add the faintest edge of pain to the pleasure of his hand.

He withdrew his hand from me and placed it over mine on his cock. I could feel the stickiness of myself on his fingers. He guided his cock to my entrance and pushed the thick, smooth head in, so it was just filling the opening. Then he took hold of my hands in his, and put them behind me, against the rough bark of the tree. For a moment he stood quite still, not even kissing me, his cock barely in me, looking into my eyes. Then he slid it into me, slowly, till it filled me entirely and I felt his pubic hair being pressed hard against my clit.

It was enough. I had been so excited for so long that I came at once, impaled on his long cock, held against that tree, while in the tent the wedding guests danced and the girl sang 'One of these mornings, you're gonna rise up singing . . .' (Even now, I can't hear that song without a shudder of excitement.) Kit was motionless as the throbs of my orgasm squeezed his cock and my body arched helplessly. He watched my face as I managed not to cry out aloud. Only when my eyes opened again and looked into his did he begin to fuck me with long, measured strokes. As his cock buried itself deep inside me, I could feel the linen of his trousers against my thighs and belly. The thick head of his prick scraped itself up and down the ridges inside me.

Kit lifted my thighs so my bare legs were wrapped

around his waist, my weight supported between him and the tree trunk, and moved me up and down on his cock. His middle finger stroked me behind the entrance to my cunt, where his cock was sliding in and out, slippery with my juices. I felt as if I were turning inside out.

I could feel his movements getting more urgent, and his excitement was turning me on even more. I felt his wet finger at the entrance to my anus, pressing gently, then pushing in. Lubricated by my own juices, the finger slid in all the way. I was full, front and back, each thrust of his prick rubbing now against his own finger as well as me. As he came, pumping into me with violent thrusts, I felt another orgasm begin inside me, cunt and anus contracting in unison, and a cry escaped my lips, scarcely stifled by Kit's mouth on mine.

As I placed my feet unsteadily back on the ground and we stood there, still joined, Kit laid a finger gently on my lips. 'Hush, little baby, don't you cry' came the end of the song through the thin canvas. We both smiled. Kit bent his head and kissed me again, more softly this time. In the distance I heard somebody shouting.

'Emma?' It was my sister.

'Shit!' I whispered, looking around to see where the voice was coming from. A figure was moving through the garden in our direction. It was Kevin. Kit slipped out of me and I pulled my skirt down. I made off into the darkness as quickly as I could, pulling my lace body back over my breasts as I ran. Passing the corner of the marquee, I bumped into the singer from the band, coming out through a flap in the canvas, sequinned shoes in her hand. She looked at me in surprise then, seeing my clothes in disarray, shot me a knowing grin. As I made my way round to the front of the tent, avoiding the search party sent out by Kevin, I saw her picking her way across to a van. There was something less glamorous about her – what was it? As she reached the lights of the car park I saw it – she had put on clogs to cross the muddy garden.

I wasn't ready for the looks of shock that greeted me as I went back into the marquee to retrieve my handbag. Surely we can't have been heard over the sound of the band? My sister handed me my bag and steered me straight back out. 'Come on,' she muttered, 'before Sarah's mother sees you in that state.'

'What state?' I was determined to brazen it out if I could. 'Let's just say, next time don't wear a cream suit,' she replied, almost throwing me into the back of the car. Kevin already had the engine running, and was looking like thunder. I decided not to apologise for holding them up.

As the car pulled out into the lane, I managed to take my jacket off and examine it. The back was covered in green marks from the tree. They looked just like grass stains. Ironic really, I thought, grinning inwardly. No wonder Kevin was so scandalised. Then, as we turned on to the main road and back towards London, I suddenly thought, 'I didn't even say goodbye.'

Chapter Two

A Phone Call from an Old Friend

I turned the key and walked with pleasure into my own flat, kicking my shoes off in the hall and letting my toes sink into the deep, springy carpet of the living-room. I opened the big French window that led on to the balcony to wave to my sister as she drove away, and smelt the fresh scent of the geraniums.

I was relieved to be home at last. My sister had found my scandalous behaviour very amusing, but Kevin had been rather frosty on the long drive back and over lunch today, behaving as if I had been caught torturing puppies, not enjoying a quick kneetrembler behind the tent. I flopped on to the sofa and reached across to turn on the answerphone.

'Hi, Emma, it's Jane. Are you there? Hello? Oh, well, give me a call when you get back.' My best friend – still a bit bruised from the recent end of an affair, by the sound of it. I promised myself to call her as soon as I'd had a cup of tea, and pressed the button for the next message.

'Where are you, sexy redhead? I've been watching

16

your flat and you're not there. I wanted to watch you undressing through your bedroom curtains. You know how much I enjoy standing in your garden and wanking while I watch you in the shower. I like to see you smearing soap over your tits and imagine it's my come. But you're not there, so I'll have to go home and jerk off to the photos I took of you walking around your flat naked, when you thought no one could see you.' The husky voice and the East London accent told me it was Geoff.

I can't remember how we first started this telephone sex thing, but we'd been doing it, on and off, for a year or so. He was often working abroad – this was the first time I'd heard from him for three months – but every now and then I'd come home to a blue message like this one. I would close my eyes and picture him as I listened: a big man with a shaved head and muscled body tattooed with fantastic designs.

I picked up the cordless phone and dialled his number. 'Hi, thanks for calling, Geoff White ...' It was his answerphone, of course. Even if he was in, he seldom picked up the phone when I called. I sometimes wondered whether he liked to record my messages and listen to them again later. I walked over to the window and looked out across London as I talked, relishing as always the sweep of red sky as the sun set over the city, and the distant masses of Canary Wharf and the Millennium Dome.

'Welcome home, sailor,' I whispered to his phone, taking my time over each word. 'I've been missing you while you've been gone. In fact, I got so lonely I've had to take a different man to bed every night, but when I came I always closed my eyes and saw your face looking down at me. Now you're back, I'm going to take a bath and wash all their spunk off me.

17

When I rub those bubbles over my tits I'll be thinking of you sliding your cock between them.'

When I hung up I did go and run a bath. I was aching a little after the previous night's exertions, and a long soak in hot, lavender-scented water was just what I wanted. I threw the green-stained suit in a corner, smiling to myself as I wondered what the dry-cleaners would think.

As I lay in the bath, I looked down appreciatively at my own body. My full breasts moved gently in the water, and beyond them a small patch of copper-coloured hair floated, like seaweed in a rockpool. I ran a languid hand over my slippery breasts, remembering vividly the cool night air and the brush of Kit's hand across them. I shivered, shaken even in memory by the intensity of our encounter. I was resigned to never seeing Kit again – after all, I had not even said goodbye, let alone given him my telephone number – I didn't know where he lived or what he did – I didn't even know his surname. Still, I knew I would not forget that kind of passion in a few days. One hand moved down to where my pubic hair was spreading out in the water and I ran my fingers through it and stroked myself gently. I was too relaxed to want an orgasm, but a gentle glow of pleasure spread out into my belly.

I was just getting out of the bath when the phone rang. 'Probably Jane,' I thought and, without pausing to wipe the bubbles off me, I walked, dripping, into the living-room to pick it up.

'So, sexy redhead, you've come back to your true master.' It was Geoff. 'Tell me what you're doing right now.'

'I'm naked and soaking wet,' I answered. 'What are you doing?'

'I'm thinking about your body,' he purred back,

'and I've got a hard-on that feels like it's going to explode any moment.'

As he spoke, I walked into the bedroom. 'I'm looking at myself in the mirror,' I told him. 'I'm wet and shiny, and there's a few bubbles still sticking to me. I'm slipping my hand over my breasts, making the nipples stand up.'

'Take hold of your nipple between your finger and thumb,' he told me. 'Squeeze it. Hard, the way I would squeeze it.'

I did it just as he said, imagining his big, rough fingers pinching the nipple as I watched myself in the full-length mirror. He heard my intake of breath.

'That's right,' he went on. 'Now, take your breast in your hand and push it up to your mouth. Take your nipple in your mouth.'

I bent my head and put my nipple between my own lips, sucking sharply so he could hear the wet sound over the phone. He gave a little grunt, like an animal.

'Bite it,' he said. 'Use your teeth.'

Again, as I did so I imagined him, his broad hands holding my shoulders down on the bed as his smooth, bare head moved down my body. 'I'm putting my hand between my legs . . .' I said, but he interrupted me.

'Wait! Go to your window. Open the curtains.'

I walked over to the bedroom window and opened the curtains a little. My bedroom overlooks my own garden, which is surrounded by trees. To see in, you would have to be standing on my balcony – which was exactly what Geoff was doing. A strip of light spilled across him as he leant against the balustrade, one hand holding his mobile phone and the other inside his jeans, rubbing an erection that I could see even in this light.

'So, little red ridinghead, are you going to open the

door and let in the big bad wolf?' he growled into the phone, his eyes in shadow from where I stood.

I pressed my naked body against the cold glass of the window, enjoying the chill on my bare breasts. 'No, I don't think I am,' I replied. 'Not just yet.' Instead, I began to rub myself against the glass, my breasts dragging up and down, the nipples stiff with cold and pressure. Teasing him, I slowly brought my free hand to my mouth, sucking each finger to wet it, before I put it between my legs.

Tilting my hips and parting my thighs, I pushed my pussy towards the window, using my fingers to part the lips to make sure Geoff had the best possible view of what I was going to do. Holding myself open like this, I used my middle finger to frig myself, flicking quickly across my clit, which was already swollen.

Geoff moved towards the window. 'Let me in,' he pleaded, 'before one of your neighbours calls the police.' But I was enjoying myself far too much for that.

'Not yet,' I told him sternly. 'You'll just have to behave yourself and watch the peepshow.' I began sliding the finger in and out of my cunt.

He bent his head and licked the glass where my breasts were still pressed against it. Then he pressed his whole body against the window. It felt weirdly sexy to be naked and yet not feel his body against mine. I knelt down, opened my mouth and sucked at the glass where his erection was squashed against it. He gasped, and I stepped backward, still fingering myself, as he unbuttoned his fly and released a prick bulging with excitement. I could see him rubbing his fist up and down the length of it.

'That's right,' I murmured to him, 'you jerk off while you watch the show.'

Turning my back on the window, I bent over and looked through my legs at him. I felt a surge of power, watching him outside, knowing how much he wanted to be on this side of the glass, and how everything I did was making that desire more urgent.

'Look at that,' I teased him, 'see how wet I am. Wouldn't you like to be pushing your cock in there, instead of rubbing it yourself, out there in the cold?'

With my free hand, I was fingering myself playfully, just one finger still slipping in and out. I could see myself reflected in the window, my pale image superimposed on Geoff's dark figure. My long, slim legs rose to the gentle curve of my buttocks and, between them, my finger was disappearing into the shadowed opening of my cunt. Beyond, my breasts swung heavily, the nipples erect, and my red hair hung damply around my face. The pale flash of his erection was clearly visible through the image of my rear, presented to his view. I felt a rush of excitement, realising I was looking at what he could see and also watching his reaction to it.

'You bitch,' he groaned. 'When I get in there, I'm going to fuck you so hard . . .' He was losing control. His face was distorted with arousal, and I knew it wouldn't be much longer before he shot his spunk all over the glass of my bedroom window. The thought excited me – I felt like a woman in a real peepshow, performing her sexy movements while strangers touch themselves to orgasm in the dark behind the glass.

I pushed four fingers into myself, knowing that Geoff could clearly see them stretching me to fullness. I watched him watching me, transfixed, as I pumped them in and out, thumb working on my clit.

'Oh yes,' he grunted, stroking himself more slowly, trying to delay his own orgasm. 'That's it, fuck yourself, you little whore. Show me everything. You like it up you, don't you?'

I felt my orgasm coming, like a big wave about to break. 'I want to jerk myself off while I watch you come,' said Geoff's voice in my ear, and I came, thrusting into myself, crying out into the phone.

Legs still shaking, I leant on the bed to steady myself. Then I turned to look at Geoff. He was gone.

For a moment I feared he had indeed been seen on my balcony and fled. Then I heard a sound from the living-room and remembered – before I got into the bath I had shut the French windows, but I had not locked them. By the time I got into the living-room he was already halfway into the room.

'So, peepshow girl, you'd keep me waiting in the cold, would you?' His voice was quiet but with the tiniest edge of threat. I stood still, savouring the way the tables had just been turned. He was the one in control now, and he knew it. Suddenly my familiar room, so often a haven of privacy and peace, was transformed into a mere setting for this man and his power to make me surrender to his will.

'Come here,' he ordered me. I walked over and stood in front of him. 'Now turn round; I want to fuck you.' I turned away from him and he pinned me against the back of the sofa, pushing me forward so I was half bent over it. 'Time for a real cock, showgirl,' he whispered in my ear, as his callused hand parted my buttocks and he urgently sought my entrance, still moist and tender from my own hand. I held on to the sofa as he thrust into me, his arm round the front of my shoulders, holding me still.

I felt the metal buttons of his fly, bitingly cold from the night air, being pushed against my backside with each thrust. The buckle of his belt made a dull clinking sound in time with his thrusts. He was using his legs, in their rough denim, to hold mine apart, and my bare feet, still damp, were braced against the sides of his boots. His stubbly cheek scraped against my neck as he pulled me back against him.

'That's what you want, isn't it, showgirl,' he whispered in my ear, 'a man to fuck you good and hard.' He put his free hand between me and the sofa and pressed against my clit, the rhythm of his thrusts rubbing me against his finger. I was sobbing with pleasure.

'I bet you'd like an audience for this, wouldn't you, peepshow girl?' He put his hand between my shoulderblades and pushed me down, so I was bent nearly double over the sofa back, then held me down as he pumped harder and faster into me, pounding me against his fingers in front. 'You'd like someone to watch me fucking you like a dog.' My orgasm hit me, shuddering and trembling, and it was enough to bring him to his own climax. With three deep, powerful thrusts, he shot his come into me, grunting with each thrust.

We collapsed where we stood, soaking wet and exhausted. Carelessly, he wiped the sweat off my back with his hard, dry hand. Slowly, our breathing returned to normal and he stood up, slipping out of me as he stepped back. I shivered with a sudden chill. 'Well, if you will wander around with no clothes on!' He grinned. I could feel his come trickling down the inside of my thigh.

I went back into the bedroom to get a dressing-gown, and when I returned, Geoff had produced a bottle of wine, ready chilled from the balcony, and two glasses from my kitchen. We lay on the sofa, side by side, and drank cold wine, slipping back easily into our familiar intimacy. Geoff ran a casual hand over my bare legs as we chatted. He had returned only last night from working in Australia, so we both had plenty of news to catch up on, and he was too jetlagged to want to sleep yet.

I had met Geoff at a party a couple of years before and my first impression of him was one of insufferable arrogance, a trait that I find both infuriating and fascinating. He was big, handsome, confident, and he worked as a stunt man on feature films. I spent most of the evening trying to take him down a peg or two, using all my wit and irony, only to find he gave as good as he got.

Others at the party got bored with our obsessive sparring, or frightened of the sharp edges of our tongues, and by four in the morning we were left alone, still evenly matched. He stood up, and I was surprised to feel a pang of disappointment that he was leaving, but instead he produced a coin from his jeans pocket.

'Heads or tails?' he asked.

'Heads,' I answered, and he tossed the coin.

'Tails,' he announced. 'My place it is then.'

The barefaced cheek of the man! I couldn't resist it. 'All right,' I answered, 'but I expect a cooked breakfast.'

He was full of stories that night, of near-disasters on the film he'd been shooting in Australia, of time off lying on the beach and diving in the warm, blue waters, and of the people he'd been working with. I had met a few of his friends and they were not the sort of people to whom you would offer a dare, however dangerous, unless you wanted to see them do it. Their idea of a practical joke was to put an explosive charge down your trousers, or to abseil off the roof of a twenty-storey hotel and bang on your window in the middle of the night, shouting 'Room service!'

I had plenty of news of my own. Since I'd last seen Geoff I'd been taken on as a partner with an up-and-coming architects' practice. Only last week, our bid to design a new museum had been accepted, and I was hoping that some of my ideas for the building would finally be made real. Geoff wanted to know where I had just returned from, and the subject turned to weddings.

'I hate them,' he said. 'I've got that many cousins and aunts and uncles, I spent half my childhood at weddings, dressed up in some scratchy page-boy get-up. Now I see them and they're all divorced, and I think, "You put me through all that – and for what?" Good luck to them and all, but I really cannot see the point.'

To my surprise, I found myself defending the institution of marriage to him. 'But if you take that attitude, you might as well give up on everything before you start. I think, if two people are prepared to say they're going to give it their best shot, in public, with all their friends there, the least you can do is show up and –'

'– and drink their booze,' Geoff finished for me.

'Well, there is that,' I conceded. 'You do usually get a good party. Anyway, I never went to weddings as a kid. My first wedding was when I was eighteen.'

'And . . .?' Geoff settled back on the sofa, his legs wrapped around mine and his eyes closed. He was clearly in the mood for a bedtime story, so I began to tell him one.

'I'd just left school, and my best mate got married that summer. I was head bridesmaid – long peach-coloured satin dress, the works. It was a real village wedding – a church ceremony in the afternoon and then an evening do in the local country club. Her parents were divorced and her mum had moved away, so I had to do loads of the organising, hiring the DJ and everything, sorting out the guest list. It was like the last party of our schooldays – all our friends were there, all their parents and older brothers and sisters. A few months later, half of us went away to college. That was the last time we were all together.'

'Mm-hmm?' Geoff prompted me, his rough hand

gently stroking my legs and belly. 'And what happened at this wedding?'

'Well, the funny thing was, she was my best friend since primary school, but I got on really well with her dad as well. He used to flirt with me all the time. It was great! At school I was surrounded by spotty boys, and suddenly I was getting all this attention from a handsome farmer. I loved it.'

'What did he look like?' asked Geoff, as his light touch wandered over my body.

I shut my eyes, remembering. 'He had a beautiful, ravaged face. You could tell he'd been really handsome in his twenties and thirties, but with working outdoors and drinking too much it was weathered and lined. He had amazing black hair, and he used to brylcreem it back in a sort of fifties style. I used to think, if Gene Vincent had been a farmer, he'd have looked like that at forty-five. And his shoulders were so broad – he used to come out of the cowshed when I arrived to visit Julie and he'd have to turn sideways to get through the door.

'Anyway, I turned up on the morning of the wedding, and there he was in his suit. I'd never seen him dressed up before. He looked fantastic – such a big, powerful man in a perfect black suit, white shirt, polished brogues, the lot. I took one look at him and thought, "Oh God, I fancy my best friend's dad. How weird." And, because her mum wasn't there, of course I kept sitting next to him and doing stuff with him all day. Suddenly, after all these boys, there I was with a real man beside me. And we both felt really emotional, too, because Julie was getting married. I think we both felt a bit like we were losing her, so we were sticking together, you know.'

'In the evening I had loads of stuff to do, laying out the buffet and so on, and suddenly they'd done the speeches and the cake and I thought, "Oh! Now I can

26

relax." And the DJ put this Frank Sinatra record on, so all the parents could get up, and Julie's dad looked me in the eye and said, "Would you like to dance?" like a real gentleman. So we danced to this Frank Sinatra song, real proper dancing with his hand around my waist, and I suddenly thought, "He doesn't think of me as just Julie's mate. I could actually do something about this." And I looked at him and he was looking at me the same way. But I didn't know what to do. I mean, he was forty-five; he's not going to ask if you want to go outside so you can snog in the car park, is he? So we went and sat down again, and just played with our drinks and didn't look at each other, and in the end I got up to go to the toilets, just out of embarrassment.

'I got out of the function room, and suddenly he was right behind me, he'd followed me out of the room, and we were on our own in this corridor, just looking at each other. So I thought, "If I don't do something now, nothing's going to happen", and I took his hand in mine and put my mouth up towards his. But he whispered, "No, not here", and he pulled me through this other door, and there we were in this dark room.

'As soon as the door shut behind us he grabbed me and we were kissing frantically. He was such a great kisser, after all those fumbling teenagers. I'd never known anything like it, and he was completely confident. He had his arms round me, holding me really tight to him, and one of his hands was squeezing my bum, and his tongue was everywhere, running over my lips, round my tongue. I couldn't get my arms even halfway round him, he was so huge, so I was just hanging on to his jacket, really.

'We were a bit unsteady – we were both pretty drunk, I think – and we looked around, and there were two pool tables in this room. So he picked me up, like I weighed nothing at all, and sat me on the edge of one of them. Then he started undoing the buttons on my blouse. It was extraordinary; he had enormous, farmer's hands that I'd always seen handling big machinery, but he was so delicate with those buttons. And he opened my blouse and just looked at my breasts through my lace bra. Just the way he looked made me so turned on, like I was the sexiest thing he'd ever seen. And then he started sucking my breasts through the lace, squeezing them in his huge hands.

'I managed to undo his belt and get his flies open. His cock was big, of course, like the rest of him, and I started trying to masturbate him, pretty badly I think, but he took the hint and put those big hands up under my skirt and pulled my knickers down – just dropped them on the floor. One of his fingers was working gently at the entrance to my pussy. I was really wet, but it was by far the biggest thing that had ever tried to enter me, so he had to push quite hard to get in. As he moved it slowly in and out, he whispered, "Do you want to?" and I whispered back, "Yes."

'So he put that big cock against me, and pushed it in, quite slowly, but really hard, like it was a tight squeeze. It was wonderful – not painful, but like I was being stretched open and filled up. He was holding my hips steady on the edge of the table, and I was holding on to his shoulders and making little sounds. "I'm not hurting you, am I?" he said, and I said "No, I just never felt anything so good." And then he was all the way in, and I felt impossibly full of his cock – just fantastic.

'He told me to lie down, and he lowered me back so I was lying on the table, my hips up on the edge, and still full of his cock. Then he started moving in and out, slowly at first. Because I was arched right back, I was stretched open, my clit completely exposed, and he started rubbing it with his finger as he fucked me. I could see him frigging me as he looked down at me, my legs open wide and my blouse open. The look in his eyes was pure lust. I felt the excitement building up inside me, like a small boat being dragged towards a waterfall, knowing it's got to go over the edge at any moment. I was just overwhelmed by all these new sensations – his big cock pushing deep inside me, his finger rubbing me faster and faster, and over the edge went the little boat, and I was lost, carried away on the current. I didn't even realise till a few moments after that he had put his other hand over my mouth to muffle the sound I made. And then suddenly he pulled out of me and came, all over my face, my tits, my hair, everywhere.'

I lay silent for a moment, savouring the mental picture. I could almost smell the sharp scent of his come and feel it sticky on my cheek.

'You know, sometimes you still manage to shock me,' said Geoff.

I opened my eyes and saw him watching me, fascinated. His cock was erect again, sticking up out of his jeans like a plant thrusting out of the ground. 'I know,' I answered, 'that's what you like about me.'

I slipped off the sofa and sat between his legs, stretching my head forward to take the end of his prick in my mouth. It was so thick I had to open my lips as wide as I could to take it in, and I sucked the head in and out a few times, enjoying the warm smoothness and the slight tang of my own taste on him. Then I moved up to undo his shirt and open it, revealing a broad, nearly hairless chest, patterned with tattoos from all over the world that he had collected on his travels.

I took a sip of cold wine and, instead of swallowing it, put my mouth over his nipple so the chilled liquid ran on to his chest. He winced slightly, but not in

29

displeasure. I poured a little wine straight from the glass on to his chest and raced it with my tongue as it ran down his taut, muscular belly. Then I pulled his jeans down and off. As usual, he had no underwear on.

Filling my mouth with cold wine, I used it to leave a wet trail along his thigh, and then took his whole cock inside it. The sudden drop in temperature made it jump in my mouth. I moved my lips up and down his whole length, gripping the base of the shaft with my hand. Geoff moaned, his head thrown back and his eyes shut, his hands in my hair. I sucked gently, running my tongue over the smooth head.

Geoff took a mouthful of wine and pulled my head up gently towards his face. As he kissed me, he squirted the wine into my mouth, a strong jet of liquid, as if he were coming in my mouth. At the same time, he tipped the wine that was left in his glass over my breasts. I gasped at the cold. He pulled me up further, so he could push my breasts together with his hands and lick the wine from between them, pinching the nipples in his rough fingers.

Then he let me slide down again, so as he kissed me my wet breasts were resting either side of his prick. He pushed them together and pumped his cock between them, the head sliding in and out. Geoff looked down at himself fucking my tits and grunted, 'I love that. You look so sleazy when we're doing this. If I'm not careful I'm going to come all over your face, like your mate's dad.'

I moved up and sat astride him, sliding easily on to his wet, slippery shaft. I could feel the big head rubbing against my inner folds as I rocked in time with his thrusts. He had his face buried between my breasts, his hands pushing them together. My clit was rubbing against his body as I rode him, my hands holding on to the sofa behind him to brace myself.

Feeling my orgasm building, an urgent tightness somewhere deeper inside me, I began to ride him faster, setting my own pace. I was pumping my hips into his, almost as if I were driving into him, as if I were the one with the cock. I took hold of his wrists and held his hands against the back of the sofa, looking down at his face. He was transported, his eyes half closed and his lips parted. I imagined myself fucking him, thrusting my enormous cock into him, bringing him to orgasm by penetrating him so deeply it almost hurt. I imagined myself shooting my spunk into him as he lay there, helpless with pleasure. As I imagined it, I felt my orgasm begin in my clit and explode outwards, my whole body jerking against him, my cunt contracting around Geoff's prick.

As the contractions subsided and I began to get my breath back, he moved me on to my back on the sofa, still inside me, and began his own rhythm. I was so wet that I could hear the liquid sounds as he moved in and out of me.

'Can you hear that?' I whispered to him.

'Oh yes,' he answered, looking down into my eyes.

The increasing speed of his thrusts told me he was about to come, and as he lost control and came into me, I raked my fingernails down his spine.

We lay side by side on the sofa, drenched with sweat and too exhausted to move. Geoff wrapped a heavy arm over me and nuzzled his face into my neck. He shivered as I drew an idle finger down his flank.

'Nice to have you back,' I murmured.

'Nice to be back,' he mumbled as we drifted into sleep.

Chapter Three
Strangers on a Train

Geoff was smirking. The more outfits I dragged out of the wardrobe, tried against myself in the mirror and rejected, the more he gave me the look that said, 'Serves you right for going to another wedding, when you could be coming away with me for the week.' In fact, it had crossed my mind more than once to cry off the journey to Scotland and go with Geoff on his rock-climbing trip instead.

Although we didn't have what you could call 'a relationship', we had known each other long enough to be relaxed together. Geoff was not the sort of man you'd dream of trying to settle down with, not in a million years. We made no pretence of being faithful to each other, and when one of us was working away from home, the other didn't sit at home pining. Still, he knew how to have a good time, and how to make sure I had a good time as well, and the idea of days out on the rugged crags and nights in bed with Geoff was an attractive one.

The problem was, not only would Eric, the groom, never forgive me, but I had arranged to travel up with Jane, and she would not take kindly to a long sleeper journey alone. More to the point, I didn't want to desert her to a reception where she knew nobody but Eric, with whom she'd recently ended an illicit affair. Besides, a wedding's a wedding, and if nothing else I would drink lots of champagne in a genuine Scottish castle. Knowing how Geoff felt about weddings, I didn't even bother to ask if he wanted to come with me.

When Geoff finally dropped me off at Euston with a cheery 'And keep your hands off the bride's dad!' I had only five minutes to spare before the train departed. Jane was already in our compartment, shoes kicked off on the floor, and a bottle of Scotch open on the shelf. 'I thought I'd start getting in the mood,' she told me. Looking at the dent she'd made in the bottle, I guessed she was probably quite well in the mood already. Perhaps the whole business with Eric had hit her harder than she admitted.

Jane and I went back ten years or more, and there were very few secrets between us. I had never told her that I had borrowed her car one night without asking, and she had never told me about the fling she had with my first serious boyfriend (he told me himself, after I found her T-shirt under his bed). Apart from that, we had cried and – more often – laughed together over many adventures.

I grabbed the bottle and the other tooth-glass, aiming if nothing else to slow her drinking down. Nobody wants to share a sleeper compartment with a tearful drunk, even if she is your best friend. I also didn't want Jane to turn up at the ceremony still drunk and do something like sidle up to the bride and whisper, 'You're welcome to him. He's a crap shag anyway.' That would be exactly her style.

'So, what's your plan for tomorrow?' I asked her lightly. 'Get off with Eric's father in front of the happy couple?'

'Actually,' she said with mock seriousness, 'I thought I might have sex with the bride . . . against a tree behind the marquee.' We both laughed.

'Just make sure you're not wearing a cream suit,' I reminded her.

Jane smiled a bitter smile and knocked back a large tumbler of whisky, then held it out for a refill. I poured as stingy a measure as I thought I could get away with.

'Come on then,' I invited her, 'tell me what a bastard he was.'

'Oh, it's not like that,' she sighed stoically, 'it's just . . . I mean, I never thought we were a long-term thing, but it'd be nice if he could treat me as a friend. He's hardly spoken to me since we broke it off.'

'Bad conscience?' I suggested.

Jane nodded cynically. 'That's it, isn't it. If he imagines me as the wicked seductress, he can pretend it wasn't his fault he cheated on his fiancée. Ah, well. Serves me right for borrowing boyfriends. How about you? Still seeing Geoff?'

The train pulled out of Euston and began its long grind north. As it rattled and groaned its way out of London, we worked our own way down the bottle of whisky and into a more festive state of mind. By two o'clock and somewhere past Birmingham, Jane was half asleep, lolling across the lower bunk, blonde hair falling over her face.

'What I want,' she mumbled, 'is a cup of tea. A nice cup of tea. Wouldn't that be nice?'

I had to admit that a cup of tea was exactly what I fancied, my mouth parched by nearly half a bottle of Scotch. However, it was obvious that Jane, even if she managed to walk as far as the bar, would never get served, so I found my purse and let myself out of the compartment.

The train was thundering across some deserted part

of the north of England. Keeping a hand outstretched, ready to preserve my balance if we hit a bend, I negotiated the narrow corridor, enjoying the fresh air coming through the open windows. In the lounge a few people were still sitting drinking, one couple and a few men alone or in pairs. The steward looked up from her magazine. 'Good evening,' I said, trying possibly too hard not to sound drunk. 'I wonder if I could trouble you for a pot of tea. For two.'

I sat at the nearest table while she disappeared into the kitchen. The man at the next table was looking out of the window with great interest, as if to make it clear that he had not been staring at me. He had sandy blond hair and the faintest dusting of freckles, and his muscular forearms rested on the table either side of his plastic glass of whisky. I could see his pale-blue eyes reflected in the dark window, glancing at me and then away again.

'Orion the hunter.' I addressed him directly.

'I'm sorry?'

'Orion,' I repeated. 'Those three stars are his belt, with the sword hanging down, and those two are his shoulders.' He looked surprised that I had spoken to him – but pleasantly surprised.

'Is that right?' He had a lovely soft Scottish accent, the kind that makes me go all gooey at once.

I moved across to the spare seat at his table and pointed out at the starry sky. 'And that's Sirius.'

'The dog star?'

'It's meant to be Orion's hunting dog.'

He smiled, the most irresistible crinkly smile. I stretched out my hand.

'Emma Fowler. Compartment A9.' He smiled again and took my hand.

'Hamish McQueen. Compartment A11.' He shook my hand with a grip that was firm but relaxed, and let it go just slowly enough.

35

'So you're the boy next door.'

The steward arrived with my tray, two pots of tea and biscuits. Hamish looked amused.

'What?' I asked him, as the steward departed.

'You'll be English then, I suppose? A nice cup of Earl Grey at two in the morning – so civilised.'

I stood up with my tray. 'Well, I was going to do the neighbourly thing and invite you round for tea,' I said, 'but I suppose that would be too English for you.'

As we stood outside A9 I could hear Jane snoring a drunken snore. 'Looks like I'd better play the host this time,' said Hamish softly. He slipped off to find the sleeping car attendant to open his door. I peered into our compartment and found Jane stretched out on the lower bunk, oblivious. Hamish reappeared with the attendant.

'While you're here,' I said sweetly, 'I don't think you unlocked the connecting door.'

The attendant looked a little confused. He didn't remember us being part of the same booking. Hamish's expression was a bit confused as well, but when the attendant looked at him for confirmation, he nodded calmly.

'If you could just open it now, that'd be fine,' he said. As the attendant retreated down the corridor, Hamish held open the door of his compartment with a theatrical wave. Still carrying my tea tray, I entered.

In the compartment window I could see Hamish reflected as he shut the door behind him, locked it and turned to face me. I put the tray down on the shelf by the window, but I didn't turn round. Hamish came to stand right behind me, close but not quite touching, and looked into my eyes reflected against the night sky. I felt a delicious frisson of anticipation: something was about to happen, and I was waiting to find out what.

He put his hands on the shelf either side of me, still without touching me, and bent his head so I could feel his breath just below my left ear. Softly he blew on my neck, then brushed his lips against the skin. A shudder of delight ran through me and I let my head fall forward to give him free access to my nape. I felt his lips return, brushing more confidently now, down the side of my neck and round to my collarbone. Then he swept the tip of his tongue back up my neck, leaving a tiny trail of dampness that chilled in the night air.

Very softly, Hamish's warm hand stroked up my neck to lift my hair out of the way, and he began kissing his way down my spine. Although I was looking down, I could see streetlights hurtling past outside. I felt as if I were unwrapping a secret gift, this unexpected interlude, this warm gentle man here just for me while the world outside slept. Smoothly, he found the zip at the back of my dress and slid it down, so the straps fell softly from my shoulders and the cold night air brought goosebumps to my upper body.

Now he looked me in the eye again, as his warm hands moved round to hold my waist. I could feel his thumbs touching in the small of my back, and his fingertips rested either side of my navel. Gently, he turned me to face him. As I turned, I stepped out of my dress and stood in my underwear, inches from him.

He kissed the side of my neck once more, his tongue-tip this time travelling delicately down and along my collarbone to the tender crease of my armpit. Tremulous currents shivered along to my wrists and down to my belly. Bending lower, he lapped at the side of my breast, tongue outlining the edge of my lace bra, and then down further, tracing the lower edge of my ribcage.

37

As I rested my hands on his shoulders, he took a firmer hold on my hips and lifted me up. I ducked my head as he placed me on the edge of the upper bunk, so I sat looking down at him. His hands stroked their way slowly down my thighs, round the smooth back of my calves, to my ankles, his eyes never leaving mine, as if just by gazing at me he could drink me in.

Taking a firmer grip around my ankles, he lifted my feet towards his face and took both my big toes into his mouth. As he sucked them, a wave of pleasure ran over me. I would have thrown my head back, but I was caught between the bunk and the top of the compartment, my shoulders pressing against the ceiling, arms outstretched to brace myself. I felt deliciously caught, unable to move away from his questing mouth which was exploring my toes, my insteps, sucking and softly biting, sending so many signals of surprise and delight shooting up my legs that I began to think I would come just from his tongue on my feet. The rhythmic rattle of the train through the dark countryside only reinforced the shuddering of my body as excitement began to take me over.

Suddenly he pushed my ankles apart, so my legs were stretched wide open. Plunging his head into my lap, he sucked and nuzzled at my pussy through the thin nylon of my thong, already soaked through with arousal. Now I was truly pinioned, my legs held firmly against the edge of the bunk, and my hands pushing against the ceiling to keep my balance. His tongue pressed hard on my clit, rubbing it from side to side with tantalising slowness, then ran down to where my cunt was hidden behind the shiny fabric. With my head forced forward by the low ceiling, my face was scarcely more than a foot from where Hamish's tongue was outlining my every fold. I could see every detail of his wet mouth, his full lips sucking at my clit through the thin fabric, his blue eyes veiled by long, fair lashes.

He stopped for a moment and looked up into my eyes with those pale-blue chips of summer sky. His mouth and chin were shiny with my juices. 'God,' he murmured in his soft Scottish rumble, 'you taste just gorgeous.' He bent his head up and kissed me, our first kiss full on the mouth. I could taste myself sharp and musky on his lips. Then he ducked his head again and pulled my thong aside with his teeth, so we could both see my pussy exposed, shiny and swollen with excitement.

Even more slowly, knowing perhaps that I was watching everything he was doing, he licked me up and down with long, firm strokes. The night air from the open window left a cool trail behind his warm tongue. I wanted to cry out with pleasure, but I was afraid of waking Jane in the next compartment. Hamish was keeping me teetering on the edge of orgasm, trembling with delight. He seemed to be teasing me, refusing to speed up his strokes to bring on my climax. I was longing for him to plunge his fingers into me, knowing I would come at once, but his hands remained on my insteps, adding to my excitement with gentle scratches along the soles of my feet. His tongue continued its merciless demolition of my defences, now flat against my clit, now lapping delicately at the very lip of my pussy, now taking a leisurely stroll down to the puckered rim of my anus. I felt as if I were floating, my body washed along helplessly on warm currents.

At last, Hamish began to flick at my clit with his tongue, quicker and quicker. All my excitement was gathering in my belly. I shut my eyes and heard myself whispering, 'Oh yes.' As my body began to shake, Hamish put his whole mouth over my sex, sucking on my clit in time with my movements, the tip of his tongue resting just inside me. I felt as if I were coming into his mouth, as if he were sucking out the orgasm from deep inside me. Opening my eyes as I came, I saw him looking back at me, his blue eyes smiling with pleasure.

Hamish lifted me down to sit, still wobbly, on the lower bunk. His eyes twinkled. 'Well, I expect that tea will be brewed by now,' he said softly. 'Shall I be mother?' I watched him pour two cups of lukewarm tea from the little tin pot, his shoulderblades moving smoothly under his white shirt and his hips shifting delicately to accommodate the train's lurching. 'Sugar?' he asked. I shook my head, unable to speak, still reeling from the overwhelming pleasure of his lovemaking. He passed me a cup and sat next to me.

'Where did you learn to do that?' I murmured weakly.

'Oh, I've been pouring tea since I was a wee boy,' came the reply, the twinkle still in his blue eyes.

'Not the tea, you fool.'

'Ah, the other thing.' He smiled a slightly rueful smile. 'Seven years of marriage, that'll be. It does tend to focus the mind rather more . . .'

'Rather more than some woman you meet on a train,' I finished for him.

'That's so obviously not the case,' he retorted.

I had to concede he was right. His mind had certainly been very focused on me. I decided not to ask if the marriage was ongoing. That was his business, not mine.

Hamish took the empty cup from me and put it tidily back on the tray. 'So neat,' I murmured.

'Of course,' he replied, turning to look down at me. 'I am the boy next door, remember?'

With the same slow deliberateness he had just used to such lethal effect with his tongue, he began to undress. Button by button, the crisp smooth shirt fell open to uncover a well-muscled chest and a faint growth of sandy hair. I could almost picture him at home, shirtless, ironing it with the same unhurried concentration. He took the shirt off and dropped it on the floor, not carelessly, but the way you'd throw down a glove to issue a challenge.

This was not a strip show, more a statement of intent, like a martial arts expert limbering up before a bout – part focusing mind and body, part sending a message to the opponent. 'I can afford to take my time,' it said. 'I want to be completely ready.' I was hypnotised. Resting each shoe delicately on the edge of the counter, Hamish unlaced them and slipped them off with the socks. Then, his gaze never leaving mine, he undid his belt, unbuttoned his trousers, and let them fall. As he stepped out of them and towards me, I could see his erection pushing against his white cotton jockeys. It was huge. I felt a quick somersault inside at the thought of it.

Still seated on the lower berth, I reached up for the waistband of his shorts and slid them delicately down, feeling the downy firmness of his buttocks as I did so. His cock sprang free, a tiny drop of moisture already glistening at its tip. Steadying himself with a hand on the upper berth, Hamish stepped out of his underwear and stood before me completely naked. He was beautiful, fit without too much bulky muscle, poised without self-consciousness. And there, rising from a nest of pale hair, almost as high as his navel, his prick stretched towards me.

I put my hand under it, stroking its silky warmth, and reached toward it with my tongue, but Hamish stopped me with a touch of his hand on my cheek.

'No,' he whispered, 'I want to be inside you. Is that all right?'

'I'd love that,' I whispered back.

With a sudden swiftness, he stripped me of my bra

and sodden G-string and was lying beside me on the narrow berth. His blue eyes impossibly close to mine, he was kissing me with an intensity that took my breath away. I rolled backwards, bringing him on top of me, feeling his warmth all along my skin, and wrapped my legs around his, his downy hair rubbing against my thighs. A few freckles dusted his broad shoulders. His hands found my breasts and squeezed them, his fingers pinching and rolling my nipples till I groaned aloud. Then I felt his fingers inside me, at last, stretching me open.

He started to push his cock into me, using his fingers to hold me open till the head was inside. It was big, but I was so wet from his mouth that it was sliding in, inch by inch. Steadily he pushed himself into me, using his hands to hold my buttocks apart and his thumbs to stretch my lips open. All the time he kept kissing me, pushing his tongue into my mouth in the same merciless way that his cock was entering my cunt. I was gasping into his mouth at the size of it. I felt completely filled, and still it kept penetrating me deeper and deeper. I drew my knees up towards me, trying to open myself up still more. Hamish encircled my ankles with his hands and pushed my feet right back towards my shoulders, bending me almost double. He raised himself up, looking down at where his cock was still forcing its way into me, my new position giving an even deeper penetration. I looked down too, and saw myself stretched around his prick so tightly that my clit was rubbing against its girth. The sight was unbelievably arousing. I felt my orgasm begin, my muscles trying to contract around this prodigious shaft, but already so taut that each wave only gripped it harder and increased my excitement. Grabbing his buttocks, I pulled him into me, so with each spasm he slid deeper and finally, as I reached an intense climax, was wholly inside me.

42

Timing his movements with the waves inside me, he thrust gently, rocking his hips against me, so I could feel the head of his prick pushing deep inside me, and my clit rubbing against him with each thrust. The sensations were so powerful that, instead of dying away, the waves of my orgasm kept rolling, my body carried away on his rhythm. His own excitement was mounting, his hips moving faster and stronger, his self-control finally slipping as he pounded into me. I wrapped my legs round the back of his neck, pulling him down towards me, and saw his eyes cloud with arousal. 'That's right,' I whispered to his ear, 'come inside me. Come now.'

His whole body convulsed and, with a shiver, I felt him shoot his spunk deep inside me. With my own aftershocks he trembled two, three times, and then lay heavy and spent on my chest. We lay for a few moments, hearing our own breathing slowly return to normal, and the steady percussion of the rails.

Suddenly stiff, I tried to shift my position, and he pulled himself up and out of me. I slid from under him and stretched out beside him on the berth. Outside the window, the stars hung motionless over the night landscape flying by. The train, at least, was still keeping a relentless rhythm.

Dazed and exhausted, I lay staring out at the darkness, trying to bring myself back to reality. Hamish lay quiet beside me, his even breathing a sign that he was drifting into sleep. The anonymous sleeper compartment seemed to resonate with our passionate encounter. It was so obviously designed for the sensible business traveller – the sober decor, the narrow berths – and yet its very anonymity had made it this easy for Hamish and I to fuck without any of the usual formalities. I wondered how many others, even at this moment, were crumpling the starched white sheets and staining them with their sweat and their juices, perhaps, as I had, with a perfect stranger. Here I was, awake and savouring an intensely erotic experience, when I should be asleep, resting before tomorrow's wedding.

Tomorrow's wedding! With a sudden jolt I realised that in a few hours' time Jane and I would be woken with a knock and a continental breakfast, and not long after that I would have to look awake and presentable at Eric's wedding. If I was lucky, I might snatch a little sleep now and avoid actually falling asleep during the ceremony. I looked at Hamish. His lips were slightly open and he wore a serene expression on his face: he was asleep. Softly, I got up, pulled the sheet over him and turned out the light. Then, gathering my scattered clothes, I slipped through the connecting door to our own compartment.

Jane lay almost exactly as I had left her, eyes closed, one arm flung back over her head, mascara slightly smudged, blonde hair falling into her face and across the pillow. Now feeling chilly, I opened my bag as quietly as I could and looked for my nightshirt. I was trying clumsily to pull it over my head when Jane's voice, roughened by whisky and sleep, made me jump.

'Oh good,' she croaked, 'tea at last.' I looked at her in confusion. Tea? Tea! The tea I went to fetch a couple of hours ago, which I had in fact shared with Hamish. To Jane, the tea was probably the last thing she remembered. Bang on cue, she smiled with a drunkard's charm and asked, 'Have I been asleep long?'

'Hours,' I answered. 'In fact we drank the tea ages ago.'

A suspicious shadow crossed her eyes. 'I don't remember that.' She was wondering why I was lying to her about tea, I could tell. Sometimes we knew each other far too well.

'Not we, you and me,' I explained. 'We, me and the

44

man in the next compartment. We met in the buffet, and when we got back you were asleep, so we . . .'

She was really awake now, sitting up and looking at me sharply. As I said, she knows me far too well, and she certainly knows it doesn't take me two hours to drink a cup of tea. Her delicate nostrils flared. 'And is that eau de stranger on a train I smell?' she whispered. 'Did you get good value in exchange for my cup of tea?'

I felt myself blushing as I nodded. There was almost nothing I would hide from Jane, but to be caught naked, sneaking back in from an illicit encounter made me feel like a furtive teenager.

'Come on then, tell me all!' said Jane triumphantly. 'If I'm not getting tea, I want all the details. How big was his cock?' Just like her to cut straight to the chase.

I indicated with my hands. She looked frankly disbelieving. 'No, honestly!' I assured her. She looked at my face, decided I was not exaggerating and whistled, impressed. Then she stood up. I looked at her stupidly. 'Where are you going?' I asked.

'I'm going to have a look,' she declared, then grabbed the handle of the connecting door and walked through it. For a moment I sat there with my mouth open. For another moment, I sat mentally kicking myself. Why had I said anything to Jane? I should have known better. In normal conditions she is capable of scandalous behaviour. In her current alcoholic mist, and still smarting about Eric's impending marriage, there were no limits to what she would do. I waited to hear Hamish's shout when he saw the intruder in his compartment. After a few seconds, when no scream came, I opened the connecting door a crack and peeped in.

Hamish was still flat out on the lower berth, as I had left him. Jane was bending over him, drawing back the sheet slowly so as not to wake him. The moonlight chiselled the muscular form of his naked body with deep blue shadows. One of his hands lay on the sheet beside him, fingers slightly curled, and the other rested just above his navel, rising and falling gently with his breathing. His pubic hair was curled damply against his skin, and his cock lay relaxed on his thigh, still visibly wet with our mingled juices.

Jane was gazing down at him like a hungry traveller who has just arrived to find a feast spread before her. I wanted to pull her away from him, but I was too afraid to wake Hamish and frighten him. I watched transfixed as Jane reached out and traced the length of his prick with a single fingertip. A little pulse of excitement ran along it, but Hamish did not stir. Jane smiled and licked her finger, then drew it again from base to tip. 'Please,' I was thinking, 'please let her stop now and come back to our compartment.'

But, being Jane, of course she didn't stop. Through the slit of the door, I watched as she stroked him delicately, as that gigantic prick began to swell again and lift itself off Hamish's thigh without his breathing even changing stroke. Surely, now she would see its full size and be content with that, I thought, more in hope than expectation. Not a chance.

Jane knelt by the bed and took the end of his prick in her mouth. Her lips were stretched round it, and she slid them scarcely a third of the way down its length before her mouth was clearly full. Now Hamish stirred. He rolled his head back and a little sound of pleasure that was almost musical escaped his parted lips. His eyes were still closed, but for how long?

Jane's blonde hair fell forward on to Hamish's chest and stomach. I could see her cheeks working as she sucked, and I felt a strange disquiet. Part of me was disturbed at the thought of my best friend with this man who had just fucked me, probably tasting me on him. It seemed disturbingly intimate. We'd shared

46

many things in the past, but never a man. Well, never on the same night. It was true, we had similar tastes and our backlists had a few names in common, but we'd always kept a little bit of discretion. So part of me wanted to shut the door and not watch any more. But I didn't; I kept watching. I didn't want to admit it, but part of me found the idea of sharing a man with Jane incredibly arousing.

Just as I thought Hamish could not possibly sleep through any more, Jane stopped and stood up. A rush of relief filled me – she had made her point and was bored. I opened the door for her to come back to our compartment. Instead, she pulled her T-shirt over her head, slid down her jeans, and bent, naked, to resume her attentions. 'Jane!' I whispered urgently, desperate to get her away before Hamish realised that this was more than an enjoyable dream. Too late. His eyelids flickered, and he looked up at the naked stranger who had his cock in her mouth.

Jane removed her mouth from Hamish's stiff cock, smiled her charming smile, and stretched out a hand to shake his. 'Hello, I'm Jane,' she said, as if they'd just met at a cocktail party. 'I'm a friend of Emma's.'

Calmly, Hamish took her hand and shook it. 'I'm Hamish.' He followed Jane's glance to where I was standing amazed. 'Well, Emma,' he asked with a slight smile, 'are you going to join us, or what?'

Before I had time to think, to run away, or anything a sensible person would have done (as if any sensible person would have got herself into this situation) I stepped forward and shut the door behind me. Jane bent her mouth once more to Hamish's prick, and he stretched out a hand to me. 'So,' he whispered to me, 'I guess your friend here knows what your pussy tastes like now. Don't you want to taste hers?' Obediently, I knelt behind Jane. As I approached her sex, the sharp smell reached my nostrils and I felt my mouth start to water. I opened my lips, uncertain how to begin.

'Come on, don't be shy,' Hamish encouraged me. 'Didn't you learn anything from me?' I remembered the way he had started licking me, slow and teasing, and I drew my tongue down Jane's slit to where her clit was nestling. I felt a shiver run through her. She tasted salty and rich.

I could imagine how that felt, remembering Hamish's tongue teasing me the same way. As I licked her, long strokes up and down, I could almost feel every stroke in my own pussy. Forward to the tiny button I lapped, then back to the delicate skin behind. Flickers of delight followed my tongue, but I was clearly not distracting her from the pleasure she was giving Hamish.

His hand was stroking my back distractedly and each flick of Jane's tongue echoed in the electricity of his fingertips. I could imagine from his touch what she was doing to him: a long, firm stroke meant she was taking him deep in her mouth; light flickerings of his fingers answered her tongue flicking across the sensitive tip of his prick. This rhythm in turn was guiding my own tongue over and into Jane's sex, as I imagined everything she was feeling, my mouth behind and Hamish's cock in front.

As I grew more confident, using my knowledge of what it must feel like, I began to take the lead, boldly pushing my tongue into Jane's pussy, feeling the moist ridges just inside, then teasing her clit with a quick, delicate rhythm. From Hamish's touch and the sounds of pleasure he was making, I could tell that Jane was responding to my lead, strong when I was being strong, light when I was light. I felt a rush of excitement, knowing I was conducting this little orchestra.

I could tell that Jane, too, was getting more and more excited, her sex hot and thickened with arousal, her juices running down into her pubic hair. My face was slippery with them, my tongue as wet as if I were drinking wine. As I intensified my licking, I put a finger deep inside her and flicked it in time with my mouth, my fingertip instinctively finding the most sensitive spot within her. She moaned softly, the sound muffled by her own sucking. A moment later, I felt Hamish slide his finger down between my buttocks and into my own cunt. Now the circuit was closed, each pulse of our common rhythm answered at once by fingers and mouths, building relentlessly to a climax.

It was Jane whose voice first gave the cry of surrender, as her hole gripped my finger in waves of release. As I felt her orgasm, and my flicking finger was answered by Hamish's finger inside me, my own orgasm overtook me, and almost simultaneously I heard Hamish's voice and felt the quivering of his climax. Each ripple of excitement ran through all three of us, linked as we were, and it felt like minutes before the excitement receded. We sank into a heap, Jane and I on the floor and Hamish still lying on the berth. I shut my eyes for a moment, exhausted.

When I opened them, the sky speeding past the window was a pale grey and a watery light filled the compartment. Jane was standing over me, her hand on my shoulder.

'Emma!' she was whispering urgently. 'Come on! It's six o'clock.'

I blinked at her stupidly, wondering for a moment why I was so cold and so stiff. As I remembered where I was, I realised why she was so keen to rouse me. In a matter of minutes there would be a knock on the door of our compartment and two continental breakfasts would await us. Then it would be time to dress for Eric's wedding and get off the train and on the road to the castle where it was taking place. I giggled as I forced my aching limbs into a standing position.

'What?' asked Jane, as she pulled me through the connecting door and shut it behind me.

'I was just wondering whether Eric's bride had as good a hen night as we did.'

Jane began to giggle too, as she wrestled with the folding handbasin and dabbed at random bits of her body with a damp flannel. 'Not Philippa. She's a good girl. She'll have had a couple of spritzers and an early night, so her eyes aren't too puffy in the photos.'

For some reason this was hilarious, and when the steward arrived with two breakfast trays we were helpless with laughter.

Chapter Four

Boy on a Motorcycle

*S*omehow, I still don't know how, Jane and I stumbled out on to the platform at Edinburgh Waverley looking quite presentable. In less than an hour we had both washed in the tiny basin, administered enough make-up to disguise our lack of sleep, devoured the croissants and the dinky bowls of cereal, drunk the tea ('Tea at last!' Jane had cried, bringing on another fit of laughter. You probably had to be there.) and decided what we were going to wear.

Jane was looking drop-dead gorgeous in a bright red dress that matched her nails. 'If I'm going to be painted as the scarlet woman,' she had pronounced, 'I may as well dress like one.' I had tossed a coin, which was what Geoff had suggested 24 hours before, and gone for the silk trouser-suit, a particularly good bet since I could wear my loose silk knickers underneath. I was, frankly, still sore from Hamish's impressive attentions, and my usual G-string style would have been pretty uncomfortable.

What we both wanted was a big fry-up and lots of coffee. Instead, we had to find the minibus Eric had organised to collect guests from the station and deliver them to the romantic but inaccessible setting he had chosen for his wedding. We weren't the only ones to have rolled in on that overnight train, and a little bunch of bleary Sassenachs began to assemble outside the station on Prince's Street. There were a couple of faces I recognised, but nobody I knew well – something for which I was grateful. I didn't feel up to a proper conversation.

The minibus rolled up, bang on time, driven by Eric's youngest brother Michael. I could tell Jane was worn out – normally she'd have been making eyes at Michael, just for the sake of it. This morning she sat beside him without a second glance, in spite of the fact that he really was a younger, more handsome version of the man who'd jilted her so recently. If anything, he was rather impressed by her, but she seemed oblivious, growling at him to stop at a coffee shop on the way out of the city and, once she was equipped with the large, strong coffee she needed, sinking into a cappucino-scented heap of blonde hair and dishevelled velvet.

I found a seat in the back where I could look out at the view and not have to talk to anyone, and promised myself a nap between the ceremony and the evening party. Once we were clear of Edinburgh's dreary suburbs, the countryside was quite stunning. First, rolling hills with clumps of woodland stretched away from the winding road. As we climbed higher, the hills became more bare, scattered with sheep and a blush of purple heather. The sky also had its scattering of white, as a few clouds skimmed across the blue: it promised to turn into a bright but breezy summer day for Eric and Philippa.

A nagging discomfort kept nibbling the edges of my mind. I was reluctant to give it a name, but if I stopped concentrating on the view or the back of Michael's head, it popped into focus. I couldn't quite accept that last night Jane and I had added a whole new dimension to our old friendship. It still seemed like something I might have dreamed, but I knew that it had happened, and that she knew it too. What did it mean for our friendship? Was she embarrassed? Was that why she was playing the 'too hungover to talk to anyone' so assiduously? Or was it something she had thought about before last night? And what did I feel about it?

At some point, I knew we'd have to talk about it, but it wasn't a conversation I was looking forward to very much. I was afraid that we would never again be completely comfortable with each other. Exciting though last night had been, it was not worth losing a best friend over. What an eventful weekend it was turning out to be. I smiled to myself, thinking that Geoff's climbing trip would have had a job to equal the highs of my train journey. The minibus swung around a tight corner and the castle came into view across a steep valley.

It was immediately clear why Eric had felt it necessary to drag us all into the middle of nowhere for his wedding. The castle was fantastic. Set on top of a rocky hill, it was at once fairy-tale and forbidding. A jumble of granite towers and walls pierced with arrow-slits glowered over a grand whitewashed hall, whose mullioned windows overlooked a formal garden sloping towards us. The effect was something like a pretty, aristocratic lady being escorted by an armed guard.

Our road dropped towards the valley floor, lifting the castle even higher above us. Everyone was gaping up at it, even Jane. 'Wow,' she murmured.

'It's great, isn't it?' Michael responded, still failing to draw even a glance. He was right, though. As we crossed the little river by the stomach-jolting humpbacked bridge and began our climb towards the gates, we felt as if we were on a film set. I half expected to see Geoff and his reckless friends abseiling off the battlements.

Michael drew the minibus to a crunching halt on the gravel in front of the main entrance and we all spilled out on to the lawn. The sun was warming the air and the flowerbeds that flanked the paths breathed a delicate scent into the fresh breeze. It was impossible not to feel more relaxed. I flashed a happy smile at Jane, who swept her hair back from her face and grinned back. If she was still bothered about Eric, she was putting on a good show.

Caterers were rushing about with white cloths and flower arrangements and strapping young men were building trestle tables on the lawn. I felt a bit lost, standing there with my luggage. The castle was a fully fledged hotel, but our rooms would only be available from two o'clock. We had nearly two hours to fill before the ceremony and the desire for a substantial breakfast was creeping back. I looked around for Michael or Eric. Instead, it was Jane who appeared at my side and grabbed my bag. 'Come on,' she told me firmly, 'bags to reception and then we chat up the caterers. They won't be putting up all those tables without the aid of a bacon sandwich.'

With relief, I followed her into the dark entrance and let the porter take my bag away. If Jane had any thoughts about our encounter last night, they were not coming between us. My spirits rose. I saw her nostrils flicker as she tested the air for the smell of frying. 'This way,' she whispered, and I followed her down a wood-panelled corridor towards the clashing of pans.

Into a bright, steamy kitchen she stormed, as only Jane can, oozing irresistibility. The head caterer received her story – that we were helping the lads putting up the tables – with dry scepticism. Neither of us, after all, were dressed for manual work. 'We're Andrew's English cousins,' Jane added sweetly.

The caterer, still unsmiling, jerked his head towards a tray of bacon butties lying on one side. 'You'd better take that out for the boys, then,' he answered, without pausing in his chopping. Jane picked up the tray and smiled charmingly. As I held the door open for her to carry it out I caught a little grin and a shake of the head from our benefactor. He may not have been taken in, but his morning had been brightened.

'How did you know there was a caterer called Andrew?' I whispered as Jane took her booty past the reception desk and back into the sunshine.

'Oh, this is Scotland,' she answered dismissively. 'There was bound to be an Andrew doing something.' We each grabbed a bacon roll and Jane called the boys over for their breakfast. I couldn't tell what was attracting them more, the smell of bacon or the sight of Jane in her scarlet dress. She was revelling in the attention too – quite her old self again.

I began to feel less worried about whether we'd jeopardised our friendship. Jane was relaxed and teasing the table-builders, not at all like a woman preoccupied. Probably, I thought, last night had been just the ego-boost she needed to face Eric at his wedding. Myself, I was too tired to flirt and took my breakfast a little way down the garden.

The gardens had a French air: lawns divided geometrically by rosebeds and square-cut hedges, all designed to make the view from the house as stunning as possible. You really must have felt like the master of all you could see, living in this house and looking out across your estate. Although modern times had softened the edges of the formality, the place still had an ancient, haughty air. A light breeze across the valley stirred my clothes, blowing right through the thin silk to my skin, but the sun was warm enough to make it a pleasant frisson.

I shut my eyes, trying to concentrate on the sensation of the air on my flesh, the smells of the garden, the taste of the last mouthful of bacon, and the silence. Living in London, one of the things I appreciate most about the countryside is the lack of background noise. It wasn't really silence, of course. I could hear the cut and thrust of Jane bantering with the boys and the brisk sounds of preparation from the house. Further afield, the birds were singing as if they were so glad to be alive that their tiny hearts would burst if they tried to keep it to themselves. A woodpigeon was purring in the woods behind the house, somewhere a dog was barking, and on the road below a motorbike's throaty growl announced its approach.

I opened my eyes to see it come up the hill. As a teenager, unable to afford a car, I had gone everywhere on a terrible old 125 that threatened to fall apart at any moment. Now a car was indispensable for my job, but I still hankered for the thrill of two wheels and kept promising myself that soon I would buy myself a bike just for fun. I was becoming a bit of a joke among my friends, the way my head would turn to see which speed machine was roaring past.

The flash of red was coming closer, over the bridge and straight towards the castle. Secretly, I hoped it was coming here for the wedding. Perhaps I could get talking to the rider and convince him to let me take it for a spin. It would mean holding back on the champagne, but it would be worth it. I looked critically at the rider's technique, hoping to convince myself that I would do it better, but I couldn't find any faults. Whoever it was, they were using all the bike's speed and power, but they seemed to have the skill and experience to carry it off. By the time the bike glided to a stop on the gravel drive below me, I was feeling nothing but pure envy.

The lucky, lucky owner put the Ducati 900SS (I told you my friends laughed at me) on its stand and got off. Jane appeared at my shoulder. 'Tell you what,' she whispered, 'you take the bike and I'll have the rider.'

She knew me too well. Mind you, she was no martyr: the leather-clad figure was tall and manly, and moving very gracefully for one who had probably been tensed against the wind for miles and miles.

'Yes, but wait till he takes his helmet off,' I whispered back. 'Far too many bikers look better with it on.'

'I could always get him to put it back on for the evening,' Jane replied.

I was just thinking happily that Jane must be back on form when the rider did take his helmet off and we got a look at his face. It was Kit.

My expression must have said it all. 'Are you all right?' Jane asked, in a tone of real concern. 'Do you know him?'

'Know him?' I croaked. 'It's Kit. Kit, from Sarah's wedding.'

Jane looked amazed. 'Mr Marquee?' Her voice was incredulous. 'Here? What is he, some kind of wedding groupie?'

I couldn't believe it myself. Never expecting to meet him again, I had nonetheless been dreaming about him. Those light-brown eyes had gazed into mine in several night-time adventures, from which I had woken sweating, my heart beating fast. And now, here he was in person. I was staring hard, trying to convince myself that it wasn't him. Perhaps he had a brother? After all, we hadn't got as far as discussing our families.

Don't get me wrong: it's not that I didn't want to

57

see him again. There was nothing I wanted more. Every few days I had caught myself concocting elaborate scenarios in which Sarah for some reason invited all her most distant cousins to an occasion where Kit, as Robin's best friend, would also be found. But here? I was panicked. What if he pretended he didn't know me? That would be far worse than never seeing him again. Especially with Jane here. I had told Jane the whole story, glad for once to have something to tell that would make *her* say 'No!' and 'You didn't!' as I was always exclaiming over her exploits. Worse, what if he were here to accompany somebody else?

My own reaction surprised me. I had no idea what an impact Kit had made until I was confronted with the reality of his presence. At least, I thought, I had seen him first, before he knew I was here, and had a chance to plan my tactics. The best thing to do, I was thinking, would be to play it cool, not go out of my way to bump into him, and let him make the first pitch. That's it, I thought – leave the ball in his court; pretend you haven't seen him till he sees you. And as I thought this, he looked up, saw my face, and smiled a huge smile.

'Oh, my God!' I wailed to myself as he strode up the bank towards me, still in his leathers and looking even more gorgeous than I remembered him. I looked to Jane for moral support, but she had vanished, tactfully retreating to the posse of table-builders and the tray of bacon rolls. I was alone on this lawn with Kit.

In no time at all he was standing in front of me, looking down with that same impudent half-smile that had popped, uninvited, into my mind countless times in the last couple of months. All my plans to be cool had vanished: I only just remembered to shut my mouth as he arrived. We stood for a moment in awkward silence, our eyes questioning each other.

Then he seemed to recover his self-confidence. 'Hello, fancy seeing you here,' he said. Then he smiled again, and all my doubts melted away. It was obvious that he was as pleased to see me as I was to see him. Then he kissed me.

I thought I'd remembered just how wonderful his kisses were, but I had clung on to a mere shadow. There was no holding back at all, no awkwardness but no self-conscious technique either. Kit was putting his whole self, all the desire he felt for me, all the responses he was getting from me, into this kiss. It was as if our mouths were inventing a new language, a language of sensation, of currents of energy, in which everything we had been thinking and dreaming since our first meeting was being shared. I felt as if my body was suspended from this point where our mouths were meeting, as if the kiss was the fixed point about which we, and the whole universe, were moving.

After a couple of hours – all right, seconds – we stopped kissing and looked at each other again. I'm sure I was grinning like a fool; he certainly was. 'So,' he asked, as if we'd just met at the supermarket checkout, 'how have you been?'

'Fine, good,' I burbled. 'How about you?'

'Not bad, not bad at all.' He kissed me again. My whole body was going mad, my skin racing with tiny currents of excitement, my pussy throbbing with anticipation, my hands clasped round his waist, feeling the cold smoothness of the leather suit, holding him close. All I could think about, if you could call it thinking, was getting somewhere private with Kit, ideally a bit more private than last time.

He must have been on the same track because he released me, gasping, for long enough to ask me, 'Have you got a room here?'

'Yes,' I whispered back, 'but I can't get into it till two.'

'Bugger.' He spoke for both of us. We looked around for anywhere that wasn't in public view and, catching each other's eyes, laughed.

'Typical,' I murmured, 'not a marquee in sight.'

Although there was still over an hour before the ceremony was due to start, guests were starting to gather on the lawn before the house. I got a glimpse of Eric in his fancy suit, greeting somebody who looked like an aunt. Jane was still chatting to the boys, and I saw Eric glance her way a bit nervously. Good, that would teach him to pretend she had led him astray, when the reality was the other way around. Things were getting busier, though, and there seemed no chance of picking up our unfinished business till after two o'clock. Three of our old college crowd started heading towards our patch of garden, and I resigned myself to hours of suspense.

It was the hedges that saved us. As the approaching guests disappeared from view behind a block of ornamental topiary, Kit put his hand in mine and pulled me away behind another hedge. Giggling like children, we sneaked away as if in a maze, keeping out of view of the others, till our path was stopped by a concealed ditch.

'It's a ha-ha,' I told him. He looked blank. 'A concealed ditch,' I explained, 'to stop the farm animals wandering into the garden without any unsightly fences. They were all the rage a couple of centuries ago.'

We contemplated the ditch. It was about four feet deep, with steep grassy sides, and the bottom was dry but muddy. Kit looked at me.

'Not a chance,' I told him firmly. 'Have you any idea what it cost me to get that cream suit cleaned?'

Amazingly, he blushed. 'Sorry,' he muttered.

We looked up at the house. We had managed to put some distance between us and the other guests, so their conversations were faint twitterings on the breeze, but anyone glancing our way would see us clearly. Our chaperones were distant but inescapable. We sat on a stone bench, still holding hands, and gazed out at the view.

My hand in his was burning, a fire that sent heated blood racing around my veins. His fingertips were softly tracing spider paths on my thigh, their warmth penetrating the thin silk and drawing little flames of excitement dancing in their wake. I could feel myself getting wet between the legs, soaking the thin silk of my knickers. We were both still looking out across the valley, watching the road that wound down the opposite hillside. Cars were coming down it in ones and twos, bringing more guests to the wedding, swooping over the steep arch of the bridge and disappearing from our sight beneath the foot of the garden before we heard them crunching to a halt on the gravel drive.

Kit slipped his hand from mine and slid it across my thigh till his fingertips lay hidden in the narrow gap between my legs. Slowly he stroked them across the silk in languorous figures-of-eight. The fabric was so thin, it was almost as if he were touching bare skin. If anything the silk amplified my sense of touch even more, acting like a fine lubricant, allowing those fingers to glide across me, setting every nerve alight. I gripped the sharp edges of the stone bench till they cut into my palms, trying to keep control of my responses.

As I kept my eyes fixed steadily on the green hill in front of me, I felt Kit's fingers working their way steadily up my thighs. They were heading inexorably towards my pussy, sending out advance parties, electric shocks of excitement that jolted my clit with shudders of pleasure. Part of me was silently begging him to hurry, my cunt already moist and aching for his touch; the other part was hoping this would never end, this slow progress that was taking in every square inch of tender skin on the inside of my thighs. Kit said nothing as his touch travelled slowly, slowly, in to my centre. The only sounds were the birdsong, the growl of the cars as they arrived at the castle and the scraps of laughter and conversation that the wind blew down to us.

Kit's fingertips reached the edge of my knickers and kept their rhythm, silk now rubbing against silk. The only friction was a slight dragging where the inner layer of fine stuff was already soaked with my juices, the moisture making them cling to me. Even through this double layer, the fabric was so thin that his fingers were tracing every fold and crevice of my pussy, his strokes light but sure. I felt like a work of art being brought into being by a master craftsman, a sculptor perhaps, coaxing a block of marble to living form.

From behind, anyone glancing our way would have seen two people sitting side by side, catching up on old news, perhaps, or just enjoying the panorama before us. In fact, Kit was making love to me as thoroughly as if I were lying naked on my back, his questing hand rubbing more urgently now, pushing the fine silk into the sodden crack, stretching the wet fabric tight across my clit and pressing against its smoothness with his thumb. My legs were shaking; excitement was making my body weak. I was biting my lip to stop myself betraying with sound how good that felt. I put a steadying hand on the cool leather of his thigh.

Kit was pushing two fingers into the wet mouth of my cunt, the loose flowing garments following his thrusts, thin enough to be pulled right inside me. Every time he plunged in, the fabric was stretched tight over the rest of me, pressing hard against my button and forming a narrow cord that pulled against my anus. The cloth was soaking now, almost dripping with my juices. Still his thumb kept moving over my clit, the rhythm sending waves of pleasure up into my belly, faster and faster. Each thrust of his hand brought an answering squeeze, gripping his fingers as my climax drew closer. I knew it was close now; I could feel my hips instinctively answering Kit's movements, rocking me towards the pressure of his hand.

As my orgasm broke, I turned to see him looking at me, his golden-brown eyes fixed on me, a smile shining in them as he watched my face, enjoying my pleasure, seeing me lose control as his fingers pulled me delicately over the edge and into the deep waters of sexual abandon. I trembled with the aftershocks as he kept stroking, slower now, bringing me in to land gently, then finally putting his hand back into mine with an affectionate squeeze.

'All right?' he whispered, sounding almost shy.

'Better than all right,' I whispered back. He squeezed my hand harder. 'So,' I asked him, 'do you only do this at weddings?'

'Oh no,' he assured me seriously. 'Bar mitzvahs and twenty-first birthday parties too.' He kissed me again, a quick, respectable kiss. 'What time does this do start, anyway?' he asked.

I looked at my watch, noticing that my wrist was still shaking a little. 'Ten minutes,' I answered, suddenly panicked. I looked down; sure enough, the crotch of my thin trousers showed a dark wet mark, glistening in the sun. 'Shit!' I exclaimed.

Kit, following my gaze, pulled a guilty face. 'Think it'll dry in time?' he asked hopefully.

'Not without leaving a mark,' I answered.

He bent over, plunged his face into my lap, and sucked hard on the fabric. 'Mmm,' he said with relish

63

as he lifted his head, 'delicious.' Another quick kiss, and I caught the faintest taste of my sex on his lips. 'Now let the breeze get to it,' he told me, 'and it should just about dry before we have to go indoors.'

Just about was the word. I was scarcely dry when we walked back to the castle, but at least I wasn't advertising my excitement to the world. Kit and I strolled up the lawn to join the throng outside the great oak doors to the hall, now thrown open. Jane materialised in front of us.

'Jane, this is Kit.' I introduced them calmly. 'Kit – my friend Jane.'

'How do you do.' Jane stretched out a hand and Kit shook it.

I felt nervous all over again. What was she thinking? Did she approve? I still remembered with shame a student fling whom I'd introduced to Jane with great excitement. When I'd cornered her later and asked her, 'Well? What do you think?' she'd looked at me with genuine perplexity. 'Emma,' she'd asked me simply, 'why ...?' The awful truth was, I'd had no good answer. 'Because he was there' doesn't seem adequate, somehow.

Now, shaking Kit's hand, she was the picture of friendliness. Glancing up at him, I tried to see him through her eyes: that dark hair flopping forward, threatening to fall in his eyes at any moment; a big-featured, mobile face, showing the first flush of a tan and animated with a natural smile; light-brown eyes and long, dark, lashes; a physical grace rare in one so tall, without the hint of a stoop. Suddenly seeing him clearly, I caught my breath as his beauty took me by surprise.

'Very nice to meet you, Kit,' said Jane, putting the emphasis firmly on the 'Very nice' for my benefit.

'Lovely to meet you too,' he responded, 'but I think

we'd better get inside.' Most of the guests had already vanished into the oak-panelled hall.

'Hmm,' agreed Jane as she followed them in through the door, 'but you might like to slip into something a little more comfortable first.'

As the usher glared at us, Kit looked down abashed at his leather suit. 'Shit.'

Stillness was already descending on the room within. Urgently, Kit wrestled with his zips and extracted himself from the leather suit. Underneath it, his suit was as crumpled as you might expect.

'I was going to iron it if I had time,' he murmured in embarrassment.

'Oh well,' I answered. I could hear people moving into their places for the ceremony and didn't want another conspicuous late entry. I thrust the stiff leather suit into the arms of the usher. Too surprised not to grab it, he stood holding it in his arms, looking as if he were supporting a fainting scuba-diver. 'We'll collect it later,' I whispered, and pulled Kit into the back row of seats.

Chapter Five
The Second Wedding

*E*ric and Philippa's wedding ceremony went off charmingly. The bride played successfully to both modern and traditional factions, in an ivory-coloured suit and a hat with a little veil. Small nephews and precocious nieces read poems and a band with whom Eric had played guitar at university performed a love song that was, frankly, dreadful, and we all smiled and nodded indulgently. There was a moment when we were asked if we knew of any good reason why these two should not be joined in marriage, and I caught Jane's eye. She flashed me a wicked look and stuck her tongue in her cheek. I shook with giggles. 'What?' whispered Kit, still holding my hand firmly. I could only shake my head.

As we all followed the bride and groom back out on to the lawn, the band played another dreary, senti-mental guitar anthem. We filed past the happy couple, offering congratulations, shaking hands and kissing cheeks. Jane, just in front of me and Kit, kissed Philippa warmly and then took Eric's hand. He pulled her in for an embrace, a tender kiss on the cheek – not inappropriate for an old friend, but carrying for Jane another message. I saw her shoulders lose their tension and her free hand pat his back in silent reply. As Kit was brushing Philippa's cheek with those lips, Eric murmured in my ear, 'Who's your friend?'

'Tell you later,' I murmured back.

Kit and I headed with unerring instinct for the tray of champagne. I stretched out my hand for the comforting, cool curve of the glass, when a flash of red beyond the waiter caught my eye. Kit's motorbike. I wavered: if I had a glass of champagne, I would inevitably have two, and if I had two, I would never be able to ride that lovely red machine. Kit, glass already in hand, was smiling smugly as he followed my gaze. 'She's a beauty, isn't she?' I nodded. 'Fancy a spin?' he asked.

Luckily he had a spare helmet with him, and in no time he had the bike turned towards the gate, powerful engine revving, with me sitting behind him. I clasped him tightly around the waist, hands gripping him through the cool leather. As we swung out of the drive and up the road past the castle, the wind pierced my thin silk outfit, but I didn't care. Not only did I have an excuse to hold Kit tightly to me in public view, but I was back on two wheels, speeding along in the sunshine, banking with every bend of the road.

Kit was a good rider, too. We were racing along, swinging round the curves of the hill, but I felt perfectly safe. As we cleared the summit I looked down over his shoulder at the next valley, laid out below, and felt like laughing aloud. Even an open-topped car doesn't match the feeling of freedom you get on a motorbike, the sensation of the wind rushing past you, the smells of the countryside, the way the bike pushes itself into the contours of the road like a masseur pressing his hand into your shoulderblade.

Kit pulled in to a gateway that led on to a field,

pushed his visor up and smiled at me. 'Good, eh?' he asked.

I got off the bike and grinned back. 'Fantastic. Can I have a go?'

He looked a bit taken aback – not the response he had been expecting, I suppose. As he swung his leg over the bike and lifted it on to its stand he said nothing.

'Go on,' I continued, 'I've been riding since I was sixteen.'

He seemed to be in a bit of a dilemma. He took his helmet off thoughtfully. 'You're not really dressed for it,' he ventured.

'I could borrow your leathers,' I persisted.

He looked down, as if he were embarrassed. 'The thing is,' he said reluctantly, 'it's not actually mine. I've borrowed it for the weekend.' So that was why he was so reluctant.

'That's what I call a friend,' I said. 'Someone who'll lend you their Ducati on a sunny weekend like this.'

He looked amused. 'It's not really like that,' he said.

'Why, have they got more than one?' I asked.

'More than one?' He was openly laughing now. 'They've got more than you and I could crash in a lifetime.'

I was confused now – was this some millionaire playboy friend who collected motorbikes just so his friends could ride them? Kit took pity on me.

'I've borrowed it from Ducati,' he explained. 'I'm a bike journalist. I just tell them there might be a newspaper article in it and they bring one round to my house.'

I couldn't believe my ears. Not only did this man get paid to ride motorbikes, but even when he wasn't working he could ride the latest machine for nothing! How lucky could one man be?

'So,' Kit murmured into my ear, 'you see why I can't let you take it on the public highway.'

He started kissing his way round my throat, but I was not to be deflected.

'OK then, let's take it somewhere off-road and I can have a ride there. There must be a car park round here somewhere.'

He sighed. 'There isn't, not for miles. I'm not just saying that; I was looking for petrol on the way up – this place is the outback.' He seemed to be thinking, wondering whether to say something, but instead he pulled me into his arms and began kissing me, his hands caressing my back and arms through the thin silk.

Once again, I felt as if his tongue could touch my whole body, ripples of excitement running along my legs and arms and resonating inside my belly. I could only run my hands over his leathers, held too close to find the zip and get any closer to the warm flesh beneath. His hands slid down to my buttocks and took a firm hold, almost lifting me off my feet. I could feel my excitement rising again.

'Why don't we go back to the hotel?' I whispered to him. 'Your room should be ready by now.'

He looked stunned. 'My room? Haven't you got a room?'

'Well, yes, of course,' I answered. All the guests had rooms, it was part of the deal. That was how Eric and Philippa could afford the trappings of Scottish lairdhood.

'Well, why can't we go to your room then?' he persisted.

I felt a stab of doubt. He was here with somebody else after all. That was why he had to take me out of view of the other guests to kiss me. His wife – or whatever – was back at the castle waiting for him. Humiliation and rejection flooded me like a cold river.

'My room's a twin,' I explained. 'I'm sharing with Jane. What's the problem with your room?' If there was somebody else, I wanted to know now.

He looked mortified. 'The thing is,' he said quietly, 'I haven't got a room. I suppose I was gambling on being able to share yours.'

I watched him closely. Was this some outrageous attempt to cover up, or could he be serious?

'How did you get away without booking a room?' I was sceptical. 'Didn't your invitation say you had to have one? You didn't tell Philippa's mum you were planning to share mine, did you? She knew I was already sharing.'

Now Kit was really suffering. He looked positively miserable, as if he would rather be anywhere in the world at this moment.

'This is going to sound really bad,' he mumbled, 'but I never had an invitation. I'm not really invited. I ... er ... I only came because I knew you were coming.'

I stared at him. If this was a lie, its very shamelessness was stunning.

'That's why I borrowed the bike,' he continued. 'I was asking everyone about you, and all Sarah could remember was some family do when she was a kid. She said you turned up on your motorbike covered in oil, and everyone else was in their best frocks. I thought maybe, if you were still into bikes, I could ... er ... I could persuade you to travel back with me on this.'

I could only stare.

'Stupid, I know.' He was looking at his feet now. 'I mean, you've probably got loads of luggage with you and ... well, I didn't even know if you were here on your own. I'm sorry; you must think I'm a complete idiot.'

'But – you don't even know where I live.' I couldn't think of anything more sensible to say.

'London, isn't it?' Kit looked into my eyes again, like a man who's laid all his cards on the table and has nothing left to lose.

Silence. Nothing but frantic birdsong. I contemplated this man I hardly knew. Was he a liar? A madman? Or was he really so desperate to see me again?

'Let me get this straight,' I said. 'You were not invited to this wedding, but you have gatecrashed it because you knew I would be here. You gambled on my being here alone and being sufficiently pleased to see you that I would invite you to share the room that you were gambling I would have booked.' Even to myself, I was sounding like something from a courtroom drama. 'You even borrowed a Ducati and rode it all the way here, gambling again that I would be impressed and that I would choose to travel back to London on the back of a motorbike, instead of in the comfortable sleeper compartment I have already booked.'

'Yes,' Kit muttered gruffly, now looking exactly like a naughty schoolboy in the headmaster's office.

'And you expect me to believe that, do you?' I asked him sternly.

'No, of course not,' he said. 'That's why I wasn't going to tell you. How was I to know you were a mistress of cross-examination?'

I laughed. What else could I do? If Kit was a madman, he was the most attractive madman I was ever likely to meet, and if he was a stalker, he was a stalker with a Ducati. There was only one sensible course of action.

'Right then,' I told him, 'I'm coming back to London with you on two conditions – one, we get me some

71

proper leathers and, two, we stop off at some deserted place where I get to ride the bike. OK?'

It was Kit's turn to look incredulous. 'After all that, you're going to do it?'

'Well, make your mind up, Kit. I thought that was what you wanted.'

He kissed me in reply, then started fiddling with the bike's panniers.

'I'm hoping condition one won't be a problem,' he said, bringing out a leather suit, similar to his but noticeably smaller.

'Oh, right, and you bought a leather suit, gambling that it would be my size,' I said sarcastically.

'Borrowed, not bought,' Kit corrected me, holding it up against me. 'And I did bring a couple in case I had misremembered your proportions.' He flashed me a dirty grin. 'Now, let's get back to that castle and see if we can sort out the rooms.'

We pulled up on the gravel again just as people were starting to move into the banqueting hall for the wedding breakfast. I've never been able to understand why it's called a breakfast, when you invariably don't get it till early afternoon. That bacon roll seemed a long time ago, and after all the excitement I was starving, but I did feel we ought to wash our faces before going in, to remove the grime of the road. In the ladies I met Jane, who had been enthusiastically covering for me on champagne-drinking duties and was twinkling wickedly.

'Been shagging in a layby somewhere?' she enquired.

'No, but we've got a room problem,' I replied. As I explained, she looked as disbelieving as I had felt, but Jane is too wise to offer friendly advice when she knows it will be ignored anyway, and simply promised that we'd sort something out after we'd eaten.

72

Then I had a sudden horrible thought. 'It's not a sit-down dinner, is it?' I asked Jane, 'because Kit won't have a place. He's not even invited.'

Now Jane was giggling in disbelief. 'Ooh, Emma's lost her heart to the leather-clad gatecrasher,' she sang drunkenly to a tune of her own devising. 'So romantic – like Marlon Brando in *The Wild One*.'

Being the sober one of us, I felt it my duty to respond in a mature manner. 'Piss off,' I told her as we left the ladies.

Our luck held – it was a sit-down dinner, but one where you help yourself from the buffet and find your own seat, so Kit passed inconspicuously. I could see Eric eyeing him curiously but, as the groom, he had too much to do to come over and quiz me. Jane had a young man on each side of her, but I knew her well enough to see that she was only flirting for the sake of it, not out of real interest. I scanned the room – I could usually spot the man that Jane would go for at any gathering, but here there were a couple of possibilities. Part of me wanted her to get off with someone just so I could have our room, but I knew she would probably be looking for a one-night stand if only to boost her ego on Eric's wedding night. They might have made their peace, but it's still a difficult moment for any ex-lover.

It was strange sitting next to Kit, being to outward appearances a couple yet knowing so little about each other. I wanted to ask him all sorts of things, but I knew it would look odd if I was asking this man about his job and where he lived, when he was supposedly here as my partner. I mean, you don't normally bring a casual squeeze to a wedding with you. I picked up what I could from what he said to other people. When college friends came over to talk, I introduced Kit and let him answer their questions.

He was working as a freelance journalist, writing

for any paper or magazine that would commission him. He lived in London, off Brick Lane in the East End. He was doing a good job, though, of turning people's questions back on themselves, so they wouldn't spot how little he knew about me. I felt like a spy, trying to keep my cover from being blown. I listened hard to Kit's replies, making sure we kept our stories straight. He was very good – he didn't actually lie, even when people asked him how we'd met ('through Emma's cousin') and how long we'd been together ('not that long . . . not sick of each other yet, are we, love?'). I found myself slipping into the pretend world where we were a couple who had come to a wedding together like normal couples do. 'So did you both come up on the bike?' someone asked me. 'Oh no,' I replied glibly, 'Kit was working, so I came up on the train and he met me here. We're going back on the bike, though.' I caught a little glow in Kit's smile at me.

Since university, where I'd seen too many of my friends lose hold on their course and even career because a relationship was going too badly – or too well – I'd steered clear of too much involvement. Someone like Geoff was perfect for me – a good friend, but no strings and no expectations on either side. One of the reasons people were so interested in Kit was that they had probably never known me with anyone that I was serious about – serious enough to bring to a wedding. I felt a bit of a fraud, but I was also enjoying myself playing at couples. What would it be like, I wondered, having someone who would say, 'What shall we get as a wedding present, dear?' I sniggered at the thought.

It was strange, too, coming into a wedding breakfast sober. Normally I have managed to down at least a couple of glasses of champagne on an empty stomach, and go through the whole thing in an alcoholic haze.

74

I've even been known, when summoned to a particularly traumatic wedding, to take a hip flask and be reeking of brandy before the ceremony was over. This time, although I was drinking wine with the food, I was still way behind most of the other guests. For the first time since my early teens I was able to listen to the speeches and notice who laughed at which bits. Jane – now drunk enough for two – laughed particularly loudly every time the best man referred to Eric's shady past – I couldn't quite tell whether she was laughing because she was involved or because she found the scenarios too unbelievable.

As the speeches ended and the party began to dissolve into general drinking and chat, I looked at Jane and realised she was not in a fit state to negotiate room bookings. I was on my own with this one and, after whispering 'I'm just going to see if our room is ready, dear' in Kit's ear, I slipped out.

As I had feared, the place was booked solid. The desk clerk was sympathetic to my story – there'd been a mistake on the form and 'one twin' should have read 'one single and a double' – but said she had nothing at all. What were we going to do? We couldn't even head off and look for a B&B till Kit had sobered up; in any case, there was an evening party that I ought not to miss. Could we really gamble on Jane making other arrangements for herself and not coming in search of her toothbrush at an inopportune moment?

As I was hovering by the desk in indecision, Michael came past. 'Everything all right, Emma?' he asked cheerily.

'Not quite,' I answered.

He seemed to feel it was his responsibility to look after the guests' accommodation and listened to my explanation, biting his lip with concern. He really was a sweetheart.

'Well, I know everything's booked up,' he agreed, 'but I also know that some people aren't planning to stay the night. Some of the Scottish relatives are going to drive home after the evening do. Let's see . . .' He leant over the desk and examined the bookings. 'Uncle George and Auntie Bella,' he cried triumphantly. 'They were asking me just now how early they could leave, and they're planning to be packed and ready to go before the party even starts, so their room will be clear for tonight.' He smiled at the clerk. 'I'm sure you'd be able to have the sheets changed, wouldn't you?'

I don't know if it was Michael's charm or relief at having her problem solved, but she said it would be no problem at all and she'd see it was done during the party.

I went back to Kit, very relieved. He was listening to one of Philippa's relatives, who seemed to be telling him about her youthful exploits as a despatch motorcyclist in World War Two. Funny how the sight of one biker seems to bring all the others out of the woodwork. 'Great big heavy things they were,' she was saying, 'not like the bikes today. If it fell over, I'd have to go and ask some nice man to help me pick it up. I remember once, I parked it in a country lane, next to a ditch, and when I came back from delivering my message it had gone! Slid into the ditch, it had. Well, there was nobody around, not for miles, and I knew I couldn't lift it out; the ditch was six feet deep! So do you know what I did?' Kit shook his head, taking my hand as I sat beside him and squeezing it. 'I rode it out!' She was shaking with laughter. 'I looked around, nothing was coming, so I jumped on it, started it up and rode it straight up the side of that ditch! Ooh, I was muddy when I got back to the base. But I couldn't tell them why. If they knew what had happened, I was worried they'd take me off the bikes and put me on to driving lorries.'

'Looks like we've got a room for tonight,' I murmured to Kit when our storyteller was briefly distracted and I could get a word in his ear.

'Great. Can we go there now?' he asked, his golden-brown eyes fixed on mine.

'Oh no,' I answered. 'It's ours, but not till after the party.'

Our eyes held a silent conversation. Would we ever really be alone together? Would we ever be able to relax together, to take our clothes off, lie on a bed and take our time? We were starting to feel like teenagers, grabbing a quick fumble when the grown-ups weren't looking. It's true, the reckless urgency of our initial encounter had added to the piquancy; but now we had both acknowledged that there might be more between us. Yet another enforced wait was starting to be frustrating.

Nothing to be done, however. Until tonight, we would have to play the happy couple. Perhaps, in the lull between dinner and the start of the evening festivities, we could at least find somewhere quiet for a conversation. Kit went in search of another bottle and Jane appeared to see how I was getting on. 'Don't worry about the room,' I told her, 'they've found us somewhere for tonight.'

'Oh good. Good, good, good.' She was very, very drunk.

'So don't feel obliged on my account to spend the night in somebody else's bed,' I added.

She put on a mock-disappointed face. 'I wouldn't have minded, just to help you out,' she insisted.

'Did you have anyone in mind?' I probed. She smirked knowingly.

Kit came back with a bottle of champagne. 'You're good at this, aren't you?' I said, as I took the bottle and poured myself another glass. 'Do you gatecrash a lot of weddings?'

'All the time,' he answered dryly.

'We gatecrashed that wedding once, didn't we?' Jane slurred as she reached across for the alcohol she so obviously didn't need. 'You remember – that hotel in Cambridge.'

It was true. When we were both students we had been on our way to dinner at a friend's house when Jane had discovered she needed cigarettes. Dropping into the nearest hotel, we'd been directed to the bar to find a wedding reception in full swing and waiters offering pink champagne to everyone. We weren't as dressed up as most of the people there, but we looked pretty close to some of the younger ones, and by the time Jane had bought her fags, I had a glass and was the life and soul of the party. We never got to our dinner, I'm sorry to say, because we stayed at the reception for hours. We only left when Jane, who had dragged some young man outside for a snog, fell in the river and had to be rescued by the groom in full white tie and tails. I think he was a lord as well. That was the night that really cemented our friendship; she never forgot that I had stayed to get her home and dried off, instead of sneaking away in the darkness to avoid embarrassment.

So that was the story Jane told Kit, although it was much longer and more rambling the way she told it, and she slightly exaggerated my heroism, making it sound as if I had waded in, not just stood on the bank and lent her my coat. Good old Jane – she knows when to talk you up to a new man. I knew the story already, of course, and I was much more interested in watching Michael, who had just come into the room and seemed to be looking for someone. He trotted over to me, and told me again about Uncle George's room. Why was he being so attentive?

78

Of course – as Jane turned her blue eyes in his direction and shot him one of her laser looks it all became clear. Once free of the burden of the Eric thing, she had noticed Michael's youthful charms and his wide-eyed adoration. Even without the added satisfaction of bedding Eric's brother, she could do a lot worse for herself. Sensing the moment for a tactful retreat, I stood up and Kit followed me out.

As I had hoped, many of the guests had retired for a rest and perhaps to change out of their formal clothes. The garden was almost empty, and we easily found a bench with another stunning view over the hills. For the first time, Kit and I were able just to talk, the urgency of our desire abated by the promise of time and privacy later on. We talked about his job, my job, our respective areas of London, films, music: all the normal things that boy and girl are meant to talk about, usually before they have illicit outdoor sex, but better late than never.

The only thing we didn't talk about was Kit being here, like this, just to see me. That was too strange, too scary. Maybe it was a story he'd made up to conceal some other agenda, but – what if it were true? If, after that one meeting at Sarah's wedding, he had come here to see me again, risked riding all the way up to Scotland and being rejected, having to ride all the way home ... it was flattering, yes, but intimidating as well. Or was it just a good excuse for a long run on a nice bike? I didn't want to think about it now.

The sun swept lower and lower across the garden as we talked. Kit was easy to talk to; bright, funny, but not afraid to be serious. In no time we were covering trickier areas such as family and politics. We watched the sun set in glorious crimson and tangerine, but felt no impulse to move till the evening breeze made me shiver. Even then it was Kit who said, 'Come on, you're freezing. Let's go in and warm up.' As we walked back up to the castle he put his arm around me in such an easy way; I couldn't believe that before today I'd met him only once.

Having no room to retreat to, we wandered back into the hall. Beneath the minstrel's gallery instruments and a drum-kit were being set up, and the tables had been cleared to the edge of the room to leave space for dancing. 'Looks like there's going to be a band,' I said to Kit.

'Yes,' he replied, 'I know.'

At that moment, a gorgeous woman in a black trouser-suit appeared from the minstrel's gallery and came down the stairs to the stage. As she looked up, saw Kit and me and smiled a secret smile, I recognised the singer from Sarah's wedding.

'It's the same band!' I said.

'That's right,' said Kit, sliding an arm around me, 'how did you think I'd found you?' Sure enough, the singer was coming straight across towards us.

'Hi, Kit,' she greeted him. Even without the make-up and the frock, she was a stunningly attractive woman.

'Hi, Cassandra,' Kit replied. 'This is Emma.' It was the first time I had heard him speak my name.

'Hello Emma.' She stretched out a hand to shake mine.

'Hello.' I took her hand. It was cool and smooth, the nails perfectly manicured. I felt dowdy beside her.

'I'll see you later,' she said as she moved away. 'I have to get these chaps to do a sound check before the revellers return.'

Now I was really thrown. So Kit knew the singer? Even so, how had she known I would be here? And what had he said to her about me? All this, added to the fact that I felt grubby and plain next to her, made me feel a little insecure. As if reading my mind, Kit slid his other arm to encircle me and said

'Cassandra and I are old schoolfriends. Robin first met Sarah when I took him to one of her gigs. That's why Sarah wanted the band at their wedding. Like all old friends who'll never sleep together, we have very few secrets.'

I relaxed slightly. Even if he was only saying it to keep me quiet, the fact he'd noticed my unease was surely a good sign.

We made ourselves scarce while the band sound-checked, Kit having assured me that if we stayed a combination of self-consciousness and showing-off would mean it took twice as long. 'But the bar staff are still there,' I'd protested, as he pushed me out of the door.

'They don't count,' Kit told me firmly. 'At a wedding the band and the bar staff are in the same boat. They're all treated like servants, or so Cassandra tells me.' I couldn't imagine anyone treating Cassandra like a servant, even having seen her stomping through the mud in her clogs.

We met Jane, who was coming down the stairs with a smug expression and a stunned-looking Michael in tow. She'd clearly lost no time. 'Do you want to use our room to freshen up?' she offered. 'We were just going to listen to the nightingales.' Knowing Jane, that was probably a euphemism for something young Michael had never dreamt of in his wildest fantasies. I jumped at the chance of a wash-and-brush-up, though, and took the key she was waving. 'You've got half an hour,' was her parting shot.

We locked the door behind us, alone at last, however briefly. I couldn't quite believe it and stood at a loss in the middle of the room. Kit was more decisive. Pausing only to draw the curtains, he immediately began to remove my clothes, as if this might be the last half-hour we would ever have. He didn't even kiss me, but quickly and surely unbuttoned and unzipped me, pulling my arms free of sleeves and straps. I stood passive, suddenly shy now that we had real privacy. We scarcely knew each other and had never seen each other naked. I let him undress me, offering no resistance and no help. My very passivity seemed to spur him on.

When I stood naked before him, he stepped back, as if to take in my whole figure at once. 'God,' he said under his breath, 'you look fantastic.' He threw his own clothes off – there is no other word for it – and was upon me, those long, cool fingers running all over my skin, kissing me deeply, letting his mouth range over my shoulders, my breasts, my neck. I could feel his long, smooth cock brushing against me, and I was overtaken by that same urgency we had felt in the dark garden that first night. This time it was I who took hold of his prick and slid it into me, so we stood once again united, held together by his penetrating me, clutching each other so as not to topple over. Without that friendly tree to support me, I was only keeping my balance by holding on to him, and he to me. For a few moments we clung together, frantic, precarious, drowning and falling at the same time.

Kit pulled out of me and half-pushed me towards the wall, placing my hands either side of a tall mirror, so I was supporting myself. I could see my full length reflected, flushed with excitement, breasts swinging gently and nipples erect, a tiny glistening of moisture behind my pubic hair. Behind me, Kit's face was congested with arousal. I watched as one of his hands slipped across my belly and down to part the fine copper hairs, holding me open as he slid himself into me from behind. Holding me back against his thrusts with that hand, he used the other to brace himself against the wall. We were both watching ourselves as he fucked me fast and urgently, my breasts rocking in time with his thrusts, his prick just visible where it was sliding in and out of me, shiny with my juices. Eyes half closed, he was kissing the side of my neck, taking little locks of my hair in his teeth and pulling my head back towards him.

My legs were planted slightly apart and my back was arched to allow him full access to my deepest parts. I could feel him pounding at my cervix, pulling his full length out and then ramming it back up to the hilt. His hand was still on me, his finger rubbing gently against my clit, so with every thrust I got a double sensation, strong and subtle. I was so excited, after all this anticipation, I felt my orgasm building inside me like a storm. I was watching myself get carried away, watching the excitement overtake me, and the watching was only increasing my excitement. I started to make rhythmic sounds, and Kit whispered, 'That's it, come now, come for me now, come on, Emma, you want to watch yourself come . . .'

Orgasm washed through me like a tidal wave. My whole body was shaking, my hands slipping down the wall till Kit caught one of them and held it there. I saw myself climax, my body arching involuntarily, and my cunt contracting around Kit's prick. Watching me, he increased his own thrusts, losing all control as he plunged into me, holding me steady with that hand, his eyes locked on mine in the mirror as he too came, quivering with release.

My arms gave way and I leant forward against the mirror, its glass a welcome coolness to my fevered skin. Kit rested against me for a moment, then lifted his head to lick away a drop of sweat that was trickling cold down my back. 'Mm, salty,' he murmured. 'Have we got time for a shower, do you think?'

'I can't go anywhere without one,' I replied. We staggered into the bathroom. Luckily, whatever Jane had got up to with Michael, she had left us some clean towels. Kit started the shower, stood beneath it and stretched out a hand to me.

The shower was perfect – hot and powerful. I shut my eyes and enjoyed every sensation as Kit shampooed my hair, working his powerful fingers through to the roots, and then rinsed it clean. Then he worked his way down my body, rubbing the shower gel up to a lather with unhurried strokes, as if he were enjoying every square inch of my skin. I was still humming from our intense fuck and my skin was so sensitive that every touch was like a kiss. I was running my fingers all over him too, enjoying my first opportunity to explore him without clothes.

He was slim, but not skinny, with the muscles of a man who doesn't work out but is not afraid to lift something as heavy as a motorbike. A few curls of brown hair lay in the centre of his chest, with a light scattering spreading out and a distinct line going down to where his cock was nestling in its own dark curls. With his wet hair plastered to his face he looked somehow younger, more vulnerable perhaps.

Our wet, soapy bodies slithered over each other. The novelty of full-body contact was unbelievably exciting: we couldn't get enough of it. Amazingly, I felt Kit's cock stir and start to swell again, as it was pressed against my slippery belly. I rubbed myself against him deliberately, and felt an answering rush as it lifted itself up and pushed against me like a hungry animal. I slid down to my knees, my breasts pressing slickly against his prick as I moved, and took the end in my mouth.

The water cascaded over my head and face as I sucked, running down my body and Kit's legs. He tasted clean, almost soapy, and felt as smooth as polished wood. I took him deep in my mouth, as deep as I could, till he was almost completely inside me. The feel of him filling me, nudging at the back of my throat, was deeply exciting. I sucked gently, running my tongue along the underside, and looked up at Kit's face. He was half-leaning against the wall, his hand on the shower-head to maintain his balance, a look of curious fascination on his face. As I suckled on his cock I ran my fingers through the hair on his balls, lifting and squeezing them softly. He said something I couldn't make out, because of the noise of the shower, something that could have been 'Oh God,' or 'Don't stop . . .'

I changed my rhythm, now slowly sucking his length into my mouth, now pumping my lips up and down it fast, as if I were fucking him. I could feel his buttocks tense with excitement in my hand, as I ran it over their soapy curves. Kit's eyes were closed now, his lips were slightly parted and his hands were flat on the tiled wall, as if he were trying to hold still. I intensified my movements, feeling the answering throb in his balls as his orgasm drew closer.

Suddenly I heard an insistent knocking at the room door. Jane's voice was clearly audible over the running water. 'Emma! Emma!' she was shouting. 'Let me in; I know you're there!' Our half-hour must have been up, but I was going nowhere, not till I'd given Kit the same kind of pleasure he had given me.

I felt Kit's spine stiffen, and I slipped one soapy finger into his arse. His spunk exploded into my mouth as he came, unable to stop himself thrusting into me. It ran, hot and salty, into my throat and spilled down my chin, mingling with the warm water. He knelt beside me, kissing me, tasting his own come on my lips and tongue, the water running off our faces.

Jane was still shouting outside. Reluctantly, we turned off the shower and pulled on the soft cotton bathrobes. While Kit dressed in the bathroom, I unlocked the door to admit Jane. She gave me an accusing look. 'Sorry.' I brazened it out. 'We were in the shower. Had you been knocking long?'

'Hmmmph,' was her only response. Kit emerged, clothed if a bit rumpled, and I took the opportunity to slip away and get dressed myself.

Chapter Six
And the Band Played On

*I*emerged to find Jane and Kit ransacking the mini-bar. 'If we don't drink it now,' Jane explained cheer-fully, 'I'll only drink it later when I don't really need it and be sorry in the morning.' Indisputable logic, as usual. By the time we descended the oak staircase as a slightly tipsy trio, the band were in full swing.

Cassandra was a star, there was no doubt about it. Armed with a radio mike, she was able to leave her band playing on stage and make forays into the audi-ence, to the delight and terror of the male guests. Balding old men and spotty youths all blushed and squirmed as she sang her way towards them, fixing them with a look that seemed to pin them like a butterfly to a card. One or two of the drunker ones seemed to believe they might actually be in with a chance, but the look in her eye told us that was pure fantasy on their part.

'Shall we dance?' Kit invited me gallantly, offering his hand. As I took it, he placed the other lightly on my hip and led me expertly in the first few steps. Of course – if Cassandra was an old friend of his, he must have had plenty of practice in dancing to her music. I relaxed and let my body follow his around the floor, my mind drifting back to our last – and first – meeting, when our dance looked set to be the only contact our bodies would ever enjoy. Dancing to the same band, the same music, but how different I had felt, expecting those minutes to be the last we'd ever spend together. Now I felt as if we'd known each other for ever, the bonds of conspiracy as well as passion binding us together. We had spent all day pretending to be a couple, so it was not surprising if we were starting to feel like one.

Kit pulled me closer, so my cheek brushed the coarse weave of his jacket, and I felt his warm breath in my hair. I suppose I should have been thinking about what it all meant, his coming here, the ludicrous story about the motorbike, but I wasn't thinking at all. I was just enjoying the music and the feeling of sharing this dance with the man I'd never expected to see again.

The song ended and Cassandra spoke into her mike, but not to announce the next number. It was to welcome 'the happy couple'. All the dancing pairs, and the drinking guests along the bar, applauded as Philippa and Eric made their entrance. I was afraid we were in for more speeches when all I wanted to do was dance, but the band launched almost immediately into a fast dance tune, and Eric did the right thing by leading his bride into the centre of the dance floor. We all moved out to give them room, and it was just as well. This was clearly not their type of music.

As I watched Eric strut his stuff, I was reminded that his short period of musicianhood had been spent as axeman in the band then known as Longships Landing. It was more famous for Eric's long blond hair and the horned helmet he insisted on wearing on stage than for any rhythmic or melodic qualities. He seemed to be trying to recreate the Longships Landing's stage show on this dancefloor, as far as I could see. Luckily for him, Philippa had a basic grasp of all-purpose wedding dancing and was holding on to his hand and attempting to impart some pattern to his movements.

But what did it matter? Nobody goes to a wedding to see how well the bridegroom can dance. We were all dancing with gusto, and when Cassandra told us the band were taking a break, there were genuine moans of disappointment. Michael came over to tell me that our room was being prepared at this moment, and that they were making a special effort to compensate us for the wait, but before he could finish his sentence Jane had scooped him up and dragged him into a corner.

The buffet was uncovered and perspiring dancers thronged around it, but as we tried to join them we were intercepted by Eric. 'Emma!' he cried. 'Having a good time?'

'Lovely, thank you, Eric,' I replied, knowing what was coming next.

Eric turned his attention to Kit.

'And you are . . .?'

'Kit,' came the smooth reply, with a warm smile and a handshake. 'I'm sorry Emma didn't warn you I was coming. We thought I'd be working this weekend, and then –'

'– and then he wasn't.' I finished for him.

Eric looked even more intrigued. Although we weren't the closest of friends he'd presumably been hearing my news through Jane till fairly recently, and Kit had not figured in it, for obvious reasons. Now I had turned up with a tall, handsome stranger, and a bundle of unanswered questions. Was Kit a recent acquisition? A long-standing secret suddenly gone public? I almost wanted to tell him the truth, but I couldn't – after all, it was his wedding that this virtual stranger had gatecrashed in the hope of fucking me again. I felt myself starting to giggle at the thought, and Eric's devious mind smelt a rat. I saw his eyes narrow and I squeezed Kit's hand, bracing us both for the best lying of our life.

Divine intervention saved us: Eric spotted something over my shoulder that seemed to wipe me from his mind. A look of shock appeared on his face and was instantly suppressed. I followed his eye-line: on a bench behind me, Michael was sitting with Jane on top of him. She looked as if she were pinning him to the seat and devouring him whole. His head thrown back, he was prostrate beneath her, his hands on her breasts as if a feeble attempt to push her off had somehow mutated into caresses. Good old Jane. What timing – if she had set out to save me she couldn't have done it better, and there was a deeply satisfying natural justice about it.

'Ah, yes,' I said, turning back to Eric, who was still transfixed, 'Jane does seem to be getting on very well with your little brother. It's sweet, isn't it?' He couldn't answer. 'After all,' I continued mercilessly, 'it's about time Jane found herself a decent bloke – one who won't mess her around. I've always thought she deserved better – haven't you?' Eric gurgled something noncommittal and staggered off towards the bar.

Kit watched him go. 'I guess there's a story there,' was all he said.

As we finally sat down with plates of food, I noticed that the band seemed to have vanished altogether. 'It's always like that,' Kit explained with a mouth full of tiger prawn. 'Like I said, the band at a wedding aren't treated like stars – they're part of the staff. You wouldn't expect to see the girls who laid the tables eating with us, would you?' I'd never thought about it before, but it did seem a bit unfair; one minute applauding the band and the next minute expecting them to make themselves scarce. 'Anyway,' Kit continued, 'on the whole they prefer it that way. Gives them a chance to stop being on their best behaviour.' I followed his pointing finger, and caught a glimpse of one of the musicians disappearing on to the minstrel's gallery with more bottles of beer than a normal person with two hands could ever carry. He vanished behind the carved rood screen, behind which all the musicians were presumably relaxing.

Somehow, knowing that we had a room waiting for us, a whole night together in our own bed behind a locked door, meant that we could stay and enjoy the party without feeling any pressure to rush away. I even abandoned Kit for long enough to dance with Eric, holding him firmly in both hands and pushing him around the floor like a rod puppet to avoid injury to other dancers. He was too preoccupied to resume his questions, constantly looking over my shoulder to see where Jane and Michael had got to. Kit was twirling one of the little bridesmaids around the floor and in no time was disappearing under a delighted heap of little girls, all demanding their turn to be 'twizzled'.

As I rejoined Kit, I noticed that Cassandra was leaving the stage and ascending the stairs to the gallery again. 'She's not finished, has she?' I shouted over the band, who seemed to be playing on regardless.

'Don't worry,' Kit shouted back, 'she'll just be getting changed. She told me she likes to do a minimum of three frocks for a posh wedding.'

Over the carved rood screen we could just see her head, as she presumably struggled out of one sequinned creation and into another. Without her, the band were keeping us busy with up-tempo tunes, and soon I had to admit defeat.

'Got to take a breather,' I shouted, and dodged between the sweaty bodies to a bench. Kit tried to follow, but the bridesmaids' ambush was too quick for him and, when I turned to sit down, I saw him back on twizzling duty.

As I leant my head against the wall, a movement caught my eye, a pale flash on the gallery. Cassandra changing, I thought, but something made me look again. That was Cassandra all right, but not changing. Behind her dark hair was another, blond head. Through the carved holes piercing the wooden screen I could see glimpses of naked flesh, and whoever was behind her was doing more than unzip her frock. I was fascinated. Cassandra, the distant, unattainable, glamorous figure of fantasy, was actually getting up to something. What was more, she was doing it in the middle of one of her own gigs, and effectively in the same room.

I felt like a voyeur, but I couldn't help myself. The very concealment offered by the screen made the sight more exciting than if I'd caught her in full view. There was no doubt what was going on, but she was keeping her cool very impressively. As I watched, Cassandra rested a hand lightly on the dark wood, steadying herself. What was he doing, her mysterious blond? His head had disappeared from view, but I could see flashes of his skin, visibly darker than hers. It was too far, and too shadowy, to make out specifics, but my imagination was filling in what was hidden from my view. He was still behind her, I thought; was he kneeling behind her, licking at her, cupping his hands over the gorgeous curves of her hips? No – his head reappeared over her shoulder, and she turned to face him, a smile on those scarlet lips.

Whatever he was doing now, his head dipped out of sight, made her throw her head back with pleasure, so her black glossy hair fell behind her, covering the wood and the pinholes of pale skin. She stretched her long, graceful arms along the top of the screen, her fingertips barely touching the intricate wooden leaves and grapes, as if their cool smoothness was giving her as much pleasure as her invisible lover. I pictured him lifting her full breasts to his mouth, pressing them together to form a dark crack, into which he would plunge his tongue, sucking on her nipples, which I imagined as pink and rosy. Or was he already giving her more intimate caresses? Was he burrowing beneath her pubic hair, dark like her long tresses, flicking his tongue to send the shivers of pleasure that were making her bare shoulders flicker? I was becoming aroused at the thought, impulses shooting through my own sex, echoing the ones I was imagining for Cassandra.

'Are you all right?' I had not even noticed Kit arriving beside me. I nodded, but I couldn't drag my eyes away from the tantalising scene above. He followed my eye up.

'It's Cassandra,' I said softly. 'She's got someone up there.' Kit said nothing, but his hand around my waist began stroking my stomach, slowly, lightly, in time with the tiny movements of Cassandra's head and neck, which were all that betrayed her illicit pleasure. As I watched, captivated, his other hand found my bare forearm and his thumb slipped into the crease of my elbow, taking up the same slow stroking. The light caresses only increased my sensation of being hypnotised. My body was not my own, but a reflection of Cassandra's, feeling what she was feeling, and all I could do was watch her.

Like warm water flowing over my skin, Kit's fingers were calling my whole body to life; not just my sex, but my neck, my feet, all were tingling with excitement. I couldn't move, not till I'd seen Cassandra reach the climax of her secret adventure. The blond head reappeared, half-hidden behind hers, his tanned arms covering hers as he kissed her, veiled by her dark hair. Then he slid his hands along her arms, round her slender neck, and lifted the full opulence of her hair, revealing both her white nape and the glimpses of her body through the screen. As he kissed her, he let the curtain of her hair fall over them both, so both heads disappeared beneath its waves. I saw her arms lift, as if suddenly weightless, and she seemed to throw them around her partner's neck. 'He's entered her,' I thought, feeling the answering squeeze in my own pussy.

It was impossible to see, from the tiny scraps of pale and brown skin visible between the wood, what exactly was happening, but my body was mirroring hers, my mind supplying all the images my eye could not. He had lifted her full hips, so her legs twined around his, the white smooth ones wrapping around the darker, hairy ones. Her fine toes, nails painted red to match her fingernails, were digging into the firm muscle of his calves. Pressing her against the carvings, so her soft flesh would bear the impression of them, he was fucking her, her moisture running down over his balls, her breasts pressed against his chest. She raised her face from his, her head rocking with his thrusts. Perhaps she cried out – over the music her band was playing, it would have been impossible to hear. Then she went soft, as if released, and her arms slid down from her lover's neck.

For the first time, I was able to draw my eyes away, and I turned to see Kit looking at me. He looked as excited as I felt. 'Did you enjoy watching her?' He asked me softly.

I nodded. 'Did you?'

'I wasn't watching her,' he replied, 'I was watching you.' He took my face in both his hands and kissed me fiercely. 'Let's go to our room now,' he whispered.

'Won't Cassandra mind if we miss her third frock?' I asked.

94

He shook his head, grinning. 'No, she knows what I'm here for,' he answered. 'Anyway, it's partly her fault, isn't it?' We almost ran up the uneven wooden staircase to our room, Kit's hand holding mine as if he were afraid I'd slip out of his grasp.

The room was worth the wait. In a hearth as big as a four-poster bed, a wood fire was blazing, and along the mantelpiece – which was nearly as high as me – a dozen candles were burning in iron candlesticks. They certainly had made a special effort. A little upright sofa in slightly threadbare brocade faced the fire across a sheepskin rug, and on a side table a plate of short-bread and a half-bottle of malt whisky reminded us we were in a Scottish hotel. The bed itself was no less magnificent, its canopy draped heavily with dark-gold curtains and its white linen sheet turned down to expose a pile of white pillows.

'Wow!' Kit was impressed. 'If this is ours, I'd like to see what the honeymoon suite looks like. And so would you, wouldn't you, my little voyeur?' he said, picking me up and laying me across the bed. 'You'd like to watch them, the bride and groom, on their wedding night.' As he spoke, he was peeling off my clothes, and I was tugging at his, images of Cassandra still resonating in my brain. 'You could hide in the wardrobe,' he continued, sliding my silk knickers down my legs and turning me over to unfasten my bra. 'What would you see through the crack in the door? Your friend Eric, tearing his new wife's clothes off like this.'

He lay on top of me, now as naked as I was. His weight was pinning me down, pressing me into the softness of the quilt, so I was held between the cool bedcover against my breasts and belly, and the heat of his skin on my back. His hands found mine and stretched them out past my head, till they found the curve where the far edge of the bed fell away. His breath was hot in my ear.

'Eric,' he whispered, barely audible, 'alone at last with his wife, not knowing you're there, watching them. Thinking, "At last she's mine. She's my wife, and I'm going to fuck her." Holding her down, anticipating the moment . . .' Kit's breathing, like mine, was getting quicker, more excited. He pushed his knees between mine, forcing my legs apart. 'Waiting for the moment when he's going to fuck her.' As he said it, Kit pushed himself into me, one hard stroke that entered me up to the hilt. I let out a sob of abandonment, half-muffled by the bedding against my face.

Kit was holding the edge of the bed, thrusting into me as if he wanted to pin me to the bed with his cock. 'Go on, close your eyes, imagine them,' he was growling, 'Can you see them there? Can you see him fucking her?'

I could see them. In spite of myself, in spite of Eric being my old college buddy, in spite of my loyalty to Jane, my mind was full of the pictures of Eric and Philippa. I was feeling Kit, frantic with desire, ramming his cock into me, mashing my clit against his hand, but I was seeing Eric, his fair hair plastered to his face with sweat, his stocky, muscular body arched over Philippa's. I saw her spread-eagled on the bed as Eric held her arms outstretched and looked down at her round breasts shaking in time with his thrusts. I saw his cock disappearing into her, emerging shiny with her juices only to plunge in again.

'Can you see them?' Kit was shouting at me now. 'Can you see them?'

'Yes, yes!' I cried out as I came, seeing even at the moment of orgasm Philippa's eyes closing as Eric pumped himself into her.

As he felt me go limp, Kit pulled swiftly out of me and rolled me over, kneeling above me on the bed and looking down at my face. 'Jesus,' he said softly, 'is there no line you won't cross?'

I looked up at him. 'Not so far,' I answered simply. We stayed like that for a moment, looking at each other, each wondering what the other was going to do next. Then he threw himself back on to me, pulling my hips up towards him as he entered me once more, his mouth seeking mine.

We were almost wrestling, rolling over each other, trying to get him deeper inside me, trying to get right inside each other's bodies. Kit was pulling my legs so far apart I thought I was going to break in half, and I was digging my nails into his buttocks, pulling him into me as he fucked me, our faces wet with each other's spit, sliding over ourselves. Our kisses were getting nearer to bites, but the stabs of pain only seemed to add to the excitement. I rolled Kit on to his back so I was astride him, fucking him for a change, and he slapped my buttock hard. The sting of it made my pussy contract with shock, and then a new level of arousal seemed to kick in.

We didn't hold any position for more than a few seconds but, no matter what angle Kit was fucking me from, we kept up the same urgent speed. No pictures of anyone else now, it was just the two of us on this bed; Kit's hair whipping across my face as he pulled me on to my back, the grip of his fingers on my thighs as he pushed my legs apart, the clean acid smell of his sweat. I was thrust backwards into the pile of pillows, Kit held on to the bedpost as he thrust into me, and at last we came, drenched with sweat, trembling with exhaustion, and lay still.

Kit rolled aside, pulled a stray pillow under his head and watched me again. There was no other word for it, this serious regard, this attentive look he had given me before. 'You see,' he said, as if this explained everything, 'this is why I had to come.' I was tempted to make a joke, to laugh about him being so desperate he had to come four hundred miles to get a good shag, but for once I held my tongue: I knew that wasn't what he meant. So instead, I watched him right back.

'What do you mean?' I asked him, thinking 'don't give me that "love at first sight" shit.'

'I had this feeling about you, the first time we met.' He spoke calmly, as if he were talking about finding a common interest in football. 'I didn't feel any fear in you, any sense of holding back. I had this idea that you would say yes to whatever life offered you. But I wasn't sure.' His honey-coloured eyes were steady on mine, but he lay motionless beside me. 'It could have been the alcohol,' he went on. 'It could have been a moment of madness before you went and married an estate agent.'

Lying there, on that white bed in that candle-lit room, listening to Kit talking this way, I felt a sudden relief. I felt like a traveller in a foreign country, who arrives in a town where distant relatives are rumoured to be living and suddenly hears someone shout their name across the street. I felt as if someone had recognised me.

'It's not a romantic fantasy, or just an erotic fixation. I had to find out,' he was saying. 'Of all the women I'd ever met, were you really the only one who was not afraid of life.'

I put a hand to my face to wipe away the sweat that was dripping off and found, to my amazement, that my cheeks were wet with tears. Kit reached out a finger and wiped them away, and then he drew me into his arms. 'It's all right,' he whispered to me, 'it's all right. It's our secret. I won't tell anyone. It doesn't mean you owe me anything. I just had to know.'

Chapter Seven
The Devil Rides Out

We must have drifted into sleep, because I awoke from a disturbing dream to find the room almost dark, lit only by the red glow of embers in the fireplace. Kit was standing over the fire but, hearing me stir, looked across and said, 'I'm just trying to find some more candles.' I was shivering with a sudden chill, my body still damp with the sweat that was soaking the sheets beneath me.

'Cold?' he asked.

'Yes, suddenly,' I replied. The fire flared up, big yellow flames lighting up Kit's naked body.

Instantly, I was back in my dream, a dream in which Kit was the devil, come to steal my soul. In the dream we had been riding together on a motorbike that became a huge black horse with fiery eyes, galloping across a landscape in flames. We kept passing people I knew, who were calling out to us. 'I must get off,' I kept saying to the Kit-devil, 'I must help them,' but he only smiled and lashed the horse onward, faster and faster. I tried to slip off, but found I was tied to the horse, sharp leather thongs cutting into my ankles and wrists.

'I put the candle-ends on the fire,' said Kit. I must have looked at him blankly, because he added, 'To get it going again. To warm you up.' He smiled, a shy little smile, as if he wasn't sure how I'd take it. He was beautiful, standing in the firelight; he didn't look like the devil at all. I sat up on the bed and shivered again. 'Do you want a bath?' he asked, and I nodded sleepily.

The bathroom was as splendid as the bedroom, a long cast-iron bath in the middle of the blue-tiled floor, and a real bookshelf against the wall. I sat on the edge of the bath as Kit ran hot water and poured in some scented liquid he'd found beside it. I couldn't quite shake off the dark mood of my dream, the unformed fear. There was nothing about him that should have made me feel this apprehension, but it was hovering at the back of my mind. 'There you go,' he said, turning off the taps, and dipping a hand in to test the water. As I stepped in, I steadied myself on his shoulder, and he knelt beside the tub.

The scent of summer flowers rose heavy from the water and the warmth seeped into my bones, easing the tension in my joints. Kit rubbed my back with soap and then worked his way down each arm, pulling gently on my hands and fingers to stretch them out. We were quiet, neither feeling the need to speak, and the only sounds were the creaking of the old plumbing system and the distant bark of some solitary fox. When he had washed me all over, Kit climbed into the bath and sat facing me. Both of us had pulled our knees up and our toes were just touching under the pink-tinged water. I had the feeling he was a little wary of me: perhaps he thought he'd gone too far with his instant assessment of my character. I was still too fuddled to reopen such a deep discussion, so instead I picked up the soap, pulled his feet into my lap and started to wash them.

I don't often pay close attention to anybody's feet, not even my own. Kit's were long and slim, the arches high, but his toes ended with fleshy round pads. I worked my fingers firmly down the lines of his feet, working between the bones and sinews and tugging softly on each toe. Dark, wiry hairs sprung from the top of the foot, a little tuft on each toe. Underneath, though, his feet were surprisingly soft and supple. As I pressed my thumbs into his insteps, making small circles just in front of the pad of his heel, I felt the response rush through his body, and saw his prick stir in the water. I looked up: Kit was lying back, his wet, dark head cradled between the big brass taps and his arms hanging over the sides of the bath. He looked as sleepy as I felt. I smiled at him and saw his mouth curl up in reply.

Now I was massaging his feet more deliberately, my touch a little swifter, aiming to send those currents up to his whole body. I varied my stroke, now squeezing strongly, now the most feathery touch on the tender inside of his ankle. With my legs lying outside his, I could feel the dance of resistance and involuntary surrender as his thighs and hips tensed and shifted in the water. I stroked my own feet against the curves of his buttocks, watching the swell and rise of his member in silent answer. The smooth tip of it was breaking the surface of the water now, the tiny waves caused by my movement lapping against it, now covering it, now letting it meet the air again. I placed my foot between his legs and rubbed it gently against his prick, the way I'd rub my palm across a horse's soft wet muzzle. It pushed back against the pressure.

I stood up and saw the water disturbed by my rising wash over his cock and up his chest. After reaching for one of the dry, rough towels, I wrapped myself and stepped out on to the cold tiles. Through the open door I could see the fire burning brightly again. I held out another towel for Kit, wrapping it around him as he stepped out of the water, feeling his prick nudge against me through the gap in my own towel. Feeling suddenly aroused myself, I kissed him and slid my dry hands under his towel to touch the wet curve of his back.

We left the bathroom and sat on the rug in front of the fire, leaning back against the sofa, our arms wrapped around each other, still kissing. The sheepskin was warm beneath our bare bodies, and almost unbelievably soft. In the stillness, the cracking of the wood on the fire seemed to fill the room, like the smell of wood-smoke that was bringing back half-remembered images of teenage camping trips. We were kissing slowly, sensuously, our lips roaming across one another's face and neck.

In the orange firelight, Kit's brown eyes had turned russet, like autumn leaves, and our skins were glowing so we looked red-hot. Kit lay back on the rug and I rolled on to him, my legs astride his legs, my body stretched over his. As I kissed his face, I could feel the heat of his erection caught between our bellies. Slowly, I rubbed my body up and down against him, my nipples dragging against the hairs on his chest, my pubic hair lightly brushing his prick. He was lying back, his arms folded beneath his head, letting me take the lead.

I slid my body down his, my breasts tracing a path down his flat, hairlined belly and falling into the dip of his lap. Laying my cheek against his erection for a moment, I felt the heat on my skin, and then I began kissing it in the same slow, dreamlike way we'd been kissing each other's faces. I took his cock into my mouth and lazily played my tongue over the end, teasing every little ridge and crevice with my tongue-tip. Kit gave a little sigh of pleasure, and I half-expected to look up and see him watching me with that sharp attention, but his eyes were closed.

With my fingernail, I drew a line round his nipple and slowly down his ribs to where his hip-bone rose from the flat plain of his stomach; a tremor followed it, muscles twitching beneath the skin. I repeated the gesture, this time using both hands and all my fingers, leaving an invisible grid of sensation behind them. A quiet groan escaped Kit's parted lips and resonated in his chest.

I sat up on my heels and took his cock in my hands, feeling the slippery wetness of my spit on it. Firmly, but without hurrying, I pulled my hands up and down its length, using the lubrication my mouth had supplied. I could feel the tension growing in Kit's pelvis, but he was gripped between my legs and could not move, even to set the rhythm of my pumping. I stopped for a tantalising few seconds and felt his spine stiffen in protest, and then I knelt up and slid myself on to his cock.

Kit's sound of delight mirrored my own feeling. I had been concentrating on his pleasure, and my own excitement had been building unfed. Now I was filled with his prick, kneeling astride him, rocking gently against him so that my clit was rubbing against his body. Savouring the feeling, I lifted myself slowly off him, feeling his cock slide down against the folds inside my cunt, and then pressed myself down again, so it reached my deepest parts.

I could see from the way Kit's hands were clenching behind his head that he was enjoying this leisurely pace as much as I was. My whole body was alive with the sensations, my knees cushioned by the springy warmth of the sheepskin, my left side glowing in the heat from the fire and my right side awakened by the cool air from the dark room. I ran my hands over my breasts, palms brushing the erect nipples. I was resisting the urge to speed up, to hurry us both to orgasm.

Kit put a solitary finger on my clit, but seemed hardly to move it, letting my own rocking movements provide the pressure. Now my pleasure had a double focus – Kit's finger on my clit and his prick deep inside me. Still he lay passive, his head resting on the other hand, his eyes shut. I reached a hand round behind me to where his cock was entering me and placed a finger there to feel its wet slide in and out, pressing gently against it, so it was pushing past my fingertip each time. In spite of myself, I could feel my mounting excitement forcing the pace, my movements getting quicker. Kit must have felt the same, because he opened his eyes and sat up, drawing his knees up behind me like the back of a chair. For a few seconds we sat on our heels, interlocked, face to face. Kit put his arms around me, kissing me, and lowered me backwards on to the rug. Now it was he who was kneeling, and I was lying back, my hips raised up and resting on his thighs and my legs around his waist. I expected him to thrust harder and faster, but he continued with the same steady rocking, his prick sliding in and out as regular as a piston. He was looking down, watching his cock slide in and out of me.

Kit put the heel of one hand on my pubic hair and pushed it up, away from him, so my pussy was stretched, pulled forward. I could feel the tightness of my lips around his prick, as it continued its steady pumping, increasing the feeling of being penetrated. My clit too was pulled forward, held tight against the underlying bone, each movement of Kit's rubbing it against the soft folds surrounding it. Arched backwards as I was, I already felt exposed, lifted up to his view: now I felt completely opened to him, spread out for his enjoyment. His finger still rested on my clit, but now it was intensifying its movements, flicking across the sensitive head quicker and quicker, its swift, light motion a contrast to the slow thrusting of his cock inside me.

My body was being overwhelmed by the strangeness and intensity of these feelings. As Kit's finger struck sparks from me, the slow build up of heat within me suddenly caught, like a furnace roaring into life, and the orgasm engulfed me. My hips bucked against Kit and my whole body seemed racked by powerful waves of energy. Kit's thrusts followed mine, suddenly stronger and faster, and as the waves of my climax receded, I felt his reaching its peak and heard him cry my name as he came inside me.

In the quiet room, we could almost hear our hearts pounding. We sat cross-legged, side by side, staring into the glowing interior of the fire, as our own afterglow receded. The light of the fire flickered across Kit's face, but there was nothing diabolical about him. He looked like a very tired man, like someone who has gambled for high stakes and still doesn't know whether he has won or lost. I let my head rest against his shoulder, and his hand rubbed my knee absentmindedly. 'Come on,' I told him, 'let's go to bed.'

For the first few moments after waking, I didn't know where I was. I was first aware of birdsong, far louder and closer than I ever heard in my flat at home, and an unfamiliar smell. I couldn't remember where I'd gone to sleep, so I opened my eyes on a tiny, golden room, bisected by a single shaft of sunshine. Recognising part of the smell as blossom, and the other part as the faint traces of wood-smoke, I had the illusion that I was in a tent, before the memory of last night returned to me. This was the four-poster bed, and Kit had drawn the curtains before we fell asleep.

Nevertheless, the impression that we were enclosed

105

only by this canopy of golden cloth, and that beyond the drapes was open countryside, remained with me. Lying beneath the heavy covers, I breathed deeply, drinking in with the fresh, scented air the feeling of anticipation I had as a child, waking in the summer holiday with another endless day of sunshine ahead of me. Limitless possibilities were mine, and unknown adventures lay all around, waiting for me to go out and seek them. I stretched my limbs under the sheets, the nebulous excitement flowing through to my toes and fingers like a cold rushing stream.

I sat up on the bed and stuck my head out through the curtains. The sun was filling the room with daz-zling, golden light, reflecting off the smooth wooden floor so it seemed that bed, rug and sofa were floating in a sea of fire. Outside, the sky was blue, not a cloud in sight, and the green curve of a distant hill was just visible over the windowsill. I was filled with the desire to be out there in the sunshine, filling my lungs with the fresh air, and then, with a jolt of happy surprise, I remembered that today we would be speeding through the countryside on Kit's motorbike. I couldn't contain myself any longer and threw open the bed curtains, so the sunlight poured across the white covers and into Kit's sleeping face. He stirred, screw-ing up his eyelids against the light, but did not wake. I lay down, my face next to his, and whispered, 'Kit, Kit, wake up. Wake up, we have to go.' His eyes opened cautiously and, as he focused on me, he smiled blearily.

'What time is it?' he croaked.

I looked around the room, but could see no clock. Kit was hanging over the edge of the bed, feeling around on the floor for his watch. 'Emma,' he groaned, his voice pained, 'it's half past six! What are you doing waking me up?' His face wore an expression of real injury, as if I had done something truly unforgivable. A tiny sliver of guilt pricked my joy, but I persisted.

'Come on, get up,' I urged him, 'it's beautiful out there. Let's get on your bike.'

'Noooo,' he wailed, burying his face in the pillows. 'Shut the curtains and go back to sleep!'

I thought about getting under the covers and waking him the way Jane had woken Hamish the night before, but if he really was that tired, it seemed cruel to deprive him of his sleep. Instead, I did as he asked and drew the curtains back to shield his face. I couldn't go back to sleep myself though, so I dressed quietly and tiptoed down the stairs and out of the front door. The sun was already warm on my face and arms, but the grass was still wet with dew and icy cold to my bare feet. There was no sign of human activity, though a cat paused in its washing to watch me as I walked across the lawn to smell the honeysuckle that was climbing the corner of the house.

Remembering our breakfast on this lawn, less than twenty-four hours before, I wondered whether Jane was sleeping beside Michael in the room that would have been ours. I would have liked to talk to her, to get a friendly perspective on my strange adventure and hear about hers, but I was too impatient to be off. Jane would probably be in bed till noon, and even then would only emerge, like a bear from hibernation, in search of food. By that time, Kit and I could be racing through the bleak splendour of the Pennines. His bike sat on the drive, dew sparkling on its chrome and red curves. 'I should have brought the keys down,' I thought, 'then I could have taken it for an early morning spin, and Kit would never have known.'

'Oh no you don't,' came Kit's voice from behind me. I turned to find him standing on the doorstep, already in his leathers. I laughed: he had thought of my plan before I had.

'Don't worry,' I said as I walked back to him, 'I didn't think to find the keys.' To my surprise, he was holding the panniers and his helmet, and looked ready to go.

'Where's your luggage then?' he asked. My luggage – I hadn't thought of that. How was I going to get a suitcase back to London on the back of a motorbike?

'Dear Jane,' I wrote, 'I am going home with Kit on his motorbike and will see you in London. Please look after this suitcase and when I get it back I will buy you a drink. Love, Emma.' I stuck the note through the handle and wedged the case across the door of her room, so she couldn't leave without falling over it. Unless, of course, she had climbed out of the window and landed in a flowerbed – which wouldn't have been the first time.

'You'd better get me home by tonight,' I told Kit as he zipped me into the leather suit. 'I haven't even brought a toothbrush.' He just grinned as he handed me my helmet and gloves.

'Is that why you had to wake me so early?' was all he said in reply. As we rolled down the drive, leaving the sleeping castle behind, I felt a rush of adrenalin.

The golden light slanted across the hills, casting long, violet shadows that dwarfed the clumps of trees which had created them. The sky seemed vast, unbroken by a single cloud, and there was scarcely a car on the road. If the rest of the world had fallen under a spell and was sleeping for a hundred years, we could scarcely have felt more alone. Not lonely: more as if the day were a secret gift for the two of us to enjoy privately.

Had we wanted to talk, the helmets and the rushing wind would have made it impossible, but there was no need for words. Here we were together, moving in

108

unison as the bike banked for each curve in the road, my hands resting lightly on Kit's waist as I gripped the bike – and his hips – with my thighs. When we passed something of particular oddness or beauty, a nod of the head or a point of my finger would do to share it: a pollarded tree standing absurdly in the middle of a loop in the stream; a ruined barn whose stone was radiant in the shallow-angled sunlight.

I thought I could have stayed on the back of that bike for ever, but when Kit turned off the road and parked outside a café, I realised how cold, stiff and hungry I was. We hobbled across the car park, legs seized up from holding the same position for over two hours, and the warm air that hit us at the doorway sent a welcome blast through our chilled bones. Kit ordered two cooked breakfasts and we sat dazed, stunned by the wind and the speed of our journey.

'Enjoying it?' Kit asked, but not till he'd had his first mouthful of coffee. I nodded behind my own mug, which I was clutching in both hands, trying to wring every drop of warmth out of it and into my numb fingers. 'We'll hit the coast soon,' he went on, 'then you'll be able to have your turn.'

I tried to inhale my tea, choked and spluttered, and had to be vigorously banged on the back. 'What's the matter?' he asked as I wiped my face dry. 'You haven't changed your mind, have you? I thought that was condition number two.'

'Of course not,' I protested. I hadn't forgotten, or changed my mind, but I had expected Kit to try and wriggle out of it, and had been biding my time till I got the opportunity to insist.

'Good.' He smiled at me, an oddly triumphant smile, as if he'd just won some bet with himself.

Fortified and warmed, we set off again, the roads tending downhill now, and the wind less bitter. The sun was high in the sky and shining almost in our faces as we headed southeast. As we topped a rise, the sea spread out before us in the distance, a shimmering band along the horizon. Feeling again like a child on the first day of the holidays, I squeezed Kit's waist with excitement, and he spared a hand to squeeze my knee in answer. When we got nearer the coast, we lost sight of it, but now the smell was there, drawing us on.

Nobody else was in the car park when we swung in through the gate: a long strip, barely a hundred yards wide, but nearly a mile long, it led straight on to the beach on its seaward side. On a sunny Sunday in June, I was surprised not to see family cars parked, or at least some older couples out for a Sunday drive. 'It's always quiet here,' said Kit as we dismounted, 'that's why I chose it. I've come here before for photo shoots. We park the bike against the sea, give it a good rub over with a rag, and then shoot it as the sun comes up.' I liked the thought of Kit here in the faint dawn light, positioning a bike, polishing the dirt away, waiting for the right moment to capture it in its glory. Moments like that have a strange intimacy, the intimacy of the work that somebody loves.

'What are you doing?' he asked, as I took my helmet off. 'I'd keep that on if I were you. You may be good, but I'd give it one lap with your lid on before you start showing off.' Seeing my confusion, he gestured at the bike. 'She's all yours.' He sat on a log that was marking the limit of the parking area. 'Just don't let her tempt you on to the public highway.'

Now the moment had arrived, I felt a sudden pang of nerves, but not about the bike; I was confident I could ride that and any other bike you can name. What made me nervous was the thought of Kit watching. Being able to control any machine with two wheels and a motor that had been ruined by some teenage mechanic – as I'd spent my teens doing along

110

miles and miles of country lane – was one thing, but I'd never had to impress a bike journalist with my riding technique before. I was damned if I was going to let him know that though.

Pulling my helmet back on, I walked decisively back to the bike and took a quick look at the controls. They don't vary too much as a rule – not to look at, at least – and there was nothing unfamiliar. Kit, to his credit, offered no advice or instruction but sat calmly watching me as I swung my leg across the seat, tested the weight and balance of the bike, and kicked the stand up out of the way. Although I hadn't ridden for well over a year, it felt more natural than anything I'd ever done. As the engine roared into life, my heart leapt with anticipation. Looking, out of habit, over my shoulder, though there was nowhere for anything to appear from, I let the powerful engine take hold of the bike and pulled smoothly away.

Kit was right, she was a beauty. Even on my warm-up lap of the car park, she took the corners gracefully, allowing me to hold her power in reserve. Feeling more confident, I took a second circuit with a bit more speed, trusting myself to take the tight U-turn at the far end, or to take evasive action if a car full of trippers should, after all, be coming through the gate as I reached it.

As I turned the bike's nose towards the open gate, I felt the sharp bite of temptation – to keep pointing that way and be out on the road I could see curving away, taking the same sweeping bends that had brought us here, feeling the rush of accelerating up the undulating hills that we'd just rolled down. There was nothing to stop me. I even knew, in my heart of hearts, that Kit would forgive me, that he was half-expecting it.

In fact, it was that knowledge – that Kit was ready for me to take the bike off without permission – that stopped me. I didn't want to prove to him that I always had to do the daring thing. What I wanted was for him to see my other side, the side that would keep a promise. Anyone could be brave on impulse, when all that was at stake was a good time; sticking to your guns when things are dull and difficult, that's what sorts the men from the mice. So I turned her nose back up the car park, towards where Kit was sitting, and racked up through all the gears as quickly as I could, to reward myself for being so trustworthy. The feeling of that speed, the power that responded to the lightest turn of my wrist, was like a drug. Exhilaration coursed through me as I flew along that car park, lifted on wings of metal and petrol. Even in that limited space, I could have ridden for hours. The only reason I came to a halt alongside Kit was so he could share my pleasure. It must have been clear in my face, because he was smiling back at me before I spoke. I wanted to tell him all the things that were great about riding that bike, but all I could manage was 'Thanks.' How on earth people like Kit manage to write pages and pages about an experience so beyond words is a mystery to me.

Having killed the engine, I was about to get off the bike, but Kit stopped me. He took my helmet from me and slid his arms around my leather-clad body. His own leather suit was undone and the top part hung down behind him, sleeves dangling. Against my armoured chest, his own felt almost naked, warm through his T-shirt. The way he kissed me was proof that my ride had excited him as much as it had me. Once more, I moved to dismount, but he held me still and, instead, swung his own leg over the pillion seat behind me, so he was standing pressed against my back. His arms still round me, he was undoing the zips that held my suit together, jacket and trousers. I tried to turn round and kiss him but lacked the flexibility in my stiff leathers. I was also hampered by the sheer height of the seat: with my feet planted on the ground, it was snug against me.

Kit unfastened my leather trousers and tugged at the back of the waistband, pushing me forward over the bike's petrol tank. I reached for the handlebars to steady myself. Kit was struggling to pull down the stiff trousers. 'Put your feet up on the footpegs,' he told me. As I obeyed, my rear lifted clear of the seat and he managed to get it free from the leather. Now I was even more immobilised, my legs pinned against the bike by the tightness of the waistband. I felt Kit's hand pull my G-string aside, and then his cock was pushing into me from behind, his hands gripping my waist to steady both me and the bike. I pushed back against his thrusts, my arms braced against the hand-grips, but still each forward push pressed my clit against the hard metal of the petrol tank, cushioned only by the top of the leather trousers.

The excitement of the ride and the pleasure of Kit's fucking were mingling in my bloodstream. Closing my eyes, I imagined that I was still moving, that the throbbing in my pussy was from the bike's engine as well as from Kit's prick and the hand he had slipped into the front of my G-string. I pictured us riding along like this, Kit making love to me as I took us along the winding roads, accelerating uphill to press me back against his cock, then braking downhill so he would slam against me from behind. Many times I had dismounted after a fast bike ride, my body tingling with excitement, but now the fantasy was as near to reality as I could get.

Whether Kit had the same fantasy, or whether it was just the sight of me on his bike, flushed with exhilaration, I don't know. Whichever it was, he was hot, already close to climax. I felt my own building inside me and pictured it as a steep, mountain road.

113

Up the road we were roaring, faster and faster, the engine screaming as I opened up the throttle and the revs built up to their limit. I could see the top of the hill clearly and as I came, mounted on Kit's thrusting cock as if it were part of the bike, we reached the top of the road and saw a landscape spread out below us.

Kit helped me restore my clothing and I was finally allowed to get off the bike. 'Don't worry,' he said, seeing me glance around the car park in case anyone else had arrived while we were preoccupied. 'I told you – nobody ever comes here. Except us, of course.' He grinned at his own pun. Undoing my jacket to try and cool down a little, I leant back against the bike.

'You realise I'll never be able to get on a Ducati again without thinking of you?' I said.

He smiled wickedly. 'That was the idea.'

We were both warm from too much exertion in too many thick clothes. Where I had taken off the leather jacket, I was actually steaming. The sound of the sea on the shingle beach drew our eyes, and we exchanged a look.

'Got a towel?' I asked. Kit nodded. 'Fancy a dip?' We had no swimming costumes, but what the hell – if nobody had caught us having sex in the car park, there was no reason to worry about them spotting us naked in the sea.

The breeze was fresh as we left our clothes in a little pile a few yards from the water's edge, but to our overheated skins it was delicious. The water was even colder and we hopped about, screaming and splashing like kids, before wading further out. In up to my knees, I was trying to pluck up the courage to immerse my whole body, when Kit charged up behind me, lifted me off my feet and threw me into an oncoming wave. It hit me, cold and powerful, and suddenly I was floating, eyes and mouth full of salty water. 'You bastard!' I managed to shout before the next wave rolled over me, but Kit too had lost his footing and was bobbing about, feet making contact with the stony bed and then losing it again with each wave.

I swam along the line of the beach in a sloppy crawl, more concerned with keeping the sea water from going up my nose than with good technique. It was wonderful to stretch out my limbs though, giving free play to muscles that had scarcely been used since last summer. Kit appeared to be floating along on his back, feebly attempting to propel himself by flapping his arms about. We could see along the coast for miles in both directions, and it all looked deserted. A distant fisherman the size of my thumb was sitting by his two rods, gazing out towards the shimmering horizon, but in the other direction only seagulls broke the smooth sheet of shingle meeting sea meeting sky.

I swam up and down until I felt tired and then staggered out to where Kit had already dried himself and was getting dressed. He looked great – wet and windblown, relaxed and glowing from the cold sea. He threw the towel to me, so I could wrap it round me against the wind, all the colder now I was wet. While I tried to work my numb fingers around buttons and hooks, he sat throwing stones into the surf. 'Now what?' he asked, looking up at me, squinting slightly against the sun.

'Lunch,' I replied. 'Take me where you go after your photo shoots.'

He smiled. 'That's not lunch, that's breakfast,' he corrected me, 'and an early breakfast at that. But I guess they must do lunch.'

The place was divine: a beach-side café a few miles down the coast. There were already a few bikes parked outside and I felt the warm glow of camaraderie as we walked in and were greeted with nods of recognition. I felt included, one of the nameless broth-

115

erhood of bikers, who would greet you, ignore you while you ate and then share another nod as you left.

After our swim, we were still too cold to sit out on the terrace, but we picked a window table where the sunlight shone warm through the salt-caked glass and made the worn formica shine.

'I know where to take a girl when I'm trying to impress her,' Kit murmured as I fiddled with the red plastic tomato crusted with old ketchup.

'It's perfect,' I answered, just in case he was seriously worried.

We looked out at the blue sky and watched the waves lap against a little landing-stage where two girls were sitting, dangling their skinny brown legs in the water. I felt completely carefree. The low chatter in the rest of the café rose and fell like the ripples scintillating on the water's surface.

'Come far?' asked the waitress as she brought two huge plates of sausage and mash.

'Scotland,' I replied, expecting to see her eyebrows go up. She was unphased. Maybe we weren't the only ones to be stopping off from a long trip.

'And where are you headed for next?' she asked, wiping a few crumbs off the table.

'London,' said Kit.

'Looks like you've got a nice afternoon for it,' she said as she left us.

Chapter Eight
The Watcher Watched

My telephone was ringing, but there was no way I was going to answer it: I was tied to the bed. Blindfold and naked, I was stretched out, my hands pinioned to the iron posts of the bedstead and my legs pulled apart by the ropes holding my ankles to the sides of the frame. My hand gave an automatic twitch at the first ring, only to encounter the immovable barrier of the thick cotton rope, and I heard Kit's low laugh.

It was little more than a week since Kit and I had arrived back here on his bike, almost dropping from tiredness, and fallen into my bed, and he had scarcely been out of it since, except when we were on the bike or one of us was working. I was sure that eventually I would get sick of having him around so much, but it hadn't happened yet. We were still surprising each other. That's what had happened this evening, when Kit had appeared with a delicately wrapped parcel tied up with pink silk ribbon. I had opened it, expecting lingerie or maybe perfume, only to find four short lengths of soft rope and a black silk blindfold. Kit sat silently watching me. When I looked up at him in

117

confusion, his face remained expressionless and he simply asked, 'Aren't you going to try them on?'

So I lay listening to the phone's insistent jangle, my whole body tense as I waited to hear the answerphone take the call. I knew who it would be, who was back from his climbing holiday and calling to talk dirty to me: Geoff. I couldn't even get to the machine and switch the speaker off. How would Kit react? He wasn't under the impression that I hadn't been seeing anybody before he turned up at Eric's wedding, but that didn't mean he would expect to hear Geoff's voice describing in graphic detail what he was planning to do to me.

'Who is it?' Kit's voice made me jump, right next to my ear. His hand, which had been wandering lazily over my skin, without warning pinched my nipple and made me gasp. 'It's a man, isn't it? Do you want to speak to him?' At that moment, I heard the tape click into action as the answerphone started.

'So, sexy redhead,' came Geoff's husky whisper, 'what are you up to? Are you out, or are you in there? All the curtains shut, that's not like you . . .' I strained at the ropes, knowing even as I did so that it was futile. Damn, why hadn't we talked yet about other relationships? I was afraid that Kit would not be able to cope with this, and that I might never see him again. Geoff's low voice continued: 'I'm thinking about you. Are you in there, lying on your bed, playing with yourself? I'm picturing you there, naked, and my cock's getting hard. Have you got a man in there? Is he fucking you right now, is that why you can't get to the phone?' I felt utterly helpless. Then the plastic of the phone was cold against my cheek.

'Answer him,' came Kit's voice.

'Emma?' Geoff was asking down the phone.

'Answer him,' repeated Kit. 'Tell him what you're doing.'

118

'Geoff?' My voice was shaky.

'Emma? Are you all right?' Geoff sounded concerned.

'Yes, everything's fine.'

'Is there someone there with you?'

'Yes.' I could feel the tension in the crackling silence.

'And what are you doing?' Geoff's question was so soft I could hardly hear it. Kit's breath was hot on my cheek.

'Tell him,' he whispered.

'I'm here with Kit,' I told Geoff. 'I'm blindfolded and I'm naked, and he has me tied to the bed.'

'What's he doing to you?' Geoff asked. Hearing his voice, I could almost smell him, the faint musk of fresh sweat mingled with the sharp scent of arousal.

Kit's mouth was ranging over my breasts, his tongue leaving cool wet trails behind it. 'He's licking my breasts,' I told Geoff. 'Now he's biting my nipple and squeezing the other breast with his hand.' Hearing me describe to Geoff what he was doing seemed to rouse Kit to greater excitement. He was sucking and licking at the tender hollow of my armpit while his hand moved down to my pussy. 'He's pushing his fingers into my cunt,' I relayed to Geoff, 'two, three fingers. He's stretching me open . . .'

I felt as if my only function was as a conduit between Kit and Geoff, as if Kit's only aim was to arouse the man at the other end of the phone line, and I was simply the go-between. This, with the way the bonds were pulling my legs wide apart, and the disorientation of the blindfold, turned me into an excited, helpless object, waiting for whatever Kit decided to do to me next. The feeling of being completely out of control was immensely liberating. It was as if I was not really here, not really participating, as if I were merely observing my body's responses to Kit's lovemaking.

Unable to see, I was experiencing the other senses with an intensity I'd never known before. The smells of Kit's body and the sounds, wet or percussive, of his smallest action were vividly close. The faintest touch of his skin on mine was electric, drawing currents of energy to the point of contact. His tongue was moving delicately around the very brink of my sex, and nothing else in the world was real, and yet, at the same time, the crudeness of the words I was using to describe it made it seem anonymous and pornographic. 'He's running his tongue around the edge of my cunt,' I was saying into the receiver, which lay on the pillow by my mouth. I felt as if I were talking about someone else. 'She's getting so wet from his licking that she can feel her own juices trickling out,' I could have said.

'Open the curtains,' came Geoff's command. I stopped in surprise: he had been virtually silent since I started my commentary. 'Your man,' he repeated, 'get him to open the curtains. I want to watch him fuck you.' He was outside again. While I was laid out here, describing what was being done to me, he had been only yards away through the glass, imagining the scene from my description, and from what he knew so well of me, my flat and my body.

'Open the curtains,' I told Kit. A questioning silence, as he stopped his caresses. 'He's outside, on the balcony,' I explained. 'He says he wants to watch you fuck me.' I felt the bed shift as Kit's weight left it. An audience at the other end of the phone was one thing, but an unseen listener is very different from a voyeur who is physically present. I found the idea extraordinarily arousing: my body was turning to liquid at the thought of Geoff watching as Kit possessed me. Geoff obviously found the idea equally exciting, but what about Kit? 'So, here's *your* line, Kit,' I was thinking.

'What are you going to do? Are you ready to cross this one? Or is this the moment you bale out?'

The curtains slid open with a soft ssh, and I felt a tiny chill in the air. Kit had done it. Though I couldn't see Geoff, I could picture him, leaning back against the parapet, the light from the bedroom spilling across his shaved head and the pale smudge of his hand as he held his cock. I heard him sigh down the phone. 'Oh, that's beautiful,' he whispered. 'You, all spread out for public view like that. And your man Kit, he's got a lovely cock there, hasn't he? I bet you can't wait to get that shoved up your cunt.'

Now it was his turn to give me the commentary. Blindfold as I was, I was seeing myself now through his eyes, lying powerless and unseeing while Kit stood over me. 'What's he doing?' I asked Geoff, only to hear his low, mocking laugh.

'That's for us to know and you to find out,' he whispered back. 'And anyway, what's the point of asking? Whatever he's going to do to you, you can't stop him, can you?' The thought was so exciting that I felt I might actually come without even being touched. The image of myself presented to Geoff's eyes, lying at Kit's mercy, was more sexy than any pornographic photograph I'd ever seen.

The bed rocked again with Kit's weight, and I heard his voice above my head, but he still didn't touch me. 'There,' he was saying, 'now it's your turn to be watched. You like it when you're doing the watching, don't you? Now let's see what kind of a show we can put on for your friend.' There was a tiny thread of menace in his voice, which only added to the antici-pation that was convulsing my sex.

'He wants to see me fuck you, does he?' whispered Kit, his thumb tracing delicate circles around my clit til I was trembling on the edge of a climax and almost begging him to bring me relief. 'Let's see if this is

121

entertaining enough.' Without warning, he rammed himself into me, so hard that I felt my ankles being tugged against the ropes restraining them. Instantly I was shaking with an intense orgasm, all the tension that had been building up exploding throughout my body, waves rushing outwards from my cunt and resonating in my limbs, still held taut by the ropes.

As the waves of release jerked my wrists against their bonds, I heard Geoff's voice, like a voice inside my head, saying, 'You're so beautiful when you come, when you feel that shaft going into you and you can't do anything but lie there and take it . . .' As his words conjured the image for me, I felt another climax overtake me.

'Go on,' Kit was panting, 'tell him what you're doing.'

'I'm coming,' I sobbed into the phone, as my bones turned to water and my skin to fire. 'He's fucking me and I'm coming.'

'That's right,' Geoff's low murmur answered me, 'he's fucking you, but he's looking at me. He wants to see how much I'm enjoying it. He's making sure I can see every detail, every inch of him sliding in and out of your wet, slippery pussy. You've done well this time, showgirl, laying on a double act for me.'

I thought this orgasm would never stop: every time it began to recede, Kit changed his rhythm and I felt another peak hit me. 'Oh, God, I'm still coming,' I was crying out to Geoff, 'can you see it? Can you see me?'

'I can see you,' he answered, 'I can see every part of you.'

'Of course he can see you,' came Kit's voice. 'He's watching everything I'm doing to you, and he's wanking himself off as he watches. Come on, let's give him a show he'll remember.' With that, he flung himself on me in a frenzy, pounding into me, holding on to the iron bedstead so he could drive himself home, and I felt his climax shooting hot and strong inside me.

My pussy was still throbbing with the last flames of my own climax as Kit pulled out of me and was gone from the bed. 'Kit,' I called helplessly, 'where are you going? Geoff?' But even as I spoke his name, I heard his phone click off. What were they doing? Were they both going to leave me here alone? The room was silent. Drained and sore, I lay waiting for I knew not what. The reality of what we had just done was beginning to hit me. Kit and Geoff both knew about each other now, and knew rather more about me than I might have chosen to tell them. What's more, the circumstances of their encounter had been completely beyond my control. I pulled against the ropes around my wrists, but they held firm.

The bed rocked once more with the weight of a second occupant. Relieved, I waited for Kit to untie me, but instead I felt a soft, warm tongue drawing a line up the inside of my leg. My skin was alive again with the sensation, almost too sensitive to bear the cool, light touch. Involuntarily, I strained to escape the questing tongue, but my bonds held me too tight. I couldn't believe that Kit was still wanting to make love to me, after the frenzied passion we had just shared. Slowly, I felt the tongue's wet path make its way up my thigh and pause momentarily at the hollow where my pubic hair began.

'Go ahead – she's all yours,' came Kit's voice from behind my head. Instantly, I was rigid. If this wasn't Kit licking his way up towards my exposed pussy, who was it? Reason told me it was Geoff, invited in by Kit in a reversal of roles, voyeur turned performer. Nevertheless, the blindfold gave me a vulnerability that made anything possible: for all I knew, this silent man was a stranger, someone off the street to whom Kit was offering me in a perverse act of revenge.

Whoever he was, he put his mouth over my sex, still juicy with Kit's come, and plunged his tongue into me. My whole body convulsed, and for the first time I struggled in earnest to break free of the ropes. 'Don't mind her,' came Kit's voice, calm and quiet. 'She likes nothing better than to be used by someone she's never met.' If it was Geoff, he and Kit were playing this game all the way. The mouth continued its work, suckling on my clit, running the tongue around and over my lips and darting in and out of me. I was trying to find something familiar in the tidal wave of sensation, something to reassure me that this was really Geoff, but all I could think of was the image of an unknown man from the street, still wearing his coat, pressing his face into the spunk-soaked pussy of a blindfolded woman.

'See?' Kit's voice continued. 'She's loving it, the dirty slut.' I couldn't disguise it: the expert cunnilingus being practised on my defenceless body combined with the idea that Kit really was offering me for a strange man's pleasure were overwhelming me with excitement. Even my own struggles against the ropes only added to the feeling of being the helpless object of their desires. I knew that I was on the verge of coming. The thought of having an orgasm with this man was somehow worse than just being used by him, as if I would be giving final proof of my sluttish weakness. The idea of losing control of my body's response in such a humiliating way gave the final twist to the degradation of my mental image, and that was enough to bring on the orgasm itself. Tugging uselessly on my bonds, I felt my body respond in spite of me and heard my own voice crying out, 'Yes, yes.' Kit put his mouth over mine, kissing me deeply, so as my climax subsided I felt two mouths on me. All the nerves that ran from my mouth to my sex were short-circuiting with the double stimulation, sending after-shocks ricocheting through me.

Then both mouths were gone, and I was again lying still and powerless, straining my ears to know what would be done to me next. The second man was still on the bed, but neither he nor Kit spoke for a few seconds. Then Kit said, 'It's up to you. You can fuck her like that, or we'll turn her over and you can fuck her face down.' Hearing him talk about me like that to another man, as if I wasn't there, was strangely arousing. The man said nothing, but he must have made some gesture, because I felt two pairs of hands on me, untying my wrists and feet and holding them firmly. I made a brief attempt to break loose but, weakened by the rollercoaster of pleasure, I was no match for the two of them. Swiftly, they picked me up and spun me round, so I was face down on the bed, my legs hanging over the side. As my arms were stretched out sideways and my wrists were re-bound, my sex and thighs enjoyed the relief of not being stretched open, but not for long. As soon as my hands were secure, I felt my ankles being pulled apart again, even wider than before, and tied to the legs at either end of the bed. I was in an even more humiliating position, face pressed down into the mattress, legs wide open, and my pussy offered up to view.

I was so wet with arousal that I pictured my juices dripping out on to the floor. Now he was going to fuck me, this strange man, stand behind me and take me like an animal. The housemaid position, they called it, and that was how I felt, like a servant being enjoyed by the master and the master's friends. For all I knew, there could be more of them there, standing silently, looking at my wet, aching hole and waiting their turn to enjoy it. My pussy was hungry for a cock, longing to have a big, stiff shaft rammed up it. Kit was right, I didn't care whose it was. They were taking their time, knowing how frustrated I was, enjoying the spectacle of me so degraded and defenceless.

Whatever they wanted to do to me, I couldn't stop them. I wanted them to fuck me, either of them or both, but my whole body was at their whim. By lifting up my head, one of the two men could push his cock into my mouth, even while the other was fucking me. Or, instead of filling me, they could force a prick into the delicate entrance of my anus, penetrating its virgin depths. Running the pictures through my mind, I almost wished that Kit was filming the scene, turning it into a real pornographic performance.

Close behind me, I heard the rattle of a buckle as the second man undid his belt. Surely it was Geoff. Instead of a cock, three thick fingers were pushed abruptly into me, and I tried in vain to force myself back on to them. They taunted me by holding still, refusing to even fake the thrusting of a hard prick, and I did what little I could to rock against them and ease my need. Kit gave his low laugh again, behind me now. 'You see?' I heard him say. 'She can't wait to get your cock inside her.' The creak of the chair told me he had sat down, and I imagined him making himself comfortable, preparing to watch the other man's prick entering me.

The fingers withdrew, and I couldn't prevent myself giving a little whimper as I was left empty again, but a second later it was penetrated by the man's erection. He entered me, but only just, and then he stopped again. He was torturing me, I knew, making me wait for my fulfilment, enjoying the complete power he had over me. He moved delicately in and out of me, never quite leaving me, but never going deeper than an inch or so, till I could hardly stop myself begging him to fuck me properly.

What was Kit thinking, I wondered, seeing me being teased like this? I pictured myself through his eyes, my upturned rear exposing my wet, flushed sex, and my breasts flattened against the mattress. Could he see the exact point where the man's prick was disappearing into me? I felt my pussy contract at the thought, and then I heard him say, 'Yes, she likes that. You fuck her slowly, mate, take your time. You can do what you want to this one, she loves it all.' Once again, the feeling of being talked about as if I wasn't really there made me reel with guilty excitement.

The man behind me pushed himself a little further into me, and then stopped moving, leaving me desperately trying to move against him. Kit laughed again, but the man remained silent. Once again, he began his small thrusts, pulling out at times so the head of his prick rubbed against my most sensitive spot. I felt myself answering his rhythm, another orgasm building within me. Wordlessly, I willed him to speed up, but instead he brought me to the brink of climax and then stopped dead. I was sobbing with impotent hunger, my face muffled against the mattress. 'Oh yes,' Kit was saying, 'that's nice. That's so nice to watch. You make her wait for it.' I knew he must have his own cock in his hand, stroking it as slowly as the man was fucking me, enjoying the sight as much as Geoff had enjoyed his view through the window.

All at once, the man slid his length right into me, filling me, and at the same moment he pushed his thumb into my arsehole. The double penetration seemed to reach so far inside me that I felt as if I were turning inside out. His prick was motionless, pinning me in place, but his thumb was flicking inside me, setting off electric sparks that seemed to come from somewhere deeper than I'd ever felt. Around the two firm shafts my orgasm broke, like waves against two rocks in a storm. I could feel my cunt and my anus contracting in unison, gripping both thumb and prick as I came.

'That's beautiful,' Kit's voice was saying, the hoarse whisper betraying his excitement. 'Look at that tight little arse, how it loves your thumb. We could share this one – you fuck her cunt, and I'll stick my cock up that sweet little arsehole.' The idea shook me to the core, and the aftershocks of my climax were so strong that I felt more intense sensations overtake me. As it did, the man behind me pulled his thumb out of me, took hold of my hips and thrust himself mercilessly into me, slamming me against the mattress so my clit was hitting the edge. Utterly unable to move, I was carried along with his rhythm, the waves of my orgasm breaking again and again till I thought they would never stop. Even after he had reached his own climax, exploding into me with force, I was still shaking with pleasure.

I lay over the bed, exhausted and soaking wet with sweat and our intermingled juices, with no energy even to wonder what was going to happen next. Still not a word from the other man as he pulled out of me and moved away, but Kit murmured, 'Look at her. Look what you've done to her. She wanted a good fucking, and she got one.' Another silence, but instead of trying to hear whether they were still in the room, I lay passively waiting.

The front door closed and I heard Kit come back into the room. I wondered whether he had reached his own climax watching me with the other man, or whether he would now complete his own pleasure on me. Perhaps he would sodomise me, as he had said while he watched us. I lay limp, waiting to find out, but what I felt was him untying my ankles and wrists, pulling off the blindfold and lying beside me on the bed, his arms around me.

Neither of us spoke. My eyes were still closed and I rested my head on his chest. I felt as if we had both faced a decisive battle and emerged victorious. There were so many things to be talked about, but this was not the moment to talk. Instead, I blinked in the unaccustomed bright light and smiled at him. He smiled back and stroked my back tenderly, then took my wrists in his hands and gently rubbed at the marks where the ropes had pressed into my flesh.

Chapter Nine
No Longer Simple

The London sunshine dazzled me. I shifted my chair round the table so I could see Geoff's face without being blinded. His cigarette smoke was drifting across the table, mingling with the smell of the coffee and the slightly decaying scent of a Soho street in summer, conjuring perfectly the atmosphere of energetic decadence that I loved. Geoff was watching the people passing by, his quick eyes taking in their gait, the way they walked close to their companion or kept a distance, their mannerisms. It was Geoff who'd introduced me to this pastime; 'Old Compton Street TV,' he called it. I couldn't sit at a pavement café anywhere now without observing the passers-by, or without thinking of him.

Although I often called him and arranged to meet up like this, for a coffee and a chat, there was something else in the air today. We hadn't met since the night when he and Kit had played their strange and dangerous game with me, and neither of us had referred to it on the phone. We sat drinking our cappuccinos and basking in the sun, waiting for the right moment to talk about it, each hoping the other would find an easy way to raise the subject. In the end, it was Geoff who stubbed out his cigarette and turned his eyes to me, raising his eyebrows in enquiry. 'So,' he said simply, 'tell me about Kit.'

I went through the whole story from the beginning, how we'd met in the church, the instant spark, the improbable reunion and the pretended coupledom, right up to the parcel with the ropes. Geoff was possibly the only person to whom I could have told the whole story: even Jane got a slightly edited version – designed to make me look better, of course. As he listened, he said nothing, just nodding sometimes, smoking in that careful way of his and sipping his coffee from time to time. The only thing I didn't tell him about was the strange conversation in the castle, late at night, about not being afraid of life. That was too private and too freaky, but everything else was there. He let me finish, nodding again as if to accept the truth of my account, and then he asked me, 'But what about now?'

I didn't understand the question. He screwed up his face, working hard to express himself more clearly, and leant across the table towards me. 'What we did the other night,' he said, 'what does it mean? If Kit is another one like me, just a friend that you fuck from time to time, then it doesn't mean anything, it's just another game. But he's not, is he?' Geoff looked at me, his head on one side, waiting for my answer. I didn't want to have to think about this, not yet. I'd really only known Kit for two weeks, apart from that first encounter, and we had managed very well so far without dissecting our relationship too much.

'If you mean, am I in love with him . . .' I started, but he shook his head with a cynical smile.

'No,' he interrupted, 'that's not what I mean. Any-way, I don't think love at first sight goes too well with letting some guy come in through the window and fuck your sweetheart.'

'Then, what's the problem?'

'He looked at me, a dark shadow of sadness clouding his eyes. 'The problem is,' he spelt it out as if to a child, 'things have changed for you, and if they've changed for you, they've changed for us. When I called you, it's always been between you and me. How can I call you now, when I know that there's three of us in the equation?'

'I thought you enjoyed it,' I offered, weakly.

Geoff grinned his old wicked grin. 'Not half as much as you did, you dirty slut,' he responded.

'Then . . .?' He interrupted me again.

'Yes, yes, we all three enjoyed it, but that was a happy accident. With you and me, we do something like that, we enjoy it; next time we meet for a coffee, nothing's changed. You and Kit, you do something like that, it's like . . .' He sighed, searching for the words. 'It's like the stakes are higher. You two, the morning after, things had changed, hadn't they?'

I sat silent, remembering how delicately Kit and I had talked, lying together in my bed as the sun moved across the window, not just about Geoff, but about what the experience had meant to us. It was true, Geoff and I would never have discussed things that way, sharing frankly how the fear and the power had fed our appetites. I nodded, reluctantly admitting to Geoff that Kit was not just another friend.

'You have to tell me how things stand, Emma,' he said softly. 'There's something there. I don't know what it is, but . . .' He seemed at a loss for words. Abruptly, he stood up, kissed me affectionately on the cheek and pulled his jacket on. 'You have to find out, sexy redhead,' he said, 'and when you've worked it out, give me a call.' Before I could reply, he was off down the pavement, his light step belying the bulk of

132

his muscular frame. 'He seems dead nice, by the way,' he called back as he vanished around the corner.

The busy street rushed on around me, vans and bikes roaring by and a steady trickle of pedestrians picking their way past my table. My coffee was long finished, but I didn't want to move. Geoff had spelt out to me what I had feared from the moment the phone had rung, that nothing was the same. I hadn't wanted to trade my independence for a steady relationship, and so far there had been no demands on either side to give up our freedoms; nevertheless, with Kit there was an intensity that drew us together. He had made no request for me to be monogamous: indeed, he seemed to relish the involvement of others in our games, but that was just it – they were our games.

With a jolt, I understood what Geoff was saying. If I carried on seeing him, he would be involved not only with me, but with Kit as well. Did we really want that? And was it fair on Geoff to bring him on, for the crowd scenes as it were? Sitting there in the grubby heat of a Soho afternoon, I realised that anything I did now, I was doing in relation to Kit. We had set out on a journey together, and wherever it took us, I was going all the way.

Disturbed and excited, I didn't go straight back to work, but called round at Jane's studio. She was in the middle of photographing a young actor and I sat quietly in a corner while she cajoled him to pout and smoulder for the camera. I had to stay out of her eyeline while she was working, or we would catch each other's eye and get the giggles. He was a pretty young man, dark and slightly Mediterranean looking, and I could tell there was a little more than pro-fessional encouragement in her flirting, but he had eyes only for the camera lens. 'Oh well, he's probably gay anyway,' said Jane as she shut the door behind him. 'So, what's your news?'

'I've just had a coffee with Geoff,' I told her, and she laughed.

'That's not news!' she scoffed. 'What you mean is, you've just told him about Kit.'

'Sort of . . .' I decided not to go into the details of how he and Kit had met.

'What did he say?' Jane called from the little kitchen where she was getting orange juice out of the fridge.

'He said I'd have to tell him how things stood.'

'And?' She emerged with two glasses. 'How do they stand?'

I took a glass and walked over to the low sofa in the corner. Why had I come to see Jane, of all people? She was guaranteed to ask the questions for which I had no answers.

'I don't know,' I answered peevishly. 'I've only known the guy a couple of weeks. We haven't even had our first row yet.' Jane plonked herself down beside me. 'Anyway, what about you?' I asked her. 'Seen anything of Michael lately?'

Jane rolled her eyes wickedly. 'Oh, yes. What a sweetheart! Much, much nicer than his big brother.'

'More malleable, you mean,' I accused her.

She looked coy. 'Well, you know,' she offered with a sly smile. 'Get them young and train them, that's what I say.'

A sudden melancholy hit me as I sat beside her, looking down at our feet on the fake-tigerskin rug. Before we went to Scotland, everything had been so simple. Now the easy old arrangement with Geoff had been shaken up and I couldn't even talk to Jane about everything, the memory of our encounter on the train still hanging in the background. I must have sighed aloud because Jane squeezed my hand and said, 'Don't worry. Things will work themselves out; just

134

give them time.' I squeezed her hand back and gave her a rueful look, a bit embarrassed at being so unappreciative of life's gifts.

'Don't tell me you regret any of it,' she went on.

'Of course not,' I replied. 'It's just a bit more ... complicated than I'm used to.'

'Yes, your life was getting far too easy.' She stood up decisively. 'Come on, neither of us are going to get any more work done today. Walk round to the lab with me and then we'll go for a beer.'

With Jane I could always laugh at myself, and if that meant she was pouring beer down me at the same breakneck speed she was drinking it herself, that was a price worth paying. It was after midnight when I peeled myself out of the minicab and picked my way carefully up the steps to my door. The flat was dark and when I stepped inside there was no sign of Kit. Part of me was relieved: we had spent only a few waking hours apart since our return from Scotland, and I had to admit that I needed some thinking time. Besides, rolling in drunk after a night out with Jane rendered me very poor company. Through the relief, though, a dark thread of insecurity wove its way. Did Kit think I had gone off to spend the night with Geoff? Worse, had he gone to see somebody else? I had no right to expect faithfulness, but the thought of him being with another woman drew a cold knife-blade down my stomach. I stabbed at the answerphone's flashing button and heard Kit's voice.

'Hi, Emma, it's Kit,' he said, as if that voice could possibly belong to anyone else. 'I guess you're still out. Look, I'm knackered, so I'm turning in soon. Don't call me if you get in after eleven – I'll talk to you tomorrow. Bye.' I sat in the darkness, listening to the ringing silence after the message ended. So, he was asleep at home. Strangely, though I accepted – reluctantly – that he might sleep with someone else, I

135

knew he wouldn't lie to me about it. What was happening here? How had this man got under my skin like this?

In the bedroom, Kit had remade the bed before he left. When I had gone out early, leaving him there, I hadn't really thought that he might not be there when I returned, although I knew he had his own flat. That was the problem, I decided, rolling gratefully under the duvet: I was taking him too much for granted. We should try and spend some time apart, see some other friends. That would be the sensible thing to do. Drifting off to sleep, I automatically reached out to put an arm over Kit's back, only to remember with a start that he wasn't there. 'See?' I mumbled to myself. 'That's exactly what I mean.'

Kit rang me in the morning, just as I was getting out of the shower, and I stood dripping on the kitchen floor while I spoke to him. The speech that I had rehearsed, about seeing a bit less of each other, seemed ridiculous as soon as I heard his voice, warm and alive, offering to pick me up on the bike after work and go for a meal by the river. 'Why am I making this difficult for myself?' I thought. There was plenty of time to deal with problems once we had them. Kit didn't ask me where I had been last night, and he didn't even make me feel that I ought to tell him. In fact, I mentioned Jane so many times, it must have been obvious that we had spent time together, but he made no enquiries.

Before I'd had time to dry myself the phone rang again. Assuming it was Kit remembering some last-minute thing, I picked it up as I headed into the bedroom with my towel, but nobody spoke, and nobody answered when I said, 'Hello?' I could hear sounds at the other end, the rustling of something close to the phone and the muffled voice of a woman.

'Jane?' I said, remembering that she had once called me accidentally on her mobile, when the recall button had got stuck against her keys. It sounded as if that was happening again. 'Jane!' I tried again, but there was still no response.

Then I distinctly heard Jane's voice say, 'Mmm, yes, that's good.' A man's voice said something I couldn't make out, and she laughed and repeated, 'That's good.' What was she doing? Was it young Michael, continuing his training? In spite of myself I was listening, trying to make out what was going on. The rustling was renewed, and then Jane told him, 'Run your tongue down there. That's it, just below . . . oh!' He had hit the spot. The memory of my own tongue running down her sex hit me like a powerful kick, and I was suddenly afire with sexual need. I could visualise Michael, his fresh young face buried in the fine blonde hair of Jane's pussy, his boy's hands on her breasts, and the image was making me wet.

Dropping the towel, I laid my damp body on the bed and, with my free hand, traced the path I was imagining for Michael's hand: across my breasts, brushing the erect nipples and pushing the full, firm weight of them up towards my face. 'Yes, yes, there,' Jane was telling him at the other end of the phone. 'Flick it with your tongue, faster.' I licked my finger and flicked at my own clit, picturing Michael's dark head over my own sex, but at the same time vividly recalling the rich taste of Jane's body, the sensation of my tongue on her tiny peak. I wanted to be there, my mouth bringing Jane to the pinnacle of pleasure, showing Michael how it was done.

'Put your fingers inside me,' I heard her say, and pushed my own inside myself. They were Michael's thick fingers, plunging into me with the vigour of youth, but they were also my fingers thrusting into Jane. In my imagination it was my hand finding the exact spot inside her that was making her gasp in time with his thrusts. 'Faster,' I was willing him, 'she needs it faster,' and my own hand was pumping into me the way I wanted him to pump into Jane.

There was a muffled exchange and then Jane said clearly, 'Now, fuck me.' I was burning with excitement, my pussy running with my own juices, my hand making wet noises each time it thrust in and out of me. Jane's bed began to squeak, the old iron frame rocking under the weight of their two bodies as Michael did what he was told and fucked her. Closing my eyes, I could see her long, slim legs wrapped around him, her arms flung out behind her, fists clenched with excitement. His firm young body would be ramming into her with animal passion, his muscular arms holding him up so he could look down at her, watch her breasts moving with each thrust, see his cock driving into her cunt. His face would be contorted with lust, the wish to please her now overtaken by his own needs, the desire to possess her, to find his own climax inside her and fill her with his spunk.

Though I lay on my back, my own cunt ploughed by my fingers as Jane's was by Michael's cock, I was imagining myself on top of Jane. It was my body over hers, making that bed squeak with the power of my thrusts, looking down to see her face helpless with arousal. I imagined having a cock that I was plunging into her warm, slippery pussy, the pussy I had tasted that night in the sleeper compartment. It was I who was going to take her beyond her control and watch her tumble into the free-fall of orgasm.

'Oh, oh yes,' I heard her sob as she came, and I felt my own orgasm rise with hers. My thrusting fingers felt the waves of my climax grip them, and at the same time I heard Michael's strangled shout as he released himself into her. The creaking of her bed slowed and stopped, my own pleasure subsided, and I heard more sounds of sheets being pulled about. Michael asked something, his quiet voice still impossible to make out down the phone, and Jane answered him: 'Not bad, not bad at all.' There was intimate laughter, making me feel suddenly more like an eavesdropper than I had during the act of sex. I turned the phone off and lay on my bed, alone again.

Did Jane have these fantasies about me, as I did about her, I wondered. The rough towel on my skin brought back faint echoes of the excitement I'd felt. I knew Kit would find the idea of me with Jane an arousing one, but I was not sure I wanted my best friend to become part of a situation that was already complicated. Better to leave it this way, a fantasy fed by the occasional accident. Or was it an accident? I stopped drying myself and looked across at the phone. It was easy to make a call by pressing the recall button without knowing, that was true – but that meant it was also easy to press it knowingly, but without your lover being aware of it. Had Jane deliberately let me eavesdrop on her and Michael? I laughed to myself as I began to dress. There really were no limits to what that woman would do.

Chapter Ten
A Cut-Throat Razor

As I waited for Kit on the corner of the street, I smelt the first edge of autumn in the air. The evening was still warm, but a trace of frost was sharp in my nostrils and the musty scent of dying leaves came faintly on the breeze. Though it was barely seven o'clock, a ruddy sunset was spread across the sky, silhouetting the chimneys and roofs below. My bare legs, feeling the cool air, told me the summer was nearly over, the hot, lazy afternoons behind us for another year.

I saw my car pull round the bend in the road and I watched Kit park it expertly a few yards away. We were fast becoming the couple we had pretended to be at Eric's wedding, preferring each other's company to our own and using each other's vehicles – though most of the bikes I had been enjoying all summer were borrowed ones, not Kit's own battered machine. I surprised myself still, hearing my own voice say things like, 'I don't know – I'll have to see what Kit's doing.'

Luckily for me, Geoff had got another film quite soon after our discussion at the Soho café and I had been spared my explanation while he was away. We never stayed in touch very much when he was working, though I still got the typical Geoff postcards: front bearing a photo of some tropical paradise, back listing the explosions, fireballs and plate-glass windows he'd been through that week. When he came back, I knew things would be pretty clear: Kit was a big part of my life now.

It wasn't just habit and companionship, I thought, as I watched Kit struggle with the temperamental lock on the driver's door. There was still an electricity between us that was irresistible. Other men had set my body alight, so their slightest touch would drive me to a frenzy of desire, but Kit had reached into my mind. Seeing him walk towards me along the pavement, I felt a frisson of anticipation. It would be hours before I was alone with him, but every moment we spent together was part of our long game, our exploration of the furthest borders of ourselves.

He put his hands on my head and kissed me as soon as he reached me. His face was cold: he'd been driving along with the window open, as he liked to do, trying perhaps to emulate the breeze of the motorcycle. I wanted to take him straight back to the car and home to bed, but I knew this evening had been difficult enough for him to arrange.

'You're early,' he said with evident pleasure. 'You'll have to wait while Eddie cuts my hair now.'

'I don't mind,' I answered as we walked up the street, 'I can watch. I was finished early and I thought I'd come straight here.'

The blinds were down on the barber's shop and the sign on the door read CLOSED, but Kit knocked on the glass.

'Does Eddie normally open out of hours?' I asked as the lights in the shop flickered to life.

'Depends who's asking,' Kit replied, rather smugly,

I thought. 'I told him it was a special occasion.' Kit was busier than I was at the moment, working shifts for a magazine to cover for maternity leave, and had not had a day off in three weeks. He'd managed to get this weekend off to go to his niece's wedding, but not the time for things like the suit and the haircut.

The door opened and Eddie smiled out at us. 'Two of you?' he asked, seeing me beside Kit.

'No, just me,' Kit answered as we walked into the shop. 'Emma wouldn't let a barbarian like you cut her hair.' Kit had been coming to Eddie's shop for so long that they treated each other like close friends, teasing included.

'No, it's only savages like you that need barbarian haircuts,' said Eddie, winking at me in the mirror as he put a cloth round Kit's shoulders. He was not particularly handsome, but he had a sparkle that was attractive in a dark and mischievous way.

From my seat behind Kit, I watched and listened as Eddie got to work with his comb and scissors on Kit's hair. There was no talk here of where you were going for your holidays: Eddie always had a new story about his family, either in London or back home in Italy, or about his dodgy mates who had done some deal or other. I loved to be an observer in this masculine world, seeing Kit among men, how he joined in the banter and cracked jokes with the rest of them.

Eddie was talking about unusual customers: 'One guy comes in every week – completely bald.' As I opened my mouth to ask why a bald man would come to the barbers, he explained: 'He's got a wig. Brings the wig in, I style the wig, he goes away happy. The thing is –' Eddie had got carried away with his story and stopped cutting, moving round to where Kit could see his gestures '– he won't sit out here while I do it. He doesn't want everyone to see his head without the wig, so he sits in the storeroom while I do it –' he had

142

his audience now, and he was keeping us in suspense '– with a tea towel on his head! In case anyone walks in by accident. Poor bugger.' This was why Eddie's haircuts took so long: he could never let work get in the way of a good anecdote. But still, it was worth it.

Eddie was doing a beautiful job of Kit's head: I could see why Kit had insisted on squeezing in a haircut here and nowhere else. Kit's fine, chocolate-brown hair was falling in smooth layers, showing off the lovely curve of his skull. I could see Kit's face in the mirror, and he shot me the occasional burning glance. I wondered if he was enjoying the haircut, the feeling of Eddie's quick fingers running through his hair and over his scalp. In spite of Kit's jibe, I had let Eddie cut my hair before now, and had found the strong, decisive touch of his hand an interesting change from the women who usually cut my hair.

As Eddie swapped scissors for the electric clippers, I remembered the buzzing sensation on my own neck, where Eddie had finished my short style with clippers. Seeing Kit arch his head forward, offering his nape up to Eddie, I felt a shiver run down my own neck. The cold plastic of the guard, vibrating as the blades clipped, had sent a quiver down me, all the way to my sex, and my hands beneath the nylon cover had touched myself there in answer.

'There's another guy,' Eddie was continuing, 'comes in every Saturday for a shave. Doesn't seem to shave at all the rest of the week; he's got practically a full beard when he comes in. Same every week: full shave with a cut-throat razor, hot towels and everything, and that's it till the next Saturday.'

'Perhaps he's got a mistress,' offered Kit, 'and she doesn't like him scratchy.'

Eddie laughed. 'That's it!' he said. 'Goes to work all week looking like he's not had time to wash, then on Saturday it's all polished up for the mistress. I like that. It's true, women don't like to be cut to ribbons, do you?' He addressed me directly, catching my eye in the mirror.

'No,' I agreed, 'smooth is definitely better.'

'It's fair enough,' Eddie went on. 'I mean, you shave your legs for us, don't you?' His glance took in my smooth, brown legs, swinging from the leather chair.

'Not just for you,' I contradicted him. 'I like my legs smooth.'

'And your armpits,' added Kit, watching me intently in the mirror.

'Yes, legs and armpits,' I replied, wondering where this was leading to. Kit knew that I shaved my legs and armpits and waxed my bikini line. He also knew that we had talked in passing about my shaving off my pubic hair altogether, and that I had not completely dismissed the idea.

'So, do you ever get women coming in here asking you to shave their legs?' Kit asked Eddie. I left my chair and came to sit on the edge of Eddie's counter, watching him use the clippers on Kit's sideburns. Eddie laughed in reply, but something in his face responded in spite of himself.

'You would, though, wouldn't you?' I pushed him, self-consciously crossing my bare legs as I spoke and running a hand up one satin calf to the knee. 'I mean, if mine weren't shaved, you could do them with a cut-throat razor, couldn't you?' In the way Eddie's eyes flickered up my legs, I knew that Kit and I had lit a spark in him.

'Yes . . .' he answered hesitantly, 'I could . . .'

'It would be easy, wouldn't it?' interjected Kit. 'She'd have to sit here in this chair and put her legs up on your shoulders. Or I could hold them for you.' I saw a look pass between them, a look that said to Eddie, 'It's all right, we can talk about my girlfriend like this. I don't mind.'

144

Eddie's eyes passed over my legs again, bolder this time. 'Yes, he said, in a voice that was a dare as well as a joke. 'Next time you come, you bring your legs hairy and I'll use the cut-throat on them.'

'You're on,' I said, and slid back on to the counter, my knees apart so Eddie could see the shadowy hollow at the top of my skirt. I was wearing a flesh-coloured G-string, so it must have looked to him as if my thighs just faded into darkness. I looked at the cloth covering Kit from shoulder to lap and wondered if he was as aroused as I was. Eddie turned the clippers off and reached for the razor. Standing behind Kit to trim his hairline and sideburns, he was looking me straight in the eye, apparently oblivious to the fact that Kit could see him in the mirror.

'So, you can use that razor to shave anything, can you?' My question was not so much a dare as a direct invitation. Eddie nodded, his eyes not leaving mine, as he brushed away the stray hairs from Kit's face and neck.

'What she's trying to ask you,' Kit added in a low voice, standing up and shaking the cuttings from the cloth, 'is – would you shave her completely?' Eddie looked at Kit, disbelieving. 'The hair between her legs,' Kit confirmed, 'her pubic hair. Would you shave it all off, now, while I watch?'

I sat silent, looking at the desire and confusion fighting in Eddie's face, feeling my pussy grow wet at the thought.

'We'll pay you, of course,' Kit went on, leaning back against the counter so we formed a triangle, Kit and I leaning back here and Eddie at its apex behind the chair. He glanced at us both, as if seeking final confirmation, and then he gestured at the chair as if in answer.

I sat on the leather, still slightly warm where Kit had been sitting on it, and leant my head on the rest

145

as Eddie pumped the chair up to waist height, tilting it back so I was nearly supine. I put my legs up on the arms of the seat, the chrome cold against my skin, pulling my skirt up and out of the way. I felt a wonderful apprehension at the idea of this man shaving my hair off, leaving me naked and exposed, in this shop behind the drawn blinds. Kit stepped between my legs and put a hand straight on to my sex, where my G-string was already moist with my excitement, rubbing it hard and quick. 'Better get this out of the way,' he said, pulling off my thong and slipping it into his pocket. He stood looking down at me for a moment, taking in the sight of my sex revealed, my legs spread and my body tipped back in the chair. Then he moved aside, saying to Eddie, 'She's all yours.'

Eddie took Kit's place between my thighs. He had a brush in his hand and a bowl of lather, and he too stood looking down at me for a few moments. I felt deliciously vulnerable, looking up at him, my legs hooked over the metal arms. Slowly, looking into my eyes, he began to lather my sex with the stiff little brush, its bristles dragging harshly against my tender skin, pulling on the curly hair as it went. As it passed across my clit, it was almost painful, a sharp stab of pleasure piercing me with each stroke. In the mirror behind Eddie, I could see Kit's face, looking down over my shoulder at Eddie's work. It did not take him long to cover all my hair with the white foam, and he laid the brush aside and stepped back for the razor.

Kit took my wrists, holding them up against the leather back of the chair and, as Eddie moved aside, I saw myself in the mirror, wide open and pinned down, ready for the razor. A deep spasm of arousal shook me as I saw the gleaming blade approach me and imagined it cold against my skin. With his free hand, Eddie took hold of a little piece of hair from the front of my mount of Venus, gave it a sharp tug that made me catch my breath, and sliced it off. The metal barely touched my skin, the only feeling a momentary scraping sensation as the hair was gone.

I watched as if hypnotised as Eddie's swift hands moved over me, pulling and cutting, pulling and cutting. The white foam was vanishing swiftly, leaving behind it bare pink skin. As he came closer to my sexual parts, Eddie slowed down, his careful fingers finding the edges of the tender flesh and pulling the hair well away before the decisive razor did its work. His hand was roaming through my pussy, touching me intimately, but with a strangely clinical approach that made it even more arousing. His fingers moved round my clit, up and down the edges of my lips, but only pausing for long enough to strip them naked. I watched in amazement as a completely unfamiliar landscape unfolded under the blade, my clit exposed to view, lying between two simple folds of pink flesh. The hands moved down, out of my sight, and I felt them continue their work down either side of my sex and finish with the tenderest patch above my anus.

Eddie stopped, looked down at his work for a moment, then up at Kit. 'Kit, could you throw me a wet cloth from the sink?' It was the first time any of us had spoken since he began shaving me. Kit released my wrists and passed Eddie a wet flannel, leaning over me to see everything Eddie was doing. As Eddie passed the cloth gently over my sex, wiping away the last of the foam, I felt more naked than I had ever been. There was absolutely nothing between my skin and the wet towelling, and every millimetre of me was in direct contact with the stroking cloth, like a big, wet tongue moving over my newly exposed flesh.

At once tender and humiliating, it set off currents of pleasure that ricocheted through me.

Eddie stepped away, and for the first time I saw the full show in the mirror. Every single fold and crease was on display and, with no hair to punctuate the sight, it looked like some exotic orchid in bloom, nothing hidden, everything for public enjoyment. I glanced up to see Kit's gaze, his arousal in his face, and saw Eddie, seemingly transfixed by his handiwork.

'Well,' Kit asked Eddie, 'what does it feel like?' No longer hesitant, Eddie put his hand straight on to my naked pussy, his touch not clinical now but predatory. He stroked his whole hand up and down my sex, slippery from my own arousal, and let his fingers slip into me. It felt as if there was no longer any boundary between inside and outside, as if all my deepest crevices had been opened out to his hand. As Eddie's fingers teased at my clit, I felt the whole surface of my sex respond to his slightest touch. I was running with liquid, Eddie's hand slithering over the pink folds as if I had been oiled.

'Yeah, she feels great,' Eddie answered Kit. 'She feels as smooth as satin, and she's soaking wet.'

Kit's eyes were fixed on Eddie's hand, and his own hands were on my shoulders, ready to hold me down, I knew, if I made any move to get up. I heard his husky whisper, 'I bet she tastes nice and clean as well.' Another look passed between them, and I felt a lurch of excitement to know that once again I was not going to be asked my opinion on anything in this game.

As Eddie dropped to his heels between my legs, he pulled my naked sex towards him, so it was right on the edge of the seat. He ran his tongue over the naked rise of my Venus's mount, his eyes fixed on Kit's. Eddie licked his lips. 'Mmm, clean and soft,' he said.

With tantalising slowness, Eddie's tongue strayed

across my newly-naked skin. I had never before felt anything so intense here, where my little patch of hair had offered a barrier to this kind of gentle touch. He was not even close to my sex, but already I was melting with pleasure, my hands gripping Kit's wrists to steady myself. He squeezed my shoulders in reply, holding me firm against the seat. Looking down, I could see every detail of his tongue-tip working its deliberate way around me. Without its familiar dress of fiery hair, it looked like somebody else's sex, but the vivid sensations told me it was mine.

Now Eddie drew the flat of his tongue over my pussy from back to front, pressing it into all my intimate folds. I was helpless with arousal, hanging on for dear life to Kit's steadying hands, looking over Eddie's dark head at Kit's face reflected behind him. Kit's eyes were not on mine, but on the spectacle of Eddie's tongue exploring my new surfaces. It was almost like a demonstration, a salesman showing him what the new model could offer to the discerning owner. As his tongue lapped at me, I knew I was going to come, giving Kit the show he was waiting for.

With his cool, hard hands on my thighs, Eddie was quickening his stroke, enjoying his power to bring me to the height of excitement, lapping his wet tongue against my exposed sex faster and faster. As I came, sobbing aloud, I saw Kit's eyes shining with triumphant pleasure, drinking in every flicker of my cunt, now laid open for anyone to see.

Eddie stood up. Without pausing, he unzipped his fly, pulled out his cock and slid it home. As he thrust into me, his fingers pulled apart the folds of my pussy, spreading me out, so I felt stretched wide open. He was looking down, and I knew that he and Kit were both relishing the sight, his erection pounding into my opening with nothing at all to obscure the view.

Eddie's powerful rhythm was driving me, inside and out. Against my own soft, vulnerable skin, the rubbing of his hair was strangely male and exciting, the roughness provoking new ripples of sensation in my naked flesh.

There was something anonymous about my own shaved sex that I found excitingly degrading, as if it were there only to be penetrated by a prick, any prick, for the gratification of the viewer. Kit was enjoying the sight, I knew, and I knew too that as soon as we got home he would fling himself on me, aroused beyond restraint. This time, though, that wasn't enough for me.

'Give me your cock,' I whispered to him. He looked at me. 'Give me your cock,' I repeated, 'I want to suck it.'

'Go on, Kit,' came Eddie's voice, thick with excitement, 'one cock's not enough for her. She wants to suck you off while I fuck her.'

I turned my face sideways on the headrest, and at once Kit was there, his prick hot and rigid in his hand. He pushed it into my open mouth, one hand resting lightly on my head as he slid it in and out. I wasn't sucking him off: he was fucking me just as Eddie was, following Eddie's pace, filling my mouth as Eddie was filling my cunt. Both men were penetrating me in the same rhythm, my mouth and my pussy receiving them as one, the same delicious fullness at either end of my body, one cock mirroring the other. Glimpsing my own face in the mirror, lips wrapped around Kit's prick, I had the sudden picture of being surrounded by men, all watching as I took on these two, enjoying the show, handling their own pricks as they waited for their turn.

'You like that, don't you,' Kit was murmuring, 'two men at once? I bet you've fantasised about this for years, two men fucking you at once. I bet you'd like more, wouldn't you? How many do you think you could handle? Three? Four? We could push another cock into your mouth, couldn't we?' He forced his thumb between my lips and thrust it in time with his prick.

Closing my eyes, I imagined another man, pressed close to Kit, their bodies rubbing together as they entered me in unison. It was true, I had fantasised about being shared by two men, and these fantasies had grown stronger and more vivid since Kit and Geoff had divided me between them, but I had never before had the chance to make them real. It was the idea of being made part of their game that had been so sexy, but the actual experience was a thousand times more intense than I could have dreamed. My body was overwhelmed by the feeling of being entered from all directions, and the new nakedness of my sex was adding to the sense that I was being touched everywhere, inside and out.

I was almost too aroused to come: I seemed to have hit a plateau of excitement on which I was floating, and time was not running as it should, so every action felt as if it were in slow motion. Eddie's thumb was pressed against my clit now, holding it down against his shaft so it rubbed me with every stroke, my juices lubricating him. I opened my eyes and saw Eddie's gaze following Kit's thrusts, as his length slipped in and out between my lips. Each of the men seemed engrossed in the other's movements, and the feeling of being merely a connection between one prick and the other washed over me and tipped me over the edge and into the torrent of my climax. Even as I came, I was aware that I was sucking on Kit in time with the contractions of my pussy on Eddie's prick.

The sight of my abandonment seemed, in turn, to bring the two men to a new level of excitement. Eddie, pushing my legs further apart against the arms of the

151

chair, was hammering into my shaved sex, an expression of glazed lust in his eyes. Kit was gentler in his pounding, but his hand on the back of my head was bracing me against his cock, which was plunging deep into my mouth and hitting the back of my throat. Eddie pumped his spunk into me with a groan, and another peak hit me and shook my whole body. The next instant, my mouth was full of hot liquid, as Kit reached his climax, and I sucked on his quivering prick, feeling his come running out between my lips and over my face.

The two men stepped back, panting for breath, and I lay looking at myself in the mirror: my legs akimbo and my pink, hairless pussy literally dripping with our combined juices. My clothes were rumpled and my face was flushed and shiny with Kit's spunk. I felt saturated with come, the metallic taste of it everywhere in my mouth, my whole body reeking of it, as if the imaginary circle of watching men had joined in Kit and Eddie's orgasms and showered me with their own spunk.

Chapter Eleven
The Stag Party

I groaned in frustration and rested my forehead on the steering wheel. After an hour and a half, we had still not managed to leave London. 'So much for leaving after the rush hour finished,' I sighed, and Kit shrugged philosophically.

'Friday night,' he said, 'it's always the same. Now if you'd listened to me and come on the bike – Ow!'

I thumped him hard. As he was well aware, it was I who had wanted to travel on the motorbike, foreseeing our last fine weekend before the autumn rain set in, and he who had insisted on my car. He wanted, for once, to make a respectable impression on his family by not arriving in a leather suit. It had, in fact, provoked our first-ever row. 'I see, so it's all right to make me the scandal of my family and stop Sarah's mother ever speaking to me again, but we have to make a good impression on your family, do we?' I had shouted. He had no real defence, though he did point out that Sarah was a distant cousin, while this bride's father was his own older brother. We galloped through a list of minor grievances before both of us apologised, confessed what was really bothering us,

153

apologised again and laughed at ourselves – and then we went straight to bed with renewed passion.

So we sat in an endless queue of cars on the north-bound road out of London, crawling forward a few yards, stopping, and crawling forward again, every junction a minor victory. In the dark, the streams of head- and tail-lights looked almost Christmassy, like two garlands of fairy lights draped up and down the road. We had hoped, by leaving late, to get to tonight's hotel in an hour or so, ready for a good night's sleep, and to arrive fresh and early at his niece's morning wedding: at this rate, we would crawl in long after the bar had shut and go to bed tense and exhausted. We might as well have stayed in London tonight and set off early in the morning, I thought, as yet another traffic light turned from red to green and back again without our moving an inch.

Kit was doing his best to keep me entertained, telling me jokes he'd heard at work and making up stupid songs about other drivers who annoyed us. 'Oh, I drive an old silver Bluebird,' he warbled, 'that's why I drive so slow, because I know that red means stop and green means ... oh, sorry, did it change? I wasn't looking. Now, which gear am I in . . .?' He was making me laugh, but after a full day at work, a lightning bag-packing session and a rushed meal, and nearly two hours of the most enervating driving, I was longing for a break.

'Tell you what,' I said, 'Once we get to the M25 I'm stopping for a cup of tea.'

The car park at the services was surprisingly full, considering that it was nearly eleven o'clock, and the building was still echoing with overtired families on their way out of London for the weekend. I remem-bered South Mimms service station from childhood journeys, when I had always wondered what the mimms were, imagining them as small creatures living

154

in the landscaped verges. It had been renovated since then, though, and was almost unrecognisable with its new coat of glass and shiny steel. Normally I would have started a rant about pseudo-modernist architecture, but I was too tired. Instead I paid through the nose for a cup of tea and two plastic-wrapped biscuits and sat staring out of the window at the rows of vehicles in the gloom.

'I'll drive for a bit if you like,' Kit offered, and I smiled my thanks.

Watching the people in the car park, I thought with affection of Geoff. 'South Mimms TV,' I murmured to myself.

'Look.' Kit pointed. 'There's a row about to start.'

A man and a woman were standing by a small, white car, the man searching his pockets while the woman stood drumming her fingers on the roof. We could almost hear their voices: 'I know they're here somewhere . . .' 'Of course they're there somewhere, you locked the car with them, didn't you?' they'd be snapping at each other. The man looked truly dejected, and the woman more and more angry.

'What's the betting they turn up in her handbag?' asked Kit.

'Not before she's told him all the things she's always hated about him though,' I answered. Having finally had our first row the day before, we were able to observe with patronising indulgence.

We forgot our own fatigue as we watched the varied stream of humanity trickling in from their vehicles. Some, like us, were obviously weekend trippers, and a couple of motorcyclists rolled in, their bikes loaded up with baggage. There were still some professional drivers taking a break from their vans, and weekly commuters heading home to the Midlands. It was getting so late, though, that we were starting to see people on their way home from an evening out, mostly nipping in to use the shop and the toilets, or perhaps to phone home and blame their lateness on the traffic. A group of young men spilled out of a minibus, their exuberance bursting out in horseplay as the driver locked the doors.

'Stag night,' said Kit, as they moved towards the building in an energetic bundle.

'Which one's the groom?' I asked, trying to pick out the one who should be the butt of the others' humour.

'There.' Kit pointed at the car that had pulled up alongside the minibus, out of which a young man dressed in a French maid's outfit was staggering, helped by a couple of friends. That was the groom, all right. We watched in amusement as he was guided through the doors and into the gents. The rowing couple found the keys – in the woman's handbag as we had guessed – and drove away. We finished our tea and stood up to leave.

On our way out we crossed the foyer and passed right through the middle of the stag party. I exchanged some good-natured banter with them; they were very young, scarcely out of their teens and full of gang bravado. 'Hey,' one of them called after me, 'are you a natural redhead?'

'Want to find out?' I shouted back over my shoulder. We were in the shop before the groom emerged, resplendent in his lacy apron, and as Kit bought a paper I watched them sweep him out to the car park in their lively pack.

Our route back to the car took us right past the stag party's vehicles. There seemed to be some argument going on about what they were doing next, with much pointing at the groom, who was now slumped over the bonnet of the car looking green. To the apparent disappointment of the younger members, the groom was loaded back into the car and driven away as we drew near, while the rest of the party milled about the open doors of the minibus. Walking just ahead of Kit, I felt them turn their attention to me, so I played up to them, sashaying straight towards them so they'd have to part to let me through. 'All right, darlin'?' said the one who'd called after me before. 'Come to show us if your collar and cuffs match?'

I could have made a cutting riposte and walked on, but I decided to call their bluff and stopped right in the middle of the gang. I was emboldened by the knowledge that I now had no pubic hair to match my head, and that it would stun this bunch of youths into silence if they knew. 'Why,' I asked the ringleader, a short blond man in a polo shirt, 'haven't you seen a woman's muff before?' As I'd hoped, the others burst into laughter, enjoying their friend's humiliation. Kit caught up with me and, seeing him, the boys drew back and we walked on.

Kit slipped an arm around my waist. 'You do like to tease the boys, don't you?' he whispered. 'Poor little things, they'll all be going home as stiff as pokers, with you showing off to them like that.' He pulled me to him and kissed me deeply, pushing his hand down the front of my jeans. I was wearing no knickers, and his cold hand drew a shiver of excitement from my hairless sex. Knowing how turned on he was by the thought of me provoking the stag party, I found the idea even more tempting.

'You're right,' I whispered back between kisses, 'it's not fair, is it? Perhaps I should go back and fuck the lot of them.'

His hand squeezed my sex, already growing wet with excitement. 'Good idea,' he said, turning me round with a hand in the small of my back and marching me back to the minibus. It was my turn to have my bluff called.

The stag party was still trying to organise itself back into the minibus, young Mr Blond apparently fighting one of his friends for the front seat. They stopped as they saw us arrive, looking a little worried: afraid, perhaps, that Kit had come to defend my honour with his fists. 'Evening, lads,' he said pleasantly, to a ripple of replies. 'On a stag night?'

'That's right,' said Mr Blond, reasserting his status.

'Done anything good?' continued Kit. They were regarding him with suspicion, but could find nothing to object to.

'We went to a comedy night,' one of the others offered.

'And?' Kit was fishing for more.

'And Nick's had too much to drink and they've taken him home, so that's it.'

'That's a shame,' Kit sympathised. 'Not really the way you want a stag night to end, is it?'

'No,' came the chorus of disappointed young men.

'Tell you what,' said Kit, as if he was offering a packet of cigarettes around, 'you could fuck my girl-friend if you like.'

The stag party exchanged glances, wondering if this was a trap to give Kit the excuse to punch one of them. Kit pushed me forward into the middle of the circle, and I let my eyes roam round theirs with a challenging stare.

'What's the matter?' I said as they rested on Mr Blond. 'Aren't you man enough for me?'

In reply, he stepped towards me, kissed me on the mouth and squeezed my breast with his hand. From the way his tongue entered my mouth, I could tell there was genuine arousal there as well as showing-off. My heart was beating fast: could I really handle this situation? Teasing them was one thing, but I knew Kit was waiting to see me go all the way. Mr Blond released me and stood staring.

'Anyone else?' invited Kit, sitting casually on the rear step of the minibus.

There were six of them, the other five hanging back nervously. In the driver's seat I glimpsed an older man, probably a professional driver hired for the night, watching curiously in the rear-view mirror. For once, Kit was leaving it to me to run the show, and I looked round at my audience provocatively, enjoying their fear.

'Come on,' I challenged them. 'Don't tell me you've never shared a woman before.' Still they hung back, glancing at each other for encouragement. 'You.' I pointed at the tallest of them, a lanky youth with short black hair. 'Come here.' He obeyed, watched by his friends, and I drew him to me with an arm around his waist. I could actually feel him trembling.

'Don't be scared,' I whispered to him, too quietly for the rest of them to hear, and I pressed my lips against his. He offered no resistance, opening his mouth to my tongue, but he remained completely passive as I kissed him. Only the heated swell of his erection betrayed his enjoyment. I rubbed my hand over it and heard a whimper in response. 'Nice stiff cock,' I said, loud enough for the listening gang around us. 'Mind if I get it out?' He made no reply at all, but I felt an answering leap beneath the rough cloth of his trousers. I was expecting more ridicule for him from his fellow stag-nighters, but they seemed stunned into silence. As I unzipped his fly and put my hand inside his boxers, I could feel their eyes burning into me, willing me to go further. I didn't even care about Kit watching me: tonight I was playing to the gallery.

The collective intake of breath as I took a firm grip of Mr Tall's prick and pulled it out into the night air was almost a gasp. Mr Tall himself had his eyes shut, a slight frown on his face as if he were trying to convince himself this was really happening. His erection was gorgeous, long and thick, the foreskin pulled

159

back to reveal a proudly curved head, at whose tip a drop of moisture was already hanging. 'Beautiful,' I said. 'Now, wouldn't you like to shove that into my wet pussy?' I felt a spasm run through him: he was using all his self-control to stop himself from coming at once, shooting his spunk all over the front of my T-shirt.

'Go on, Andy,' said Mr Blond, trying to prove he was cool about the whole situation. 'Give it to her, mate.'

Still holding his hot prick in my hand, I backed towards the open rear doors of the minibus. Kit moved out of the way, standing aside as I led Andy into the vehicle. The others crowded around the open doors, watching as I pulled down my jeans and kicked them off with my shoes. I could just see Kit's face behind them in the darkness, keeping one eye on me and another on the car park: having ruled out arriving by motorbike as too disreputable for his family, he wasn't keen to attract attention for indecent behaviour in a public place.

The minibus was an old one with a bench seat down each side so, as I lay down on one, I knew all the young men watching could see my shaved pussy, opened up for their view as I opened my legs. 'Come on then, Andy,' I invited him, 'I want to feel that cock inside me.' He stumbled towards me, his head bowed to accommodate the low roof, and knelt between my legs. I took hold of his erection again and guided him into me. Wet and newly smooth as I was, he slid in easily, with a soft groan, his hot young prick filling me deliciously. Over his shoulder I could see the faces of his friends, at once disbelieving and excited. I myself could hardly believe that this was happening, that I was actually having sex with a complete stranger in front of five of his friends. It was a long-time fantasy of mine to perform to such an audience, but I had never expected it to become reality. With Kit in my life, there seemed to be no limit to what I might do. Realising that this was really taking place, the rest of the party pushed through the doors and crowded into the minibus, some sitting on the seat and some standing, hunched beneath the roof.

Andy lacked technique, but his sheer animal enthusiasm was exciting, and he ploughed his big cock into me wildly, so I had to hold on to the edges of the narrow seat to avoid falling off. One of my legs was hanging off the side of the bench and the other, lifted up out of the way, was resting on Andy's shoulder. The sensations of his uncontrolled thrusting against my naked sex along with the awareness that we were providing a live sex show to his friends were incredibly arousing. The watching faces were openly enjoying the sight of Andy's cock moving in and out of my naked cunt, and I saw a couple of the voyeurs taking out their own cocks and wanking as they watched. I felt myself drawing near to climax, but before I reached it, Andy gave a cry and came inside me, his whole body racked with tremors. As they subsided, he slid out of me and stood up, looking down at me with an amazed expression as if he couldn't believe what he'd just done.

I lay, soaking wet and burning with arousal, wanting nothing more than another cock inside me to finish what Andy had begun. 'Your turn.' I addressed one of the masturbating youths, and he spared only a quick glance round his mates before he was on top of me, pounding into me with urgency. This one was heavier than Andy, his body thrusting against mine so hard that my head was banging against the end of the minibus, but I didn't care. Here I was with a queue of men waiting to fuck me, and the feeling of desirability mingled with degradation was overwhelmingly sexy.

I pulled him hard against me so that his thrusts

161

rubbed my clit, and I came almost as soon as he entered me, moaning aloud so he grunted to me as he pumped away: 'That's it, you like that, don't you?' He was more confident than Andy had been, his hands kneading my breasts through the thin T-shirt. I rolled my head sideways and saw that all of them were now playing with their erections, except Andy, who was leaning back against the steamed-up window, and Kit, who stood in the open doorway, hands in pockets. I knew his coolness was just a pose, that underneath he was finding the whole spectacle as much of a turn-on as I was, but his apparent indifference only added to my feeling of being a slut.

Number two climaxed with a cry of 'take that, you little slut', and number three was instantly there to take his place. These boys had warmed to the game and were competing with each other to fuck me in the showiest way. Number three put my legs over his shoulders and gripped my thighs to his chest, driving his cock deeper into me than the two before him, his free hand steadying himself against the wall of the minibus. He seemed to be deliberately slowing his thrusts, putting off his own climax till he could prove his manhood by bringing me to mine. 'Come on, you slut,' he was urging me as his fingers worked on my still-tender clit. 'Come for me now, come on, do it for me.'

The others were feeling braver now, and Mr Blond shouted to him, 'What's the matter, can't you make her come?'

'I can make her come,' he answered through clenched teeth. His eyes were fixed on mine, and suddenly I felt a stinging pain as he slapped my arse hard. The shock provoked a contraction in my cunt and brought on my orgasm, and he came as I did, slamming himself so hard against me it almost hurt.

Number four pulled me off the bench and on to the

floor, entering me so quickly that the tremors of my last orgasm were still echoing through me. Pushing my legs wide apart, he fingered me as he slid himself in and out of me. All the young men looked down to see me, pink and exposed, spread out for their gratification like a centrefold. Number four was kneeling between my legs, controlling his thrusts and varying the speed and depth of his penetration.

I was on a rollercoaster now, my new orgasm beginning before the last one had time to fully subside, the faces of the men looking down adding to my arousal. I felt that prick after prick could enter me and I would lie here, one endless climax rolling on and on, my body's responses quite beyond my control. Kit's eyes were on me, drinking in the sight of me offering myself to this crowd of men.

Number four stayed inside me longer than the others before him, but in the end he too spurted his come into me and stood back for number five. This lad looked so young that I couldn't believe he was one of the group, but his technique betrayed the deceptiveness of his looks. Fair and cherubic he may have been, but he was no angel, judging from the expert way he turned me on my side before entering me, one of my legs braced against his shoulder and the other held down against the metal floor. As he rammed his long cock deep inside me, I could feel the stretch as he pushed my legs wider and wider apart, yet his serene expression remained unchanged. He fucked me till I felt I could split open, all the while stroking my smooth mound and clit, now slippery with the spunk of the four men before him, and gazing into my face. I was still helpless with pleasure, gasping, my cheek pressed against the cold, dirty floor of the minibus. This seemed to be lasting forever, this seraphic violation. Even when he did come, filling me with a few hard thrusts, and stood looking down at me, I did not regain my self-control for several seconds.

I lay, wet and trembling, looking up at Mr Blond, the only one of the six who had not yet enjoyed me. He was taking his time, perhaps conscious of his place at the top of the bill. 'Well, well,' he said, 'you were determined not to let me find out if you were a natural redhead, weren't you?' He dropped to one knee and shoved two fingers into my soaking pussy, his thumb rubbing across my naked clit. An involuntary convulsion ran through my body. He looked up and around the faces of his gang, then back at me. Kit was forgotten, standing patiently outside while these boys played out their own power struggles over my supine body. 'The thing is,' said Mr Blond, standing over me, 'I don't know if I want to stick my cock where you dirty animals have had yours.' I could feel the tension between the youths: was their leader trying to bottle out? He looked down at me again and, bending forward, took hold of my hair and pulled me up to a sitting position. 'No,' he told his friends, 'I think I'd prefer a blow job.'

Obediently, I leant towards him, my mouth open, and Mr Blond shoved his prick into it. I sat passively as he thrust into me, his hand in my hair holding me still, merely sucking a little as his smooth, warm shaft slid between my lips. He was demonstrating to his friends how completely I was subjugated, knowing that they were all captivated by the sight of him penetrating my mouth. I wished Kit could see the full show, but I knew that what he could not see he would be imagining. Sated as I was by all that fucking, the sheer outrageousness of the situation kept me glowing with degraded arousal. If Mr Blond was top dog here, I wanted him to prove it by filling my mouth with his spunk, outdoing the rest of the gang in pure selfish lust. Kit's expressionless face gazed in through the open door, his arms folded, looking so relaxed that he could have been waiting for a bus, not for a total stranger to come in his girlfriend's mouth. Mr Blond glanced back at Kit, without missing a stroke, and his eyes narrowed as he whispered to me, 'Is that how your boyfriend gets his kicks, then? Watching you act like a whore?'

The word hit me like an explosion inside. Suddenly feeling exactly like a prostitute being pimped out as part of the stag night entertainment, I felt a stab of guilty pleasure that pierced my sex. My hand moved towards my clit, looking for relief, but Mr Blond kicked it aside with a tap of his foot. 'Oh no,' he said, 'you're not here to enjoy yourself. If you want something to do with your hands, you can jerk me off.' Doing as I was told, I put a hand to the base of his cock, gripping it in time with his thrusts, and ran the other over his balls. As his movements gathered pace, my own excitement grew within me, and I longed for someone to service me as I was servicing him. Mr Blond's rhythm grew more urgent, his prick sliding deeper into my throat with every thrust till he ejaculated into the back of my mouth, grinding his pelvis into my face, his hand in my hair an immovable control.

With the back of a hand I wiped away the spunk that was running down my chin, looking up at the six young men. They seemed uncertain what to do now, their lust satisfied and their sense of normality returning. My instinct told me that the longer I stayed there, the more they would feel that they had done something beyond the pale, and the more they would blame me for it. Even as I thought that, Kit threw my jeans at me and I got unsteadily to my feet and put them on. The boys drew back to let me pass, part fearful and part appalled, as if I'd shown them a part of themselves that disgusted them. Before we'd even got back to my car, we heard the minibus speed away into the night.

I was reeling with excitement and with a sense of unreality. Had I really had sex with an entire stag party, or was it a fantasy? Kit's hand, firm on my arm, was guiding me across the near-deserted car park. Whatever had happened, I knew he had been there with me. We reached the car but, instead of unlocking the doors, Kit pushed me back against the bonnet and kissed me with violent passion. I responded with the same hunger, my hands struggling with his belt in the quest to assuage the need our game had awoken. Roughly, he forced my face down on to the cold metal and tugged my jeans down around my knees, leaving my pussy exposed, offered up to him. Into my aching cunt he drove his shaft, banging my naked clit forward against the car, so the whole thing rocked on its wheels with the power of his thrusts. Neither of us spoke, our physical urges too strong to leave time for anything else. In a matter of seconds we both came, me crying out with the strength and swiftness of my climax and Kit quivering inside me with a violence I'd never known. We stood for a few minutes in the dark car park, our arms around each other, kissing deeply, sharing something way beyond words. Eventually it was I who said, 'We'd better go. We've got another hour's drive ahead of us.'

As Kit drove, speeding along the empty road, I sat in the passenger seat staring out at the night sky. It seemed strange to me that it was Kit, the man who liked to share me with the world, who had got such a hold on me and I on him. Was he right? Was it freedom from fear that gave us this bond? And if he was right, how far could we really go before we found our limit, and, when we did, what would be the price?

* * *

Luckily, the hotel was one of the impersonal, business-oriented chains that let you check in at any time of the day or night. As soon as we were in the room I stripped off, saying, 'I'm just going to have a shower.' Kit blocked my way into the bathroom.

'No,' he told me, 'I want you as you are, smelling of all those men and their come.'

I looked at him uncertainly. I felt vulnerable, standing naked but still sticky, caked with spunk and with my own juices while he was still fully clothed. Kit ran a hand over my mouth, where the taste of Mr Blond still lingered. I felt a new stirring of excitement as I saw the look in his eyes.

'You've been a very dirty girl, having sex with all those men, haven't you?' I nodded docilely. 'I think you need to be punished, don't you?' I nodded again, this time with real consent.

Kit looked around the room: in front of the built-in desk was an upright chair, rather like a dining chair. 'Bring me that,' he said, pointing to it, and I obeyed. 'Now, get me the bathrobes from the bathroom,' he ordered. When I had brought them, he pulled out the tie belts and discarded the robes themselves. 'Bend over this chair,' he told me. I offered no resistance as he bound my ankles to the back legs of the chair, pushed me forward so I was leaning over the chair's back, and tied my wrists down to the front legs. He had made sure I was sideways on to the hotel room's big mirror, so I could see what a subservient position I was in, rear sticking out and head bowed, hands and feet immobilised. 'There,' he said in a voice of quiet menace, 'that's the right way for a naughty girl to stand, isn't it?'

'Yes,' I replied, apprehension and anticipation making my voice shaky.

I was longing for Kit to touch me, my body alive with the electricity of delicious humiliation, but instead he walked around me, examining me as if I were an animal for sale. Wherever he was, I could see him in the mirror, walking around with his hands in his pockets as before. I could almost imagine him leaving me here and going downstairs to sit in the bar, punishing me by keeping me waiting. He would sit on one of the low sofas, sipping a glass of wine and flicking through a newspaper, all the time knowing that I was here, unable to move, awaiting his punishment.

Leaning over my shoulder so I could hear his steady breathing, he stroked a light hand over the curve of my buttock, making me shiver, then, without warning, he slapped it hard. I felt as if it were burning, all the nerve endings singing out in shock, but Kit had gone straight back to gentle stroking, and the heat was gone in a few moments. In the mirror, I could see a red hand-print where the blow had landed. 'Like that?' he asked.

'Yes,' came my whispered reply. The slap had energised my skin, awaking every inch of it so the slightest touch seemed to draw after it little flames of arousal.

Kit continued with the light stroking, his hand wandering all over my buttocks, up to the hollow of my back and down to the crease where my thighs began. I was almost hypnotised by the delicate touch when another slap made me gasp. He continued to stroke and slap, waiting each time till I had relaxed before surprising me with another blow, letting me know I was at the mercy of his whim. With every spank, the tingling spread, till I was sensitised everywhere, aroused and waiting for him to enter my defenceless cunt, tilted up ready for him by my enforced bending over.

Kit removed his own clothes, folding them carefully and hanging them in the wardrobe, taking his time. When he was naked I could see that he had a big erection, but still he didn't make any move to touch me with it. As I stood, quivering with anticipation, he lay on the bed and turned on the TV in the corner of the room. 'Let's see what they've got on the pay-per-view,' he said, flicking through the channels till he found the porn film. An improbably lip-glossed blonde was lying by a swimming pool while two men fondled and sucked her enormous breasts. Kit stroked his prick thoughtfully as he watched. 'Look, sweetheart, there's another dirty slut who thinks one man isn't enough for her,' he said to me.

He was tantalising me, ignoring me while he watched the on-screen action, running his hand up and down his length while I was unable even to touch myself to relieve the ache growing inside me. As I watched the woman offer herself as the plaything of the two men, my own breasts thirsted for Kit's touch. At last he got up, and my hopes rose, but he walked past me to the bathroom, saying only, 'I need some lubricant for this.' Was he going to leave me here all night while he took his pleasure alone? Was this the punishment he had in mind?

He didn't lie back on the bed, however, but stood beside me, slathering cream on to his prick, so close to my bowed head I could smell its clean, fresh scent, underlain by his own manly scent of sweat and aftershave. 'Smells good, doesn't it?' he mocked me, working his hand along the slippery shaft so I could hear the wet sounds of the cream. 'Not like you, reeking of all those men.' He walked round me, sniffing. 'Let's see ... pussy – positively sticky with come ... Mouth...' He bent his head and ran a predatory tongue over my lips and into my mouth. 'Mmm, tastes of some man's spunk...' He stood in front of me, his slick erection only inches from my mouth, but just out of reach. 'Tut, tut, tut,' he said, shaking his head in

169

mock sorrow, 'is there nowhere clean for a nice boy to put his cock?'

He looked at me. We both knew what he meant, but he let it hang in the air before he turned off the TV and walked around me again in a leisurely semicircle. Picking up the bottle of lotion, he squirted a good palmful into his hand. 'I guess there's only one place left,' he whispered, as the cold cream touched my arsehole and made it pucker in response. He worked it around the tiny opening and then slid a well-lubricated finger inside. As he touched new, hidden points of sensitivity, I groaned with pleasure, the tight ring of muscle relaxing as he flicked his finger inside me. Kit pushed another finger into me, then a third, filling me in a way I had never known before, stretching me open.

I could see him in the mirror, a look of concentration on his face, his hand disappearing inside my rear hole in a slather of lotion. With his other hand he was stroking more of the lubricant up and down his own length. Tied to this chair, I was unable to move, either to resist or to hurry his penetration. Kit pulled his fingers out and spread my buttocks apart with his hands, a single thumb still circling the puckered edge of my smallest opening. I was longing to find out what his prick would feel like, entering me where his fingers had just been, but a little seam of fear ran through my desire, fear that he would hurt me when he forced his way in.

Braced against the chair, I felt the head of his prick pressing against my anus, which tensed involuntarily to keep him out. Kit was holding the back of the chair, pulling against it to apply a slow, steady pressure, forcing the slippery helmet into the tight ring of muscle. I watched him doing it to me, the sinews on his arms revealing how hard he was working to push himself into me, the visible length of his prick a challenge: would he really be able to enter me that deeply? Inch by inch, his thick shaft worked its way into me, bringing with it an extraordinary feeling of being opened up, a profoundly satisfying fullness of penetration, and also a sense of debasement. I felt as if there was now no part of my body that was not Kit's to possess and violate.

Another slap shocked my flank into a twitch of response. I felt my pussy shiver and my bumhole contract sharply with the blow, gripping tightly against the thickness of Kit's cock. A moment later, in reaction, it released its hold, and Kit took his chance to slide all the way in. I watched our reflection in disbelief as the whole length of his cock vanished into me, touching me deep, deep inside. He was in me, right to my core, the automatic clenching of my sphincter serving only to grip him tighter and confirm his presence in my most intimate crevice.

Slowly, gently, Kit worked himself in and out, one hand still holding the chair and the other now caressing my pussy from the front. Under his hand, still slippery with lotion, my clit throbbed with urgency, and deep within me an answering throb was following the pace of Kit's prick as he rocked it into me. I felt as if he had put his hand into the centre of my body and found the very root of my pleasure. I sobbed with arousal as he buggered me, trying in vain to push back against his thrusts, his hand slithering freely over my hairless pussy, his fingers working round my clit and into my cunt. Kit's own excitement was growing, his movements becoming less controlled as he forced his length in and out of me, pushing through the tight ring of my bumhole.

Now sharp instants of pain were hitting me as Kit abandoned his gentleness, but I was beyond caring. As I watched us in the mirror, Kit taking me more brutally than I'd ever seen him before, I came with a

171

violence that left me hanging on to the chair for support. I had never felt an orgasm come from so far within, and every wave of my climax only squeezed my inner muscles around his shaft, urging him towards his own peak. Grunting like an animal, he rammed himself into me with a few powerful strokes, and I felt his ejaculation deep within me.

Kit pulled himself out of me, leaving me feeling strangely empty and a little sore. I was still shaking, resting on my hands on the seat of the chair, trying to get my breath back as Kit untied me.

In the shower, I rested against him as he washed me, rubbing the soap all over my body and rinsing it off with the spray. Once dried, he picked me up and carried me to the bed, laying me on it gently and wrapping me in his arms beneath the soft duvet, so I drifted off to sleep in a warm cocoon of affection.

Chapter Twelve
The Third Wedding

We seemed to have been asleep for only minutes when room service woke us with our continental breakfast. I forced myself to go to the door and take the tray, leaving Kit lying face down in the bed. The smell of the coffee kick-started my senses as I pushed down the strainer in the little cafetière, but he still made no movement. 'Come on,' I urged him, shaking him hard, 'there's no point in turning up all respectably dressed if we turn up late.' He groaned and pulled the covers over his head.

Even with all my badgering, most of the guests had filed into the registry office by the time we joined the tail of the crowd. Kit waved over my shoulder at his brother, standing in the front row with the bride, as if to say, 'Look – here on time and wearing a proper suit!' I put out my hand and accepted a running order from the usher. It was Mr Blond.

Our eyes met momentarily, then we both looked away and pretended we'd never met. Kit hadn't noticed and was cheerfully leading me down the aisle to sit with his family. His niece, Eleanor, was a tiny, dark girl, her elfin looks only adding to the impression

173

that she was far too young to be getting married. Her father, Kit's older brother, leant across to shake my hand and introduce himself. 'Bruno,' he said in that same deep voice. 'You must be a good influence on him: I've never seen him look so smart.' Not as good an influence as all that, I thought, as I smiled back. Or is it part of the duties of the bride's uncle to lend his girlfriend to the groom's party?

'Where's the lucky man?' Kit was asking Eleanor. 'I thought you were supposed to keep him waiting.'

'He's on his way,' she answered dryly. 'Apparently he woke up an hour ago on his floor in a French maid's costume.'

I saw a bolt of realisation strike Kit, but he managed to keep his face straight. 'Sounds like quite a stag night,' was all he said.

The errant bridegroom made his entrance, his lacy apron exchanged for a smart suit. We noted with relief that neither the best man nor the witness was among the previous night's minibus party. The wedding happened with the abruptness that always surprises me about a civil ceremony, and before we knew it we were outside on the pavement again. Kit and I hovered with the rest of the bride's family, trying not to notice that all six of the gang had made it, transformed by smart clothes and best behaviour, but recognisably the same lads. To my relief, not one of them would meet my eye. 'Fingers crossed,' Kit whispered, 'they're more embarrassed than we are.'

After the photos had been taken, Eleanor and her new husband, Nick, led us across the road to the hotel where the wedding breakfast was due to be held. It was an imposing stone building with an ornate facade, the antithesis of the impartial block where we were staying. Automatically, I glanced across the road to see the railway station, recognising it as one of the embodiments of civic pride designed to impress and

174

welcome the traveller who had alighted from the train. All provincial towns probably constructed one during the age of steam, marking the new importance of a place that could now be reached at speeds unimaginable only a few years before. The iron rails cutting across the countryside must have been the information superhighway of their day.

The reception area seemed to have changed hardly at all since then, except that the brass light fittings on the walls were now electrical, not gas-fired. Elegant staff shepherded us across the deep, red carpet into the banqueting suite, a long room with high windows looking across a little square with a fountain. A long table was set with a white cloth and gleaming silverware, with waiters in immaculate uniforms standing along it, white cloths over their arms. I could see now why Kit was so worried about making a bad impression: his was obviously a family that liked to do things properly. We looked for our name-cards and stood behind our chairs, waiting for all the guests to be ready. When everyone was in place, the gentlemen seated the ladies and the best man proposed a toast to the bride and groom. 'The bride and groom,' we all echoed, raising our champagne flutes to where Eleanor and Nick stood glowing with happiness at the head of the table.

I was thankful that they had seated us together, not only because it minimised the risk of embarrassing encounters, but also because I was a little intimidated by Kit's family. His mother, a serious-faced woman with grey hair cut in a stern fringe, was interrogating one of her younger in-laws on current trends in aviation. Her voice carried right along the table, and Kit pulled a mock-scared face at me. 'Sorry,' he whispered, 'we're all petrolheads in this family. She used to fly biplanes before she was married.'

'Where are the truly innovative designs of today?'

she was asking the cowed youth. 'Even the space shuttle looks like a conventional plane. We're in the twenty-first century, for heaven's sake!' No wonder Kit found normal women a shade reticent.

I was on my best behaviour, laying on the charm and laying off the drink, determined to maintain my reputation for being a good influence at least till the end of today – unless, of course, one of the groom's young friends got drunk and decided to brag. The atmosphere of luxury was seductive. I was not used to being waited on quite so attentively, but I thought I could definitely get used to it. Every time my glass was nearly empty, a bottle appeared at my shoulder, and my empty plates were whisked away so smoothly that I scarcely noticed it. All the waiters were young and smart, but there was one who was more than smart: he was gorgeous. His hands were long and slender and his features fine, but he moved with a very masculine grace. In the autumn sunlight, his skin glowed dark mahogany, so dark it was almost matte, as if it had been dusted with cocoa powder. He walked towards the kitchens with an armful of crockery, and I couldn't take my eyes off the smooth back of his neck.

Kit saw my eyes following the young man out of the room and pinched my thigh under the table. 'Don't waste your time,' he whispered. 'He's obviously gay.'

'Why obviously?' I retorted. As a matter of fact, the young waiter had lingered at my shoulder a little longer than was professionally necessary, and I had caught his soft brown eyes straying over me as he poured my wine.

'Haven't you noticed?' Kit went on, rather pleased with himself. 'He's been flirting with me.' I was amused, but my competitive spirit was roused.

'What do you bet me?' I challenged him.

'Hmm . . .' He narrowed his eyes, thinking. 'Tell you

176

what,' he proposed, 'if he's straight, when we get back to the hotel room you do whatever you want to me, and if he's gay, I get to do the same to you.' This was irresistible, a contest with a sexual game at the end of it. We shook hands on the bet.

'But how do we decide who's right?' I wasn't prepared to take the young man's word for it, knowing full well that Kit would bribe him without hesitation to lie to me.

'I guess the race is on,' he said triumphantly.

The rest of the meal was much more exciting, with both of us watching the young waiter's every move, and both of us flirting with him whenever he passed near us. It was ideal: all the fun of the chase while knowing that, at the end of it, it would be a new game for me and Kit.

'Thank you ... what's your name?' I asked the waiter as he refilled my glass yet again.

'Alex,' he purred, with a coy smile. As Alex's long lashes dipped over his eyes, I was already planning what I would do to Kit when my victory had been acknowledged.

The speeches, like the rest of the wedding, were impeccable, and the best man's speech was a model of good taste. To listen to him, you would have thought that the groom had not misbehaved since the age of eight, though the waking up in a maid's outfit did merit a mention. Kit and I risked a knowing glance at the thought of what else had happened on the stag night. With the toasts finished and the cake cut, Kit took advantage of the hiatus to slip out to the gents, and I made friends with his cousin, a shy but pleasant man sitting on my right. Kit was right about the petrolheads: this man turned out to be an engineer working on sports car engines. It was interesting to hear about his work on pistons, but not so interesting that I didn't greet the arrival of coffee as a welcome interruption. 'Excuse me,' I said, standing up as the waiter put our cups in front of us. This time it wasn't Alex serving me. Casting a quick eye across the room, I realised Alex was not there. Alex was missing, and so was Kit. I had only intended to slip out to avoid more talk of valves and V-twin engines, but now I knew I was racing against time.

Out in the reception area, I looked around for the gents. Boldly – no time for niceties here – I walked in, surprising one of the elderly uncles at the urinal. 'Sorry, wrong door,' I called as I left; no corner there where Kit could have been working on Alex. Where could they be? I tried to read Kit's mind, to work out where he would have headed. Of course, he would never have gone somewhere like the gents, where I wouldn't find them; unless I caught them together, he could never prove he had won. So ... where would he expect me to look? Adrenaline was racing through my veins. Somewhere nearby, Kit was risking family disgrace by trying to seduce one of the staff, and waiting for me to catch them in the act. My pussy quivered at the idea. I still wasn't convinced that Alex would be interested in Kit, but either way I was looking forward to finding out.

The sounds of pots and pans told me the kitchen was nearby, and I found the door towards the rear of the reception area. Another 'Sorry, wrong door!' ruled that out – it was open-plan and there was no corner where two men could indulge in indecent behaviour. Next to the kitchen, though, was another door marked STAFF ONLY, which looked as if it might lead out to the yard. I opened it and stepped in.

There was Alex, standing with his back to the door, one arm leaning gracefully against the wall, his trousers clearly round his knees, and there was Kit, kneeling in front of him. At the sound of the door, Alex turned towards me with a guilty look, and Kit's expression turned from alarm to satisfaction as he saw it was me. 'Alex, this is Emma,' he said, making sure I could see that he had Alex's erect prick in his hand.

'Oh, we've met,' I answered smoothly. I wasn't beaten yet.

Realising that I wasn't immediately throwing a fit, Alex watched uncertainly as I locked the door behind me and moved carefully towards them between the shelves of tins. This was some kind of storeroom, and there was barely space for three of us to stand without somebody's knee being pressed against the steel shelving. 'Alex,' I said in mock reproach, 'fancy borrowing my boyfriend and then starting without me!' Kit was still kneeling, his face only inches away from where Alex's prick was rising in a proud curve. I found a sack of rice to sit back on and folded my arms. 'Now, do carry on,' I told them.

Kit was only too willing to obey, bending his head to slide his lips over Alex's erection. It gave me a strange shiver of arousal to see that familiar face penetrated by another man's cock, those lips I had kissed so many times open to receive the long, brown shaft. Alex was leaning against the shelves behind him, arms outstretched to rest on the shelf supports above. Looking down to watch Kit's mouth going to work on him, he looked like an angel coming in to land. Then he lifted his eyes to mine and ran a deliberate tongue round the merest edge of his soft lips. A shiver of desire ran through me.

With my eyes fixed on Alex's, I ran a hand across my own lips and down my throat, sweeping it slowly across my breasts. Seeing the fire in his gaze, I brought my fingers slowly up to the top button of my blouse and began to undo it. Button by button I unfastened it, revealing my smooth, tanned skin inch by deliberate inch. When it was completely undone, I opened the blouse like the covers of a book, giving Alex a clear view of my breasts, pushed up by the ivory lace bra. He responded by placing a long, slim hand on the back of Kit's head and pushing himself more forcefully into Kit's mouth, all the while looking not at the soft lips receiving his thrusts but at my exposed throat and cleavage.

The blouse fell to my sides and I placed my hands under the lace cups, pushing them up so my breasts were squeezed out of their covering. Dropping my head forward, I was able to run my own tongue over the taut curves. I could see it in Alex's eyes, that he was imagining his own tongue doing the same, tasting the salt of my fresh sweat. My fingers pulled the nipples out for his titillation, pinching them into stiff, pink stalks. His eyes were devouring me, his own movements growing faster with his rising excitement. I knew he was being aroused by me but I knew, too, that if he came in Kit's mouth, I stood to lose a bet.

Brazenly, I stepped up to Alex and kissed him deeply on the mouth. He grabbed my breasts, squeezing and stroking them. Kit redoubled his efforts, determined to keep his advantage, but when I hitched up my skirt, Alex was quick to respond. His long fingers were inside my G-string in seconds, slithering over my slick, wet sex and into my pussy. 'Fuck me,' I whispered as I kissed his neck, and he obeyed: his cock, wet with Kit's spit, slid past my underwear and into me up to the hilt. I was pushed back hard against the sharp edges of the steel shelves as he thrust into me, his mouth on mine. Triumphant, elated, I gasped with the force and depth of his penetration, glimpsing behind him Kit's indignant face.

Alex had his hands under my buttocks, squeezing them, pulling me in to him as his thrusts gathered pace. I felt my own climax drawing near, the added element of competition giving it a sharpness that made it all the sweeter. Alex could feel it too, and he seemed to be holding himself back slightly, waiting for me to come. My bare thighs felt the cool touch of a second pair of hands, as Kit slid his arms round Alex from behind, one of his fingers finding my aching clit and echoing the rhythm of Alex's thrusts. Simultaneously, I felt a sharp tug on my thighs and a deep, uncontrolled thrust from Alex, as his spine stiffened. He seemed to be overtaken by a sudden frenzy, his hips jerking wildly as he came into me, groaning with pleasure. Over his shoulder, Kit's face was blazing with victory and arousal. 'That's what you wanted, isn't it?' he was murmuring to Alex. 'You fucking my girlfriend while I fuck you.'

As I understood what was happening – that Alex was the filling in our sandwich, that Kit was fucking me through him, his own climactic thrusts mirrored by Alex's cock in me – I came with a dark intensity that shook my whole body. Kit ploughed into Alex's arse and I saw the younger man's eyes roll back in abandon as he in turn was filled with hot spunk. His double pleasure echoed back to both Kit and me: it was our eyes meeting over his quivering shoulder, our game that was being played out through his ecstatic body.

Kit and I managed a convincing return to the wedding party as the lovesick young couple, holding hands and smiling bashfully. Bruno grinned indulgently as he handed us fresh glasses of champagne. 'Been enjoying the fountains?' he asked with a twinkle.

I tried not to choke as Kit replied with a straight face, 'Yes, very impressive.'

It was still early when we returned to our hotel room, having slipped away from the evening party. Apart from the older relatives interrogating Kit as to his work prospects and casting meaningful glances at me, the only people we knew were the six boys from the groom's party, and we had no particular desire to jog their memories. Besides which, unspoken between us lay our bet and the still-disputed prize. Kit shut and locked the door and we stood facing one another. 'So,' he began, 'are you ready for me to claim my prize?'

I couldn't believe the impudence of the man. His prize? When Alex had so clearly chosen my pussy in preference to Kit's open mouth? 'You really expect me to accept that he's gay, when he couldn't wait to get his cock inside me?' I retorted. 'Or –' I began to undo my blouse as I spoke '– are you saying I'm not a woman?' Kit sat on the upright chair, and the memory of myself tied across it for his pleasure sent a tremor through my sex.

'I don't think there's any doubt about that,' he said softly, and his eyes coolly drank in my undressing. I was deliberately teasing him, reminding him through his own enjoyment of the way Alex's gaze had burnt into my semi-clothed body even as Kit sucked his cock.

'The fact is, though,' said Kit thoughtfully, folding his hands behind his head, 'he was fucking you, but what made him come was my cock up his arse. Wasn't it?'

In Kit's trousers I could see the rise of his erection, as he recalled the tight opening of the young man's arsehole giving way to his invading shaft. I was entirely naked now, but Kit was acting as if he wasn't interested in me, as if all that was turning him on was the thought of Alex's body.

'Hmm,' he sighed, closing his eyes, 'when I slid my prick into that snug little arsehole, he came like a firehose, didn't he? That firm little rear was jerking away as soon as he felt me up him. But then,' he went on, opening his eyes and looking at me with an expression of arrogant challenge, 'he's not the only one who likes to feel me in there, is he?' I felt my face

182

burning, the memory of that shamefully delicious penetration vivid and hot.

'So what?' I dismissed his argument. 'Lots of men like to experiment: that doesn't make them gay. You were the one who was sucking his cock,' I said, moving towards him till I was standing between his thighs, my bare breasts brushing against his face. 'Doesn't that make you gay?'

In reply, he put his arms around my waist and pulled me in so my naked sex was rubbing against the swelling bulge in his trousers. He took one of my nipples in his mouth and sucked gently, sending a quiver of excitement straight to my clit.

'Perhaps you're right,' he murmured. 'After all, I bet you've had that little kitten tongue of yours around a few girls, haven't you?' I trembled with the sudden memory of Jane's soft, juicy pussy opening up under my licking. 'Thought so,' said Kit, running a teasing finger up through my own moist crevice. 'So, shall we call it a draw?' My brain was protesting, wondering how we got from my theory of experimentation to the idea of a draw, but my body was weakening to Kit's touch. I nodded. 'Good girl,' he said, kissing me with a sudden passion that was both a thank you and a promise. 'Shall I go first?'

I lay in the dark, the bedclothes cool against my warm skin. As instructed, I had taken a long, hot bath – alone, Kit having gone down to the bar – and gone straight to bed, wearing the short silk nightdress I always packed and seldom wore. 'Whatever I do,' Kit had told me, 'I want you to be asleep. Don't move or respond in any way.' The warmth of the bath had done its work and, in spite of the anticipation of Kit's new game, I was indeed drifting into sleep, exhausted after last night's adventures.

The sound of the room door opening softly woke

me, and I instinctively opened my eyes before I remembered my instructions to keep them shut. I had seen nothing though, except a thin strip of light from the corridor spilling across my clothes piled on the chair. As I closed my eyes again and heard the door shut, I stilled my apprehension, reassuring myself that only Kit had the key to our room. He was moving so softly that I didn't hear his footsteps across the carpet, and only the faintest breath of cool air on my back told me he was lifting the covers and looking at me. The tiny nightdress had hitched itself up around my waist and he would be able to see my naked buttocks and legs. I managed to keep my breathing deep and steady, even as the cool draught blew across my naked pussy and made it shiver.

Another breath across the shaved skin made me quiver again, but the air this time was warmer. I felt a shudder within as I realised it was Kit's breath, that he was softly blowing under the lifted sheet. I fought the urge to move, to offer my rear to him, but instead pressed my cheek into the pillow. There was a pause, as if he were waiting to see if I would respond, and then the breath came again, a little bolder this time, tantalisingly light on my sensitive, hairless skin. My pussy reacted with an automatic spasm. Again that pause, and again another breath, such a delicate stimulation, repeated again and again till I could feel the moisture around my lower lips chilling whenever Kit's breath passed over them.

I was tense, longing for the next breath, when my sex convulsed to the touch of a single fingertip, a tentative, feather-light stroke along the edge of a lip, as if following the wetness shining in the moonlight. The finger withdrew at once, returning after a few seconds when I made no movement. This time, it strayed more boldly, tracing the petals of my sex and then slipping swiftly, like a darting tongue, into the

184

welling liquid of my hole. It was torture to feign sleep with this intricate attention setting my cunt alight. I wanted to open my legs, at least, to give him full access to my smooth folds, but I was forbidden to do anything either to resist or help him, so I lay heavy and still.

A second finger joined the first in its intimate stroking, and then a third, their touch still light and quick, now moving all over my sex, flicking in and out of me. I wanted Kit to plunge his fingers deep inside me, to exert some pressure on my clit, instead of this breath-light touching, but I waited patiently, lying unresponsive like a sleeping woman who is unaware that an intruder is touching her so intimately. A guilty pleasure washed through me, as if I were complicit in some sordid encounter.

The hand was gone, leaving only the cool night air again, washing over my wet pussy. The bed shifted, almost imperceptibly, and I felt the covers softly fall back on to my half-naked body. This time, though, they did not fall over my back; someone was in the bed behind me, a pocket of warm air between us at my back. I waited in excitement to find out what would happen next. In the silence, I heard the faint sound of a zip opening, and the next moment felt a warm touch on my sex. This touch was at once softer and firmer than the stroking fingers, a gentle but insistent pressure, pushing its way into my lower lips. My total passivity gave Kit's movements a clumsy air; there was something fumbling about them, which only added to the sense of furtive pleasure. Carefully, as if he were trying to do it without my noticing at all, he pushed his cock into me, inch by inch, till I could feel the rough cloth of his trousers against my shaved skin.

We lay still, me in a state of outward relaxation, Kit electric with tension. After so much delicate touching, my pussy was alive with urgent need, contracting around Kit's hot, smooth shaft in spite of me. With infinite slowness, he started to move, sliding it out till he was barely touching me with it and then slipping it back in with equal patience. I wanted to throw my hips back against his thrusts, to grab his hand and place it on my burning clit, to shout 'Fuck me now!' That wasn't in the rules, though: this was Kit's fantasy, and in his fantasy I was a sleeping stranger in an anonymous hotel room. Was this how Hamish had felt, I wondered, waking up in his impersonal sleeper compartment to find Jane sucking on his prick. What would it be like, if it really were a stranger and not Kit, if I were waking now from sleep to find an unexpected cock filling me? Perhaps I would be waking from a sexy dream, in which some figure of fantasy was submitting me to his will, to find that the heat in my belly was more than just imagination. I lay imagining it, that I had woken from sleep to find this stranger using me, penetrating me without my consent, and felt a strange lurch of excitement race through me. 'I'm too scared to let him know I've woken up,' I told myself, justifying in my fantasy the passivity that Kit wanted in his. 'I'm frightened that if he knows I'm awake he'll become violent, so I'm pretending I'm still asleep.'

I could almost picture the intruder, frightened in his turn by the risk of discovery, becoming more urgent in his excitement, clasping his hand over my mouth to keep me quiet. He would whisper threats in my ear as he hurried to reach his satisfaction, telling me not to tell a soul or it would be the worse for me, and other phrases half-remembered from the villains of my childhood adventure stories. This picture gave an added edge to my unresponsive state. As Kit grew more excited and less cautious, my body rocked with his thrusts, and I felt the novel sensation of complete inertia. Somehow it amplified the effect of his rhythm, my body shaken to and fro as if buffeted by waves.

When my clit felt the light touch of a finger, I could not restrain a groan of pleasure, but still I kept my eyes shut and my body inert. As I was pushed forwards against his hand by each thrust from behind, I felt again like the furtive participant in an unmentionable act. So long as I acted asleep, we could do anything, and it need never be acknowledged. I felt a rush of liberation, of anonymity, as I had with the six youths in the minibus. I was playing a part and need take no responsibility for my body's responses. As I thought this, the silent intruder increased his thrusts and the woman who was silently complying through fear was overwhelmed by a powerful climax. The complete lack of tension allowed the waves of orgasm to rack my whole body. The ripples were still subsiding as the intruder slipped silently out of the bed and I heard the room door open and close once more.

I lay in the darkness, alone again, the feeling of a secret encounter glowing within me. How had Kit known that this game would touch something shadowy inside me? Or was it really just a fantasy of his that happened to speak to my most hidden desires? Many men had excited me physically, but Kit had found so many keys to darkly exciting parts of my mind. I found myself remembering the dream I'd had in the Scottish castle, that Kit was the devil, come to steal my soul. Perhaps he was; all I knew was that I was going to take whatever he had come to offer me, and if my soul was forfeit, it was a price I was willing to pay.

There was a knock on the room door, and I shook off my strange thoughts as I went to open it. Kit smiled at my bleary face, blinking in the light, and kissed me lightly. 'Had a good sleep?' he asked cheerfully. I nodded sleepily, with an inward shiver at the idea that Kit had really been in the bar all along and knew nothing of my sleeping encounter. He dispelled the mood by lying back on the bed, still fully clothed.

'Your turn,' he said, with an expectant light in his golden-brown eyes.

'Strip,' I ordered him, 'and lie on the bed.' I left him undressing and went into the bathroom. After I had pulled off the rumpled nightdress and splashed cold water on my face, I opened the carrier bag I had brought back from the afternoon's excursion into town. In a side street near the station, while Kit was queuing in a bank, I had been amazed to chance upon a sex shop. Knowing I had only a couple of minutes before Kit rejoined me, I had gone in and asked bluntly for what I wanted, enjoying the surprise on the manager's face. Probably there were not many ladies shopping in this provincial market town who would walk straight in, smile, and ask to see his selection of double-ended dildos. It worked, though: by the time Kit emerged from the bank, I had not only selected one, but I had also bought myself a second-hand book on suspension bridges from the shop next door to disguise the bulk of the box.

I took it out of its packaging and examined it, running a thumb over the smooth ridges of the plastic. There was something surgical about it that made it more perverse, as if it was some hybrid product of a false-limb factory. I placed the cold, rigid head of one end at the entrance to my cunt and pushed it in. It was still wet from our last game and the dildo slid home as if it had been made to fit. My inner folds gripped it instinctively.

I looked at myself in the bathroom mirror. A strange hermaphrodite stared back at me, a huge pink erection curving up below full breasts and feminine features. There was not even a scattering of hair to disguise the root of the creature's cock: it seemed to spring out from between its sex lips, like an oversized clit. I was fascinated. I had often fantasised about having a prick, wondering how it would feel to have all my most sensitive parts on the outside, to penetrate another person, or to put my fist around my sex and ejaculate into the air. Now, there it was. I moved my fist up and down it, and felt the answering movements inside me set up a vibration of excitement.

Kit was lying on the bed naked, as I had told him, on his back with his arms by his sides. When he saw me come back in with my new prick, his fists clenched involuntarily, but he made no protest. His eyes asked a dozen questions, but all I said to him was, 'Turn over.' Kit obeyed, his face down into the pillow and his hands on the back of his head in a gesture of surrender. The vulnerability of his upturned bottom was fiercely arousing to my new self, my priapic self. I felt the lust for conquest rise through me. I would sodomise him, yes, but that was not enough.

On the floor lay Kit's trousers with their leather belt. I bent to pick it up, feeling as I did so the delicious pressure of the dildo on my inner folds. Kit lay motionless as I pulled the belt free, but when he heard the sharp slap of it hitting my palm in a test stroke, he jumped with apprehension. My own hand stung with a heat that was intense but soon evaporated. I could see the tension in his body as he awaited the first blow on his own skin, but still he made no sound, no movement. 'Yes,' I hissed to him, 'very obedient now. But not so well-behaved this afternoon, were we? Sucking the servant's dick in the store cupboard. Is that what a well-brought-up young man does at his niece's wedding?'

Kit didn't answer. Judging my swing to hit his buttock with the same sting I had just tested, I let the leather smack against his flesh. His whole body quivered with the shock, and I saw a red weal follow the

189

touch of the belt. 'Answer me,' I told him. 'Is that what a nice boy does?'

'No,' he replied in a low voice, congested with either pain or arousal, I couldn't say which.

'I think you need to be punished, don't you?'

'Yes,' he answered.

I was intoxicated by the feeling of power and the knowledge that Kit, who could have got up from the bed at any time and taken the belt out of my hand with no difficulty, was lying there, submitting to my commands.

I swung the belt again and heard the satisfying crack as it hit him. Again, he flinched but made no sound. Two red stripes crossed his buttocks now. I drew a curious finger along one, seeing his sensitised skin quiver at my touch. Was Kit enjoying this, or was I pushing him too far? 'Stand up,' I ordered him. With surprising grace, and keeping his hands behind his head, he stood facing me. In the mirror I saw the red marks across his behind, and facing me I saw an erection that mirrored my plastic one. It seemed Kit was enjoying it very much.

'Bend over the chair,' I told him, not allowing the enjoyment I was feeling to show in my stern face. He bent forward and held on to the seat of the chair, his posture echoing mine the night before. I swung the belt again, this time across his shoulders, knowing he could see its approach reflected in the mirror and anticipate the pain. As I expected, the flinch was smaller now that he could see when each blow was coming. Three times I let the belt fall across his submissive back and watched the pain and pleasure chase each other across his face. Three times I felt a kick of excitement when I heard the leather kiss the skin.

There was a spark of disappointment in Kit's eyes when I laid the belt aside. I laughed mockingly at him. 'Surely you didn't think that was your punishment?' I asked him. 'No, the belt is just a little something to whet the appetite, my dear. Now we move on to the main attraction.'

Making sure he could see my every move, I picked up the bottle of lotion from the dressing table where Kit had left it, and let a cold trickle run out over Kit's rear and down the dark crevice between his cheeks. The puckered opening of his rear hole contracted when it felt the cold liquid pour over it, and I saw his cock twitch in answer. Pouring more of the white fluid into my hand, I rubbed it over the big, plastic cock, relishing the way each touch pressed it against my inner ridges.

My hands looked small against Kit's buttocks as I pushed them apart and placed the end of the dildo against the little star of his arsehole. I could see fear and longing fighting in his face. 'Don't be scared,' I whispered, 'it won't hurt much. Just relax and take it like a man.' I took a firm grip on his hips and pushed the dildo into him. At first, the resistance was so strong that I thought I would never penetrate him with something so large, and Kit's eyes were closed with the pain. Instead of putting me off, however, the knowledge that I was hurting him, and that he was offering himself willingly to this pain and humiliation, rose up inside me like a flame. I pushed harder, the other end of the dildo ramming itself into me with the same force, so I was at once penetrator and penetrated. Kit gave a little whimper as I slid into him, the plastic shaft stretching him open as I watched.

Once the head of the dildo was past the ring of muscle at his entrance, there was less resistance to its entry. The smooth plastic slipped into Kit's rear as I pushed, each ridge adding to the sensations inside my cunt. His knuckles were white as he gripped the edge of the chair, but he made no complaint, his eyes fixed on his reflection in the mirror, watching me force this cock into him, steadily invading his helpless flesh. Looking down at his rear, offered up to me, I felt a surge of power and thrust my length into him more brutally, feeling his anus clench in vain against the invading shaft. I could hardly believe that he was receiving the full length of the oversized dildo, but somehow it continued to vanish inside him till my shaved clit was touching the smooth curve of his backside, slippery with lotion.

Bracing myself now against the back of the chair, I began to move in and out of him, the resistance of his tight passage setting up a parallel thrusting in my cunt. Kit was trembling, his face telling me clearly how overwhelmed he was by the sensations. 'Yes,' I murmured as I pounded into him, 'you like to be fucked, don't you? I bet you'd like that Alex to ram his cock into your hole, wouldn't you?' Kit groaned in reply, and I dealt him a slap across his flank that made his arsehole squeeze the dildo in reflex.

'Yes,' he gasped, 'yes, I want his cock up my arse,' and with that he came, quivering against my thrusts, his cock jerking in the air as his come spurted out in long threads. Seeing it, I felt as if it were really my cock up his arse, as if I too were shooting my spunk into his deepest chasm, and I rammed mercilessly into him as I came, the dildo pounding into me as I ploughed into him.

As I pulled the dildo out of Kit's hole, I saw it twitch in relief, white lotion trickling out of it as if I had indeed filled him with my spunk. The dildo looked incongruous now its work was done, and I pulled it out of myself too, throwing it into the bathroom. Kit caught me in his arms and kissed me warmly, as he often did after one of our more extreme games, as if to reassure me that our bond of mutual trust was still there. He dropped on to one knee and I tried to help him up, concerned that I might genuinely have hurt him this time. He waved me off, laughing. 'You fool,' he said, 'can't you see what I'm doing?' I was mystified, and he laughed all the more, still holding on to my hand. Then his face went very serious.

'Emma,' he said, 'will you marry me?'

Chapter Thirteen
A Difficult Conversation

Kit knelt before me, his honey-coloured eyes looking up with an openness that frightened me. 'Marry me,' he repeated softly, and he brought my hand to his lips and kissed it with a kiss that came from his soul. In the carpeted quiet of the hotel room, all I could hear was our breathing. We seemed to be cocooned, out of normal time and space, and as I looked down at his naked body, sticky with sweat and the liquids of our lovemaking, I felt a huge surge of tenderness. Perhaps we could get married; perhaps the romantic dreams that Nick and Eleanor were taking with them tonight were not too distant for us to reach out and touch.

I opened my mouth to say yes, but before I could speak, all the reasons why it was impossible came flooding into my mind. How could we get married? We would never be able to answer the simplest questions from the relatives about how we met. Who would be the best man? Geoff, regaling the guests with the story of how he and Kit first met over my blindfolded and pinioned body? No, marriage was for normal people with conventional relationships, the sort of people in whom a wedding evoked sentimental dreams of white lace, not darkly erotic images of illicit passion. Sadness and relief mingled in me as I shook my head, bidding farewell in my mind to the innocent joys that others would find on their wedding days.

Kit stayed where he was, refusing to let the moment go. 'Why not?' he asked softly. I shook my head again, impatiently this time, and was amazed to feel tears shaken from my cheeks. Suddenly I was full of rage, angry with him for pressing my nose against the glass of the lighted window that I knew was not for me. Just for a few seconds, he had shown me a picture of what might have been, and the recognition that I was not the sort of person who appeared in those scenes of bliss was almost more than I could bear. Why couldn't he have left me alone? We had been happy till now, journeying together into the wilder regions of our bodies and souls, and never missing the comfort of a normal relationship.

All I wanted was to leave him, that very second, to go out and get in the car and drive for miles through the night, to be alone and free again. I pulled my hand from his and started looking around for my clothes, blinking away the tears that were still coming. I thought he would try to stop me, to put his arms around me and keep me there; perhaps I was hoping for it. Instead he stood where he was and talked to me.

'What is it, Emma?' he asked, 'What's the matter? Have I said something to hurt you? If I have, I'm sorry, but please, tell me what it is?' I couldn't speak, my throat was tight with pain, so I just shook my head, struggling into my underwear and groping blindly for my blouse. Kit picked it up and passed it to me, as he went on, 'Don't walk out on me. If you don't want to marry me, fine. If you don't want to see me any more after this, that's OK, but we should talk

195

about it before you go.' I was sobbing now, hiccuping with tears, barely able to do up my skirt. I was longing now for Kit's comforting arms, but still he stood, naked and motionless, only his soft deep voice reaching out to me. 'Why are you running away?' he asked. 'What are you afraid of?'

Hearing him say that, I was transported back to the dark bedroom in the castle, when he'd asked if I was really the only woman he'd met who was not afraid of life. Now, it seemed, he had found something that frightened me, something from which I wanted to flee into the night. What was it, indeed? A few minutes ago we were voyaging fearlessly into places where most couples never dare venture. Now, I was full of panic and hurt. I looked at his calm, gentle face, at the body I knew so well, at the eyes looking at me with concern but above all with a frankness I'd never seen before. 'I don't know,' I said shakily, and I walked back to him and hid my face in his chest.

Now he wrapped his arms around me, holding me close and resting his cheek against the top of my head. I felt his voice vibrating in his chest as he talked to me: 'I think you want it, but you're frightened of it. You want to be with me, but you're scared that if you admit you want it, something will go wrong. Is that it? Or do you think I'm trying to trick you and turn you into somebody else?'

I shook my head, my wet face rubbing against the damp hairs on Kit's chest. I didn't know what I was afraid of, I only knew that all our bold adventuring had led us here and I was, finally, lost in the wilderness. A pang bit through me as I suddenly missed Geoff, our easy relationship that wasn't a relationship, his friendly affection that carried no conditions. Things were so much simpler with Geoff.

Kit held me as I stood and cried, saying nothing as sobs racked my body. I felt raw, letting him see me so

196

vulnerable, far more exposed than in any of our extreme sexual games. Underneath the sadness, though, there was a warm glow of intimacy. I was glad that he had uncovered this in me, and glad that I had stayed to let him share it instead of running blindly into the night. When the weeping had finally subsided, I wiped my eyes with the hanky Kit gave me and let him make me a cup of tea with the tiny kettle. We sat together on the bed, me drinking my tea and Kit – now wearing one of the bathrobes – with his arm around me. He flicked the TV on and found a black-and-white film, and we watched the private eye follow his lonely quest through the dark, rainwashed streets. Kit always knew, I reflected, when it was a time not to talk.

Drained as I was by emotions, I was turning over in my mind Kit's proposal and my own surprising reaction. The detective in the film had encountered the *femme fatale*, like him a creature of the night, like him eternally roaming an amoral world of violent passions. Was that how I saw myself? Is that why I felt that the cosy gingham world of the family was not for me? But this was a film. In real life we write our own scripts. In real life I could try something utterly unknown.

THE END, appeared on the screen, over the *femme fatale*'s last lonely sashay down the dark street. Kit took my long-empty teacup and turned off the TV. As I watched him, I felt as if I were seeing him truly for the first time. Like me, he was a person full of desires, fears and curiosity. He wasn't the devil, come into my life with a supernatural agenda to trap me, but a man, looking for his own way in a world full of conventions, just as I was. Why shouldn't we get married? We had already shown more trust for each other than many married couples ever find. I caught him in my arms as he turned round and pulled him back on to the bed, kissing his face. 'That offer you made,' I said

197

to him, 'is it still open? Because if it is, the answer is yes.'

We stayed in bed as long as we could, till the receptionist rang up and said they'd have to charge us for an extra night. I'm sure they thought we were enjoying a long morning of sex, but in fact we just couldn't stop talking. Even as we carried the bags down to the car, we were still discussing what we'd like on our wedding day. Some things went without saying: Jane would be the photographer, of course, and Kit reduced me to giggles by insisting that we should ask Alex to do the catering. 'After all,' he suggested half-seriously, 'you could say it was him that brought us together.' All the way home in the car we were planning guest lists, venues and dates. From being the most frightening thing he had ever suggested to me, marrying Kit had turned overnight into a new game for us to enjoy.

My sister was delighted, of course. I didn't mention to her that Kit was the same man with whom I had disgraced myself on Sarah's Big Day. Jane roared with laughter, having a more detailed knowledge of Kit's and my record at weddings, but told me immediately that she was planning my hen night. The only person I wasn't looking forward to telling was Geoff. With immaculate timing, he had come home just before we went away, but I hadn't seen him at all since our sunny meeting in Soho all those months ago. I tried to feel light-hearted about it, telling myself that it was quite funny, being able to announce that Kit's status was now clear as my fiancé. A cold stone in my stomach told me, though, that it was not going to be an easy conversation.

Picking my way across the smoky bar, I couldn't help but feel my spirits lift as I spotted Geoff's familiar face in the far corner. Slightly more tanned, but other-

198

wise unchanged, he was sitting quietly with a book, a pint and a cigarette and didn't see me until I was right by his table. His huge grin told me he was just as pleased to see me, and he crushed me to him in a fierce hug. Surely our friendship would endure, no matter what.

Before any serious discussion could be done, I had to catch up on his exploits and be shown his new tattoo. Geoff unbuttoned his jeans to show me a word in Arabic flowing across his flat brown lower abdomen. 'It means voyager,' he told me, as I drew an admiring finger across his warm skin. It looked as if it had just been written with a broad-nibbed pen. 'At least –' a wry smile made creases around his eyes '– that's what they told me it meant. For all I know, it could be the Arabic for "kick me".' He had been in Tunisia for months, working out in the desert on a new film that was set in ancient Rome.

'Let me guess,' I teased him, 'you were fighting lions.' He shook his head, looking, I thought, a bit regretful.

'No, they can do all that with computers now,' he said.

I didn't want to break this mood of warm reunion. The spark between us was still there, I had felt it as I touched his Arabic tattoo, and it had always fed our friendship. I was enjoying sitting beside Geoff, feeling the warmth of his thigh against my leg, smelling his clean, fresh scent. Till I had told him about me and Kit, though, neither of us could relax. When Geoff went to the bar, I knew I would have to grasp the nettle.

Geoff put the two glasses on the table and I took a deep breath. 'I've got some news for you,' I blurted out, without even thanking him for the drink, 'about Kit and ... and me.' Geoff sat beside me and waited for me to tell him. 'You, um, you wanted to know

199

what we . . .' I was faltering, my heart thumping in my chest, as I dreaded seeing Geoff's reaction. I knew we had no ties to each other, but instinct told me this was going to have a sharp impact on both of us. 'We're getting married.' I managed to spit it out.

Geoff took a sip of his beer. I couldn't drink mine – my mouth was dry and my lips seemed to be stuck together. He put his glass back on the table and raised his eyebrows. 'Well,' he said, 'I guess that clears that one up.' We sat in awkward silence. I was afraid he was about to get up and walk out but, after drinking about half his pint of beer, he smiled an odd smile, looking at me with the air of someone who has been beaten in a fair fight but taken some heavy punches in the process. I wanted to put my slim hand on his broad brown one and say that it wouldn't make any difference, that it wouldn't change our friendship, but I knew that wasn't true. At least he hadn't made any of the obvious objections, that we'd known each other only a few months, that I wasn't the marrying type.

We didn't know what to say to each other. All around us the noise of people chatting and laughing made our silence seem all the more loaded. 'You will come to the wedding, won't you?' I asked him, desperate to start piling up the foundations of some kind of new relationship from the ruins of the old one. He shook his head before he looked at me and smiled again.

'No,' he said, 'you know me and weddings. Don't really mix.' We looked long and honestly into each other's eyes. This was agony, but neither of us wanted to cut it short, knowing that it marked the end of our intimacy and even – though we didn't want to say it – of our friendship.

'I suppose it's my own fault,' he said.

'Please, Geoff,' I thought, 'please don't say you were

in love with me all along and were a fool not to say it.' He spared me that.

'If I'm not the settling down type,' he went on, 'I can't expect a gem like you to always be there when I get home. Sooner or later, somebody was bound to snap you up.'

'It's not really like that,' I attempted, remembering the extraordinary scene of Kit's proposal.

'No,' Geoff said, getting up suddenly and reaching for his coat, 'I'm sure it's not like that, not for you and Kit. But for you and me ... it makes no difference, does it?' He pulled on his jacket, leant over and gave me a swift, constrained kiss on the cheek. 'What's the point of getting married if it's not going to change anything?' And, abruptly, he was gone.

I couldn't go straight home to Kit. I had no regrets about the step we were taking, but severing the strange bond I had with Geoff had hurt, and I needed to be alone for a while. I called Kit and told him I was going for a walk, but he had a better suggestion. 'Take my bike,' he said, 'it's parked up outside your flat. I'll leave the keys under the mat, so you don't even have to come in and talk to me.' The man was an angel.

Not that it was his bike, of course. Yet another motorcycle manufacturer had rashly lent their latest product to Kit in the hope of a good write-up, and he had insisted, as he always did these days, that I should be put on the insurance as well – 'So I can take photographs of someone else riding it.' I'm sure they saw through it, but what could they say? It was an inspired suggestion, though. Even before I got back to my flat I was thinking about which quiet winding road I could sweep along, not about the raw separation from Geoff.

True to his word, Kit had left the keys under the doormat, and a helmet and oversuit locked to the bike. He knew me far too well, I reflected, as I zipped myself up and mounted the bike. Even pulling out of the drive into the late-evening traffic gave me a surge of liberation. The rush of adrenaline as I picked up speed was exactly what I needed to blow away any shadows, and to reassure me that I was not giving up my old life of freedom for one of slavery. As I drew to a stop back at my flat, my heart still pounding, I wondered whether Kit was giving me an explicit message. 'I am not trying to tie you down,' he could have been saying. 'Marrying me will not be a cage.'

I walked in and found Kit lying on my bed reading. He looked up, saw my glowing face and smiled with pure happiness. 'Thank you,' I said, climbing on to the bed beside him and kissing him softly. 'Thank you for that.'

'That's all right,' he said, putting an affectionate arm over me as I lay beside him, 'it's my pleasure.'

Kit looked surprised when I asked him, over breakfast, if he wanted to come and see my wedding dress being fitted. 'No,' he said, with a tone of mild rebuke, 'the bridegroom isn't meant to see it till the day of the wedding.'

I laughed. 'The bridegroom isn't meant to have fucked the bride the first time they met, either,' I pointed out.

'That's different,' he said confidently, pouring us both a second cup of coffee. 'If we're getting married, we might as well do all the stuff . . . you know, play it according to the rules.' His eyes twinkled wickedly. 'More fun that way.'

'All right, if that's your attitude,' I answered, 'I'll take Jane.'

I was hoping for the undivided attention of at least three dressmakers, pinning and sewing me into my dress, but the shop was unnaturally busy and the assistants seemed overrun. I had come once before, to be measured and to choose the design, and had secretly enjoyed standing in front of the long mirror in my underclothes while one girl pulled the tape measure tight around me and the other had written down the measurements she called out. I had felt like what I was, a participant in a ritual of preparation. All over the world, women gathered to prepare the bride for her husband's admiration, adorning her body with whatever ornaments were deemed most suitable. We liked to feel superior in the civilised West, but I could see no difference at all between the boned confection I had come to try on and the gold that decorated an Eastern bride.

I was glad I had brought Jane because she offered to dress me in the fitting room and call the seamstress when I was ready. It was quite a relief to get out of the hectic shop and into the stillness of the back room. Jane spread the dress out and we gazed in admiration. It was very traditional in cut and colour and, like Kit, I felt that a wedding was a chance for lots of ceremony and solemn games, and that it would be more fun to break some rules if you had played by them in the first place.

From a boned lace bodice, cut low across the shoulders with transparent lace sleeves, a full train of ivory silk spread across the floor. As I lifted the dress to step into it, I was amazed by how little it weighed: the boning gave it a springy stiffness, but the yards and yards of raw silk were as light as cobwebs. I stood looking at myself in the long mirror as Jane did up the hooks and eyes at my back, pulling the bodice tight around me. A perfect bride stared back, her curves accentuated by the tailored cut and the clouds of the full skirt making her seem to float above the ground. Feeling the pressure of the tight fit around my breasts and waist, and the loose silk brushing against my bare thighs, I was reminded vividly of my dream on the way to the wedding where Kit and I had first met. I pressed my hands against the lace, feeling the hardness of the tiny pearl beads over the soft rise of my bosom.

Jane pulled the last hook into place and stood back to see the effect. She drew a breath as the full transformation hit her: I had walked into the shop a modern young woman in jeans, and now stood here like something made of icing, a vision of ethereal femininity. 'Wow,' she breathed, 'you look absolutely stunning.' My reflection gazed back at her, part sacrificial lamb and part goddess, the embodiment of the mystery of the female sex.

Standing behind me, Jane placed her hands on my waist, using the same gesture a male ballet dancer uses when he is about to lift the ballerina high in the air. I felt as light as that, my upper body held and lifted by the dress, my lower body floating amid the cool fabric. I let my weight drift backwards against her supporting hands until I was resting against her own soft bosom and her hands had slipped round in front of me, their fingertips touching on my lacy, beaded stomach. We were both hypnotised by what I had become.

Lightly, the way a hand trailing from a boat touches the surface of the water, Jane's hands travelled up to where mine still rested on my breasts. I felt their cool softness gently pressing against my yielding flesh and slipped my own hands out of the way, reaching them behind me to her own waist, pulling her closer against me. She responded by touching her soft lips against the side of my neck, where it rose from the delicate lace of the bodice. The kiss was light but it set my skin afire, and I bent my neck forward, hoping that Jane would carry on. Her mouth planted a chain of feathery kisses around the back of my neck and shoulders, making me shiver with delight.

Bolder now, Jane's hands followed the curves of my body back down, over my waist and round my hips, squeezing the fullness of my buttocks. The silk of the train slithered beneath her touch, sliding over my skin deliciously. She seemed to be working her hands through all the silk of the skirt, rubbing it against my bare skin, and in the mirror I saw the train billowing out to either side, hiding her completely from view. Then I gasped aloud as the cool, smooth silk on my legs was followed by the warmth of her hands, stroking their way up my thighs and over my buttocks.

The bride in the mirror was standing alone, her wedding dress spread out around her like a giant meringue, but under the virginal skirt another woman's fingers were going to work, tracing paths of flame over hips and legs. I felt Jane exploring the contours of my buttocks, her fingers questing under the edges of my thong, slipping tantalisingly over my puckered arsehole and on into my moistening sex. I was already aroused by the sight of myself in this dress, and Jane's knowing touch was driving me wild. Wet with my own juices, her hand held my G-string aside, caressed my clit and found my pussy, her movements swift and sure, not heavy-handed but confident.

I parted my legs to allow her fingers better access to my most intimate folds, and felt instead her hair against my thigh and, moments later, her tongue tracing the edges of my sex. In my mind, this was starting to blend into the preparation of the bride, like the girls of the harem who were rumoured to initiate the virgins among them in this way. I was the innocent, nervous about the unknown promise of the wedding night, and Jane was the experienced woman who was introducing me to the delights of my own body. As her tongue flicked over my clit and then delved deeper inside me I felt as if these sensations were running through me for the first time, my hips trembling and my belly turning to liquid within me.

Her mouth was unlike any man's, smaller and softer but far wiser, knowing from her own body just where and how to touch me. Jane's small, slender fingers were holding me open for her searching tongue, the petals spread wide to welcome the honeybee. Up and down my electrified slit she ran her little, pointed tongue, her finger gently pushing in and out of my cunt at the same time, surprising me all the time with a new kind of touch. My legs were shaking and I had to rest a hand against the wall to steady myself as my knees went weak. 'Oh, Jane,' I murmured, 'don't stop, please don't stop.'

The sound of my voice seemed to drive her on, thrusting into me now with what felt like her whole slim hand, penetrating me deeply but with a sensitivity that found my most susceptible spot. I felt myself about to lose control and, with a hand resting on her head through the layers of silk, I welcomed the powerful shockwaves of my orgasm. Jane sucked on my clit, doubling the intensity of my climax, and as I felt my cunt convulse, she slipped one slender finger into my tight rear opening, so I felt the contractions of my orgasm gripping it just as my cunt was suckling on her other hand. In the mirror, the virgin bride's face was the picture of abandon, flushed and open-mouthed, her eyes wild, but still nothing about the pure white dress betrayed the secret pleasuring that was going on underneath.

As Jane was kissing me, her mouth salty with the taste of my pussy, there was a knock on the fitting-room door. Hastily, Jane rearranged the crumpled folds of the train before undoing the bolt. 'Sorry to keep you waiting like that,' the seamstress said as she came in. 'Now, let's see how much we need to alter. Actually, it seems like quite a good fit, doesn't it?'

'Very good,' I managed, my legs still a bit shaky.

She looked at me with concern. 'Do you need to sit down, dear?' she asked, and I nodded in relief. 'Don't worry,' she reassured me as I sank on to the chair, 'lots of girls feel a bit faint when they try the dress on for the first time. Must be all the excitement.'

Chapter Fourteen
The Hen Night

*T*he night air off the Thames bit through my thin stockings, and I allowed myself a moment of regret that we had not waited for a summer wedding. I could have had a hen night that began in warm evening sunshine, instead of being here in chilly darkness, waiting for Jane and the others to take me wherever we were going. I looked around for her, admiring as I always did the lights garlanding the riverside walks, reflected in the dark water. This was my favourite part of London, the Thames gliding through its heart, opening up the close-packed buildings to the sky, bringing light to the city centre by day and the canopy of stars by night.

I had left the planning of tonight entirely to Jane. She knew where I had to be at eleven o'clock the following morning, and what I had to be wearing, and I had abandoned myself to her care. Some of my friends had expressed surprise that Kit and I were returning to the old tradition of holding the stag and hen parties the night before the wedding itself, worried that one or both of us would fail to turn up, or be in an unfit state to last the day. 'Why not do it the weekend before?' one of them suggested. We were determined, though, to wring every drop of tradition out of our wedding. Besides, I knew that any adventure I had tonight would add extra spice to tomorrow's ceremony, and I had absolute faith in Jane's promise to deliver me in perfect condition.

Here she was, bang on time, with a group of women all dressed up to the nines, just as I was. The excitement of the evening flooded through me: my last night of bachelorhood, out with the girls for a final fling of recklessness. I knew, of course, that married life with Kit would by no means be an end to experiment and adventure, but still the occasion demanded some bad behaviour from us, and I was happy to oblige. 'Where are we going?' I asked Jane as, to my surprise, we headed not up into the West End, but across the road towards the river. She didn't answer, but another of my friends pointed to the steps leading down to the river itself.

We clambered down the stone stairs to the river cruiser, from which cheerful disco music was already blaring. Coloured lights all round the edge of the canopy gave it a fairground feel and I could smell the smoky aroma of chargrilled meat. 'A barbecue? On a boat?' I was incredulous.

Jane just shrugged. 'Why not?' she said. 'Barbecue, bar, karaoke. I said we'd take everything they had.' As I stepped down into the roomy saloon, I saw that dozens of my friends were already there. Jane had pulled out all the stops for this night.

I hardly noticed the boat chugging away from the bank, too busy having cocktails poured and being congratulated. This was what a hen night should be: just a group of good friends getting together to enjoy unpretentious fun away from other people's eyes. I was loving it already, putting my name down for the karaoke and inspecting the sausages and spicy chicken on the charcoal grill. Freed of the pressure to flirt and show off, we were able to dance as wildly as we liked, shamelessly requesting all the most uncool records of our teenage years and singing along to the embarrassing words. I didn't know what other surprises Jane had in store for me – a male stripper perhaps, or a late-night visit to some seedy club – and I didn't care. The hours were passing like minutes. Though the breeze over the river was cold, the dancefloor was soon hot and airless, and we were glad of the canopied deck on which to cool off.

I leant on the railing, steam rising from my body, looking out at the beautiful sight of the banks sliding past. As we headed upstream, the magnificent office blocks and public buildings were giving way to older houses and the river was getting darker as the sleeping buildings blocked out the street lights. The boat was slowing, turning its prow sideways on to the current, and I realised with disappointment that we were turning round. Surely the night would not be over so soon: this meant we were more than halfway home, I knew, as the current would carry us back to the jetty swifter than we had come thus far.

Jane appeared beside me, watching the bank swing round the railing and reappear on the other side of the boat. 'Enjoying yourself?' she asked.

'Oh yes,' I replied with enthusiasm. 'I don't want it to end.'

The dark houses were sliding past us again, as she smiled and said, 'Oh, it's not over yet. The best is yet to come. That's if you're still up for it.'

'You bet!' I assured her. 'I'm ready for anything tonight.'

'Good,' she said, producing a cigarette from somewhere and lighting it carefully. She held the lighter up for a moment, looking at my face in its light, kissed me briefly on the lips, and was gone back into the disco.

I knew I should follow her to where all my friends were dancing, but I waited, savouring the feeling that the banks of the Thames were being displayed for my enjoyment alone. A bump shook the deck, as if we'd collided with some floating object, but the skipper in the wheelhouse seemed unconcerned, so I thought nothing of it. I turned to go back into the saloon and was stopped by a strong arm around my chest and a big hand clamped over my mouth.

'Don't make a sound,' a male voice rumbled in my ear. My heart was pounding as my mind raced. Were we being boarded by robbers? Surely they must have overpowered the captain first, or he would be raising the alarm even now. I couldn't move at all, my captor's arm like a band of steel around me and my head pulled back so I lost my balance and was pressed against his shoulder. He dragged me back into the shadow of the wheelhouse and another man, his face hidden with a scarf, pulled a hood over my eyes. Before I could work out what was happening or form a plan, they had shoved a rubber gag into my mouth, bound my hands and feet with rope, and picked me up. I was utterly disorientated, unable to tell where I was being taken, still confused as to the identity or motives of my captors. Had I been mistaken for some rich heiress and fallen victim to a gang of kidnappers? The men were not rough, but the swift ruthlessness of their handling told me not to attempt resistance. I stiffened as I felt my body dropping, but before I left the hands of my assailants, other hands received me and laid me on a hard surface.

I was still on a boat, I could tell from the movement, and probably a smaller boat than the cruiser, since the rocking was more violent. I heard an outboard motor roar into life and was flung on to my side as the craft

211

lurched across the water. Surely no gang of attackers would draw attention to themselves with that noise? Fear was abating in me, since no actual harm had yet befallen me, rapidly being replaced by anger and bewilderment. Our voyage lasted only a minute or two before the engine spluttered back to silence and I felt the little boat bumping against something new. Four strong hands lifted me again. I was deliberately limp, offering no help to my handlers but judging it unwise to struggle when all I could achieve would be them dropping me into icy water for a swift death by drowning.

Again, I was passed to other hands, wishing with a moment of calm that I was not wearing a party dress and stockings, clothing that offered little protection for my modesty against these anonymous male hands. Not that they seemed at all lascivious: the very fact they were grabbing my thighs as if I were a mere package was somehow more degrading than if they had taken advantage of the opportunity to molest me. Who were they? Some kind of white slave traders? I felt a frisson of excited horror at the thought. This time I was placed back on my feet on another pitching deck, still with a man behind me to steady me, since my legs were bound tightly together, and to prevent any thoughts of escape. I was trying to listen, to get any clues as to where I had been taken.

The hood interfered with my hearing, as well as blinding me. We could not have travelled far, since the sounds of the river were still the same quiet gurglings mixed with distant traffic. All I could make out for a moment was my own rapid breathing, then heavy footsteps came up a few wooden steps and the man holding me said, 'Here she is, captain.'

I was right, I thought: bungling kidnappers had mistaken me for somebody rich. Instead a deep voice replied, 'Good. Take her down to my cabin and leave her there.' My sex did a quick somersault of relief and excitement: it was Geoff.

Two of the men lifted me again as if I were a bag of flour, carried me down the steps and laid me on my side on a rather lumpy mattress. As they left me, closing a door behind them, I was inwardly kicking myself. Why hadn't I guessed that this was one of Geoff's adventures? He would have had no trouble in enlisting his madcap friends to abduct me from the cruiser, doubtless with Jane's connivance, and bring me ... wherever I was. Never before had I been so literally at his mercy. As I lay, gagged and immobilised, my pussy grew wet with anticipation. This time, he was running the game. Perhaps this was the last time we would be playing, but I was going to play it all the way.

I tried to pull the hood off my eyes by rubbing my head against the pillow, but it seemed to have some kind of cord or elastic holding it in place. There was no sound at all in the cabin except that of the river lapping against the wood, inches from my head. Struggling against the ropes around my arms and legs was equally futile. Not only my wrists but also my elbows had been wrapped around with cord, so my arms were pulled back behind me and the rope bit gently into my skin. The rubber gag filled my mouth completely, holding my tongue down and my jaw open. The feeling was quite erotic, rather like having a huge rubber cock pushed into my mouth, and added to the feeling of helplessness which, now I knew that it was Geoff who had me captive, was arousing me to an astonishing degree. I was longing for him to come and enjoy the power he had over me, to take advantage of me like the pirate captain he was impersonating, but I was also relishing my enforced anticipation.

My sense of time was distorted by the darkness and the quiet, but it seemed like an hour before I heard the

213

cabin door open and lifted my head to listen. Whoever had come in said nothing, merely shut the door again and locked it. I was expecting that my blindfold, at least, would be removed to let me see the face of my master, but instead my skirt was pulled roughly up and a cold, hard hand ran over my exposed buttocks with an appreciative stroke. Was he going to leave me bound and unseeing as he explored my defenceless flesh?

The thought brought a muffled groan of pleasure to my gagged mouth, and I heard Geoff's unmistakable laugh, but still he said nothing, merely pushing his ruthless hand between my legs to feel the wetness there. His fingers caressed me roughly through the thin satin of my knickers, forcing their way between my legs, which were held tightly together by the ropes. I was desperate to feel him inside me, but I could say and do nothing except enjoy the feeling of subjection to his will. I felt a tugging at my knickers, and heard two soft snicks as a blade slid through the thin fabric. Geoff pulled the remnants off my body and my pussy was naked before him. I could imagine what he was seeing, my pale arse offered to his view, framed by the dark suspenders and stockings, my pussy in shadow but glistening with moisture. Above and below, the sight of my limbs held tight with ropes would arouse him still more.

Sure enough, Geoff wasted no more time, pushing my legs up so my knees were bent, and then turning me over so they were under me, my rear lifted in the air. My face was pressed down into the pillow and the thin straps of the suspender belt cut into my buttocks. I was whimpering with desire, this image of myself as his prize making me ache for possession by his cock. He was astride me in an instant, the cold smooth pressure of his legs telling me he was wearing his leather jeans, and the bulge of his erection pressing

214

through them against my naked arse. His legs gripped mine, holding me steady, and I heard the zip of his jeans open and felt the warm smoothness of his cock spring out against me.

Geoff rubbed himself against me, smooth shaft sliding in and out of the tight, wet crevice between my bound legs, teasing me by refusing to penetrate the hungry depths of my cunt. I was trying to push my hips back against him, but I was almost immobile in my bonds, and he merely laughed again, snapping one of my suspenders against my skin so it stung for an instant, like the burn of a lighted match. I lay obediently still, and only then did he push his cock deep into my pussy, taking me with a violence that swept me immediately over the edge into my orgasm. I heard my cries, oddly distorted by the rubber gag and muffled by the pillow, and I felt the fierce slamming of Geoff's hips against my arse as, just as excited as I was, he exploded inside me.

Before I had even returned to myself, I felt his quick, strong fingers at the bonds around my wrists, and the sweet relief as my arms were freed and the blood flowed normally again. My legs were untied next, and I lay exhausted on my back as he removed the hood from my eyes. I blinked, dazzled by the light after so long in darkness. Geoff was looking down at me, a hurricane lamp, swinging from a beam behind him, turning him into a dark shadow looming over me. He was naked to the waist, his tattoos adorning his muscular torso like a patterned T-shirt. From the waist down he was encased in leather, his leather jeans disappearing into high riding boots. The cabin was tiny, the double berth on which I lay filling half of it and a small folding table dominating the other half. Portholes on each side admitted a couple of twinkling lights from the distant banks, but the vessel seemed to be moored well away from the shore. The whole cabin was panelled in dark wood and curtains hung around the bed. It was every inch the pirate captain's cabin, and Geoff was every inch the pirate captain.

Geoff stood watching me as I took in my surroundings. 'Yes,' he said softly, 'for tonight you are my captive. Don't try to resist; my men are on guard outside this cabin and on deck and will only take pleasure in returning you to my will. In fact,' he whispered, drawing a finger over my exposed sex, 'I might let them take pleasure in rather more than that, if you do not obey me in all things. Am I clear?' I nodded, a stab of fiery arousal running through me at the thought of Geoff's 'henchmen' being given permission to enjoy my captive body while Geoff watched. 'I shall remove your gag, on the understanding that you do not scream or cry out, or indeed speak unless spoken to. Understand?' I nodded again. Geoff laughed, a sinister laugh of triumph. 'I think you like that gag, don't you? I think it reminds you of having a mouth full of cock, doesn't it?' I nodded again, ashamed but compelled to answer truthfully. Geoff laughed again as he undid the strap and removed it from my mouth. 'We'll have to see what we can do about that,' he said as he helped me sit up.

On the table I was glad to see a bottle of wine and a plate of food. Geoff poured me a glass of wine and let me eat the bread and cheese while he watched. Through one of the portholes I could see the full moon floating over the river, the white disc of its reflection shivering in the ripples, and the dark shapes of trees on the far bank. We were only miles from central London, yet I felt that we could be on an ocean halfway across the world, or even centuries away from my normal life. I had wanted a proper adventure before my wedding, and I was getting one.

When I had finished restoring my strength, Geoff took the glass and plate from me and passed them out of the cabin door. I sat uncertainly on the bed, waiting to see what he wanted from me now. 'Get up,' he told me and, when I had obeyed, he took my place, lying back on the bed, his head propped up on the pillows. 'Now, strip for me,' he commanded. As I stood hesitantly, he produced a leather riding crop from his boot and flexed it with a menacing expression. 'I said, strip,' he went on. 'Or do you want to taste the whip?' A shudder of delighted apprehension ran through me, and I began to do as he wanted, pulling awkwardly at the fastenings of my dress until I was able to step out of it and stand before him in my bra and suspenders, my pussy already naked to his eyes.

Geoff sighed impatiently. 'I said strip, not get undressed,' he growled. 'You need music, I think, or I'm not going to find it very entertaining at all. John!' In response to his shout, the cabin door opened immediately and a young man appeared in the entrance. I blushed deeply, placing my hands over my private parts as he came in. 'John, give us a tune,' commanded Geoff. Shutting the door behind him, John took a mouth-organ out of his shirt pocket and began to play a jaunty song. He was seemingly unembarrassed by my half-naked presence and sat on the edge of the table to play. 'Now,' Geoff addressed me, 'let's see if you can put on a bit of a show for me.'

Humiliated in front of this stranger, yet oddly aroused by his indifference, I began to move to the music. The tune was more cheerful sea-shanty than sultry torch song, which somehow added to the degradation. I did my best to dance sexily to the young man's playing, but I knew that I must look clumsy and ashamed as I swayed and gyrated. Knowing I had hardly anything left to remove, I spun it out, running my hands up over my breasts, lifting my hair above my head and then letting it fall over my face, dropping my head and shaking it from side to side so my hair

217

swung across my naked pussy. As I threw my head back I looked straight at Geoff's face and saw the arousal there, a dark glint in his eyes as he lay back, the riding crop twitching in his big hand.

I was enjoying myself now, and I spun round on the spot, wiggling my bare arse for his enjoyment, bending over to look at him between my legs as I did so. I still hadn't removed any more clothes, though, and a look of impatience flickered across Geoff's face. 'I said strip, not prance about,' he growled, and threw the riding crop across to John, who caught it in one hand without interrupting the music. 'Give her some encouragement, John,' he said. I felt a burning stripe across my arse as John flicked the crop against my skin. I jumped in shock, but the young man's face was unmoved as he continued to play his harmonica.

I began to strip in earnest, pulling the cups of my bra down to expose my breasts and playing with the nipples until another stroke of the crop on my thigh hurried me into unfastening the bra and casting it aside. Now I was wearing nothing but the black suspender belt and nylon stockings. As quickly as I could, while maintaining a pretence of dancing, I undid each suspender strap and removed the belt. The stockings were slipping down my thighs, and I did my best to roll them down in a sexy way while flinching under John's casual blows. The very lack of interest with which he was pushing me on was provoking me. How dare he witness this scene with no sign of arousal at all? I was playing for his eyes too, wanting to see in them the same fire that was burning in Geoff's, but he seemed utterly unresponsive.

I finished, naked, and ran my hands all over my body. John continued to play and to idly plant narrow red weals on my skin until Geoff said, 'That's enough, John.' He put the harmonica away and rose to leave, but Geoff indicated with a hand that he should stay, and he leant against the doorframe, watching. 'Now,' Geoff told me, 'bend over the table.' I obeyed, my heart pounding. The roughness of the wood against my breasts and belly excited me, but not as much as the idea of submitting like this, offering my sex to Geoff while John watched. I placed my cheek against the wood and stretched my arms out sideways, gripping the edges of the table, waiting for Geoff to come and fuck me in front of this strangely dispassionate audience.

I heard the bed creak as Geoff rose and stood behind me, my pussy growing wet again in anticipation of his prick, but he made no move to touch me. 'John,' he said, 'take her clothes and throw them out of the porthole.' I couldn't help jerking my head up, only to press it back against the table when the riding crop sang across my buttocks. I heard the porthole open and a soft splash as my clothes disappeared into the Thames. 'Just in case you had any ideas about leaving us,' hissed Geoff. 'A cold night to be wandering around naked, I think.' My skin was burning from the whip, heat flooding it and awakening every sensitive nerve. He was losing no chance to remind me that I was at his mercy.

I felt a smooth, cold touch against my cheek. It was the handle of the riding crop, leather stretched tight over wood, no thicker than a finger but with a round knob at the end the size of a golf ball. I lay still, quivering with anticipation, as Geoff stroked the end over my face and lips, offering no resistance as he pushed it into my mouth, feeling my jaw stretched open again as it had been by the gag, sucking gently on the thing as if it were his cock, the cock I was aching to feel inside me. 'Good,' he murmured, 'very good. You are finally acquiring the habit of obedience.'

The whip was removed from my mouth, but almost immediately I felt its pressure against the lips of my

219

pussy, the bulbous end forcing itself into my tender crevice. I winced a little from the sheer size of it, as my cunt was stretched round its hard, unyielding diameter, but the feeling of having it inside me was deeply satisfying. Geoff worked it in and out of me, and the smooth curve of the whip-handle scraped against my inner ridges. I knew John was watching, and the thought of his eyes following the whip as it thrust into me made me moan with pleasure. The thin handle slid easily between my wet lips, but the knob inside me was filling me as tightly as any cock had ever done and more rigidly, grinding against every sensitive inch of me.

Roughly, Geoff pulled the riding crop out of me, so I caught my breath as the ball was forced through the sensitive opening. I heard the crop bang down on the table, as Geoff dropped it inches from my face, and caught a trace of my own scent on the leather. Then his own thick shaft was inside me, plunging as deeply as the crop-handle had done, filling me with his girth. The leather of his jeans creaked as he pumped in and out of me, his hands holding my cheeks apart to open me to his cock. 'You like that, don't you?' he was saying to me as he rammed me against the hard edge of the table. 'And John likes it too, don't you, John?' He didn't wait for a reply. 'John's watching me plough into your wet little pussy, and he's got such a hard-on he's got it out and he's wanking as he watches.'

At the thought of John, cool indifferent John, pumping his fist up and down his erection as he watched me being fucked, I lost control and hit a sudden, devastating climax, sobbing as I came. Geoff didn't alter his stroke at all, driving into my quivering cunt with exactly the same steady rhythm. 'You see, John?' he said casually, as if he were remarking on the weather, 'I said she was a dirty one, didn't I?' I lay shaking across the table, and Geoff just carried on pounding into me. 'Come round here, John,' I heard him say, and felt him tangle his hand into my hair and pull my head back.

The same instant, John was standing right in front of me, his erection in my face. With Geoff holding my head at such an extreme angle, I was forced to open my mouth, and John slid his cock into it without hesitation. It was long, satin-smooth and delicately salty. Now I was being fucked from both ends, both men thrusting into me without gentleness. Another orgasm was rolling over me already at the thought of being so used, so penetrated and filled, when I felt a cruel pressure on the tight knot of my arsehole. It was a moment before I realised what it was, that Geoff was trying to push the whip-handle into my rear entrance. 'No,' I tried to protest, 'it's too big,' but John's cock was driving into my mouth and all that came out were muffled cries.

Relentlessly, the smooth, round knob forced itself through the delicate tissue. A burning pain ripped through me, followed by an extraordinary pleasure as the bulbous end broke through the barrier of muscle and was inside me. The narrow shaft slid easily through the tight opening, and the ball was deep within me, pressing against sensitive points I had never known I possessed, filling me in a way I had never before experienced. As Geoff's cock worked in and out of me, it rubbed against the hard wooden knob so close behind it and I felt the vibrations carry deep inside me. As I convulsed with a profound orgasm, John came into my mouth, his hot spunk running down my throat. 'That's what you wanted, isn't it?' grunted Geoff, as his own climax overtook him and he shot himself into me with violent spasms. 'A cock in every hole; that's what you like.'

Chapter Fifteen
The Fourth Wedding

'Wake up, Emma.' The grey light of dawn was filling the room as I responded, unwillingly, to the gentle but insistent shaking. 'Wake up, you have to get up now.'

'Why?' I complained, confused and uncertain about where I was and why I had to get up. My body was telling me quite clearly that I was warm and relaxed and should stay asleep for another hour at least.

'Because you've got to get married.'

I was wide awake in an instant, sitting up and looking around at this strange room. Geoff was lying beside me, patiently bringing me to consciousness. For a moment I thought I was dreaming, that this was my subconscious mind panicking about getting to the wedding on time and inventing a crazy fantasy in which I was with Geoff in a strange place when I should be with Kit and about to be married. Then I remembered last night, the hen party and the abduction by pirates.

'Don't panic,' said Geoff, looking at my stunned face, 'you've got plenty of time. It's not even seven o'clock yet.' The watery light coming in through the portholes confirmed how early it was, but he was right: if I was to get cleaned up after last night's debauchery, dress up in my finery, and get to the venue from ... from wherever I was, I had to get moving. I swung my legs on to the floor and Geoff thrust a towel at me. 'Shower's through there,' he said as he pointed the way. Shower? My face must have showed my doubt because he grinned and went on, 'Even pirates have bathrooms these days, you know.'

Under the jets of hot water, I woke up and thought about today. This was the day when Kit and I would make a commitment to each other, saying publicly to our assembled friends and family that we were planning to stick together. And here I was starting the day by waking, spunk-sticky and aching, in Geoff's bed. I smiled to myself as I dried my still-tender body. Perhaps it was appropriate after all, bidding farewell to Geoff this way. It was certainly truer to the nature of our friendship than the painful goodbye in the smoky bar had been.

It was apt, too, to approach the wedding venue from the river. Kit and I, looking for a setting full of romance and tradition but not hypocrites enough to get married in church, had chosen a historic ship moored on the Thames. Geoff, primed of course by Jane, had worked out exactly how long it would take us to get there, bearing in mind the tide and the fact that we would be going downstream, aided by the current of the river.

The guests were already gathering on the deck of the fine old ship as we hove into view. We must have been a magnificent sight: Geoff steering, his six sturdy friends rowing, all in clean white shirts for possibly the first time in their lives and, in the prow, my white dress gleaming in the morning sun, the glowing bride. As it happened, it was Kit's niece Eleanor who spotted us first and, as she pointed and shouted, a crowd gathered along the side of the ship to cheer as we drew alongside.

Someone found a rope-ladder to drop down to us, and Geoff stood up to help me on to it. Seeing me struggling with my train, he picked me up, told me to hold on, and climbed the ladder himself as I clung tight to him, the silk of my skirt hanging below us like a flag. More cheers erupted as he deposited me on deck, my veil slightly crooked, gave me a quick, friendly kiss and vanished over the side with a wave at the assembled throng and a special salute for Kit. I didn't turn round to watch him row away. I knew this was the last I'd see of him, and I didn't want to drag it out with a slowly disappearing speck on the water. We had shared one last night of wildness, one last morning of friendship: let that be enough.

Early as it was, tourists were already milling about onshore, pointing up at the filigree rigging which soared above us and looking with curiosity at the unmistakable wedding crowd on the deck. The ship was magnificent, brass fittings gleaming in the oblique morning sunshine and pale wood glowing. We looked incongruous here, on a vessel which seemed designed for functional elegance, each rope and cleat here for a specific purpose, and the only purpose of the ship itself to be off, around the world, its sharp prow slicing into the swell of the ocean. Perhaps, after all, it was a good place to embark on the adventure of marriage, I reflected.

We had been blessed with fine weather and were able to assemble on deck before we went below for the ceremony. My relatives were delighted that I seemed to be doing things properly, a traditional dress and an old-fashioned setting. My friends were amused, but not altogether surprised. 'You always did like to throw yourself into things one hundred per cent, didn't you?' murmured Eric, as he and Philippa stepped off the narrow gangplank. Michael darted forward from his place by Jane's side to greet his brother, and I observed with pleasure that all hard feelings seemed to be over on that score.

A thin mist was hovering on the surface of the river, wisps curling around each other as the first heat of the sun caught them. Out of the mist, right on cue, a flotilla of swans came gliding by and we all paused to watch them as they slowed, looking up hopefully for titbits. 'Too early – the buffet's not till two,' shouted Michael. They appeared to look at him in disdain before drifting on downriver.

Cassandra greeted me with a kiss on the cheek. She looked stunning, as always, but was dressed discreetly in a light-grey suit. 'Don't worry,' she said, 'I'll be changing later.' She would be singing, of course, but as Kit's oldest friend she was a guest of honour as well. 'Kit owes me for this, you know,' she murmured, smoking like a fifties film star and letting her gaze drift across the water.

'What do you mean?' I asked.

She looked faintly amused as she answered. 'Didn't you know? I had to track you down for him. All he had was your name. I was the one who had to get a guest list for every wedding I played this summer and look through it for an Emma Fowler.' She gave me a quick, sharp look. 'Lucky there's not two of you, eh?'

I went over to talk to Sarah who, beaming and heavily pregnant, was sitting by the mast. Robin was Kit's choice of best man, so he was busy organising things and had left her to rest. She squeezed my hand as she told me how delighted they both were that we had met at their wedding and gone on to find love. She had either forgotten, or was choosing to ignore, the exact events of that first meeting.

Robin and his ushers came round to shepherd us

below deck for the ceremony. The stateroom was surprisingly grand, with carved gilded wood in all directions and mullioned windows, but it was still a tight fit for all our guests. Having no parents alive to give me away, I had decided not to make a grand entrance. My brother-in-law Kevin had offered to stand in for a father, a gesture which I thought very kind but hilariously inappropriate: last time we had been at a wedding together, he had been trying to keep me away from Kit, not give me to him. I was waiting, like Kit, at the front. As I watched the space fill up, I realised that the dignified march down the aisle would only have turned into a scrum, anyway, as I fought to fit my train through the narrowing gap.

Finally, everybody was packed in and the ceremony began. As the expectant stillness fell on the assembled guests, I glanced over to Kit and felt my heart swell within me. We were really here, offering in public to commit ourselves to one another for ever. No matter how many weddings I had been to, it had never really hit me before what a pledge of hope and courage the wedding vows were. 'Will you, Emma Joan Fowler, take this man . . .'

'I will,' I said, in a strong clear voice. Yes, I will – I want it, I intend it. I want this man, who has opened up parts of me that even I didn't know were there, and who never ran away no matter what he found. I intend to stick by him the way he has stuck by me. I will.

As Kit lifted my hand to slip the ring on to my finger, I trembled at his touch. The Romans believed there was a direct link between that finger and the heart, I had heard, but my finger seemed connected with my whole body: heart, breasts and sex. I took his hand to give him the ring that Jane passed me and felt him offer it to me the way he had offered his whole body in that hotel room, with complete trust and openness. Tenderly, Kit lifted the white lace veil from my face, bent his head and kissed my upturned lips. I felt a rush of emotion and excitement burn through me: 'I am yours now,' I thought, 'I give myself to you, to keep for yourself or to share, as you wish. I belong to my husband.'

I was a bit dazed as we led the way back on deck, hand in hand. A bunch of tourists who were being turned away from the ship burst into applause when they saw us emerge and I waved back, thinking how odd it was that we were being clapped for making ourselves so happy. As everyone gathered round us for congratulations, I could only grin idiotically and repeat 'Thank you, thank you', to whatever people said. Kit seemed no better, gripping my hand as if he was never going to let it go and nodding with a beatific smile. Luckily, Robin had things in hand, organising us for photographs according to Jane's shouted instructions. The breeze was blowing my veil about, but she told me not to worry. 'That sort of thing makes the shots more interesting,' she called.

At that moment, one of the aunts lost control of her hat and it sailed up into the air, miraculously missing every single rope in its path, and landed on the water. The swans raced over to investigate, fearing an intruder, but circled it warily when it showed no signs of life. She was very good-humoured about it. 'I just hope they don't try to eat the plastic cherries,' she sighed. 'Choking a swan counts as treason, doesn't it?'

Kit's mother, whom I had met only briefly at Eleanor's wedding, came and shook my hand with a warm, strong grip. 'Congratulations, my dear,' she said in that same loud voice, 'I'm sure you'll be very happy. Don't rush off and start having babies straight away, will you?' I assured her that we were not planning any such thing. 'I'm glad to hear it,' she said, 'because these would be severely wasted if you were.'

With that, she thrust two small, heavy parcels into our hands. 'Thank you,' I said as we tore off the paper. I felt something sharp in mine at the same time as I heard the jingle of Kit dropping his on the floor. Keys – two sets of motorbike keys. As I looked up, stupefied, Kit's mother nodded towards the shore. There, glowing red and silver against the grey flagstones, were a matched pair of Ducatis.

I was speechless. So was Kit, managing only, 'Mother! I . . .' We gaped in wonder.

'Well,' she said dismissively, 'I didn't think a dinner service was really your thing.'

'Thank you,' I said, a lump in my throat. This was going to work, I knew it. Even Kit's mother knew we were not giving up our lives of freedom to become a conventional couple. The two shining motorbikes were a symbol of what our marriage could be.

There wasn't room for a sit-down meal, so Alex had provided a buffet in the stateroom below. Jane had spotted him, not surprisingly, and commented on the 'delicious catering'. I blushed, and she raised her eyebrows, murmuring only, 'I see: you've tasted it before, I take it?' as she wandered off. He was looking even more stunning than he had at Eleanor's wedding, now he didn't have to wear a waiter's uniform and was in a black silk shirt and close-cut trousers. The food was equally delicious, it was true, and the festive atmosphere was filling the ornate room.

As the eating slowed, Robin rang the brass ship's bell hanging on the wall and all eyes turned to our end of the room, the guests falling silent. Jane got to her feet. 'In the absence of the bride's father,' she began, 'it has fallen to me to make the first speech. Before I begin, however, I would like to make it clear that I accept no responsibility whatever for Emma's upbringing or moral rectitude.' There was laughter, some of it knowing laughter. If Jane had really been responsible for my morals, I would have even less of them than I had managed to acquire on my own. She spoke magnificently, moving and funny, playing to the whole audience, not just the close friends who knew me well. She looked oddly right, as well, wearing a sharply cut man's suit with a white shirt and a tie, as if she wanted to be as good a best man to me as Robin was to Kit. 'Knowing Emma as well as I do,' she concluded, 'I know it will take a very special person to make her happy, and I have no doubt that Kit is that person. I propose a toast: to Emma and Kit.'

'Emma and Kit,' shouted the assembled throng, and raised their glasses. Jane sat down and I squeezed her hand.

Kit made his speech, surprisingly serious for once, and offered the traditional toast to the bridesmaids – two little nieces who had, it had to be admitted, behaved impeccably. Robin rose for the best man's speech, and Kit and I exchanged a look of apprehension. It was traditional to tell the amusing story of how the bride and groom had first met, but that story would have to be severely edited for a family audience. 'It's all right,' whispered Kit. 'Robin wouldn't do anything to embarrass Sarah.' Sure enough, he managed to claim the credit for our introduction without mentioning the nature of our first encounter. I caught sight of Cassandra standing at the back, now changed into a devastating zebra-print frock, and she smirked at me. 'It will come as no surprise to Emma,' Robin was saying, 'to hear that Kit's reputation before he met her was . . .' the pause was long enough to raise a laugh before he finished, 'colourful. If I had been asked, at my own wedding, to point out which of the guests would be the next to tie the knot, Kit's name would not have sprung to my lips. In fact,' he spoke over open sniggering from Kit's friends, 'I would probably have bet you a hundred pounds that, before

I made a best man's speech for Kit, I would be making my first speech as father of the bride.' He indicated with pride Sarah's visible bulge, and she blushed. 'But,' Robin went on, 'nobody is happier than I am to be proved wrong on this one. Kit, you have met your match in Emma. Please join me in a rather untraditional toast: to the ability of love to surprise us all.'

Both Kit and I hated the mid-afternoon hiatus between dinner and evening party, so we had asked Cassandra if her band would play earlier, tea-dance style. Even as the last toast dissolved into excited chatter, they struck up a lively rendition of 'Elevator Boogie' and Kit and I led the guests on to the dancefloor. I knew I was not going to be able to dance freely in this dress, but I didn't care; I draped my train over my arm and let Kit lead me across the floor as he had the first time we met. I did my duty as a bride and danced with everyone who asked me, relishing the admiration I was generating in my gorgeous wrapping of lace and pearls. Kit was also sharing out his favours freely and I enjoyed watching him move so gracefully to the music.

'The next tune is one that I know has a very special meaning for the bride and groom,' Cassandra was announcing, 'so please, let them have this dance together for sentimental reasons.' The crowd parted to let us come together and, as Kit took me in his arms and the music started, I flushed scarlet. 'Summertime,' Cassandra sang, flashing us a knowing glance, 'and the living is easy . . .' I buried my face in Kit's chest, hoping nobody could see my red face. Knowing exactly what I was thinking and feeling, he put his arms tightly around me and kissed my hair where it was escaping from the back of my veil. I felt a little swell of excitement press against my belly and knew that, like me, he was remembering the passion of our first encounter.

I was loving it all, the little touches of formality and the warm feeling of being surrounded by those who loved us. I was looking forward to the moment when Kit and I would at last be alone together, but I was in no hurry; this was our day, and I was going to make the most of it, draw it out and savour every moment. The band took a break and Jane pulled me and Kit on to the deck. 'I want some shots of you on your new bikes,' she told us.

'In this dress?' I was incredulous.

'Exactly,' she told me, as she near-pushed us down the gangplank, 'that's what makes it such a good picture.' Obligingly, Kit and I climbed on to the bikes and grinned at the camera. I still couldn't quite believe they were ours, even knowing his mother's reputation as a petrolhead. 'Lovely,' breathed Jane as she snapped away, 'all white lace and shiny red steel.'

Kit smiled over at me. 'A Ducati, eh?' he murmured. 'Want me to get behind you on it?' His eyes said it all: he too was remembering the car park by the sea. I had a sudden image of Kit throwing my train forward over my head and fucking me right now on this bike, and a shiver ran right through me. 'Later,' he whispered.

We returned to the guests, but now I was afire with anticipation. Each time Kit glanced over at me, I read in his face the promise of our wedding night. No virgin expecting her groom's first touch could have been more alive with expectation than I was. That was what made me so sure I was doing the right thing by marrying Kit: every time we made love there was a newness about it, a sense of openness to the unknown. Though we knew each other better than many couples celebrating their golden wedding anniversary, I knew that tonight would be a deflowering of some new and illuminating kind.

Chapter Sixteen
The Wedding Night

Night had fallen over the river before we waved goodbye to the last guests, and the rigging stretched above us, black against the stars. The moon was out again, hanging huge and low over the lights of the towerblocks. We stood alone on the deck, enjoying the moment of stillness after all the bustle of the day's celebrations. As we looked out over the prow of the ship at the broad Thames flowing out to the sea, I truly felt that we were setting off on a voyage together.

Kit bent his head to kiss me, a languorous, deep kiss that warmed my whole body with slow fires. Drunken cheering interrupted us: on the shore a passing group of drunks were applauding. We must have made quite a picture, I thought, bride and groom in full costume kissing on a picturesque old ship. We took a self-mocking bow and then Kit lifted me off my feet and carried me below deck, to the sound of more cheering and catcalls. We had become the punchline of every dirty joke, the newlywed couple on their wedding night. This was what lay at the heart of every wedding, the moment when the groom carries the bride into his house and lays her on the bed, ready to make her his own.

Kit pushed open a little oak door with his foot and, carefully manoeuvring me through the narrow doorway, managed to kick it shut behind us. Before us was a classic four-poster bed, draped in white muslin, the picture-book bridal chamber. Brides could have been carried in and put down on this bed for hundreds of years in exactly the same way. He kissed me again, tenderly, and the next instant threw me on to the bed.

I lay back, my train spread around me, and he was on top of me at once, seemingly aroused by the sight of his bride lying on the marriage bed awaiting her husband. His hands were all over my breasts, squeezing them till the little pearls bit into my flesh and made me wince. He took hold of my wrists and held them above my head, letting his other hand delve under the layers of my skirt and petticoats. Urgently, he ran his palm over my legs, up to the top of the white stockings, snapping the garter against my thigh before going on, over the bare flesh, to where my white lace panties were already growing damp.

His fingers stroked my pussy through the fabric, as if enjoying the delicate texture of the fine covering. I was moaning and trying to push my hips up against his hand, but he was lying on top of me and I was hampered by the dress. 'That's not very virginal,' he said in a low voice. 'Do you want your husband to think you're a loose woman? Lie still and let him show you what to do.' Obediently, I lay still, simply opening my legs a little to let his hand stroke between them. He slipped a finger inside my panties and along my slippery crevice. 'That's lovely,' he murmured. 'You've never had a cock in there, have you? Maybe you've never been touched there at all – not by a boy. I bet your girlfriends couldn't resist your sweet little pussy though, could they?'

'That's right,' I whispered back, joining Kit's game. 'I asked my friend what would happen on my wedding night and she put her finger there and touched me in such a funny way. I went all tingly inside.'

'And did she kiss you there as well?' asked Kit, his fingers pushing into my pussy now, stretching it open as if preparing me for my first penetration by a man's member.

'Yes,' I whispered back, the memory of Jane's mouth against my sex vivid in my mind. 'Yes, she licked me all over there, till I felt like I was going to die with pleasure.'

With a sudden violent urgency, Kit took hold of my train and threw it up over my face, so I could see nothing. I felt him pull the lace panties down and off, and push my legs apart. I could imagine how arousing the sight must be, my face covered but my pussy exposed above the white stockings and white satin shoes. I felt his tongue plunge into me and his fingers vibrating against the slippery nub of my clit, and I cried out with genuine excitement: 'Yes, yes, like that!' All I could feel was Kit's mouth and hands and a sea of silk against my face, my hands, my legs. I was drowning in sensuous touch.

Kit's tongue withdrew and I felt instead the hot, smooth head of his cock against my lower lips. How strange that would feel, I thought, if I were really a virgin and, sightless under my own dress, I could not see what was happening. 'Oh,' I cried in character, 'what is that? What are you doing to me?' This seemed to rouse Kit to greater passion.

'This is what a husband does to his wife,' he whispered to me, 'this is how a girl becomes a woman.' He plunged his cock deep inside me with a single stroke. I felt something archaic emanating from him, an ancient joy of conquest and mastery, and some deep, submissive instinct in me cry out in response. I was

234

his now, both by legal marriage and by bodily possession, and my body was welcoming his deep within it. His shaft was driving in and out of me, our hips banging together as he sank it up to the hilt again and again, my clit meeting his body with each rhythmic thrust. He put his hands on my legs, pushing them wider apart, and I knew he was looking down to see his cock entering me, claiming me for his own. Deep within me, I felt the waves of my fulfilment begin and as I came, crying out his name, Kit's thrusts grew more frantic and he gave himself up inside me.

As he collapsed on top of me, Kit pulled away the skirt covering my face and kissed me lovingly. We lay like that for a few minutes, arms around each other, and then sat up. At the end of the bed, a camera on a tripod was pointing at us, and Jane was sitting next to it, watching us with frank interest. 'Well,' she said, 'I can see what you see in him.' I was stunned.

'You don't mind, do you?' asked Kit. 'I thought you'd like to have some wedding photos of a rather more . . . personal nature. You did look hot with your white stockings and no knickers on.'

I was taken by surprise, but I had to admit that the idea of being photographed in the act of sex was very exciting to me. After all, there was little that Jane didn't already know about me, physically as well as socially. 'Go ahead,' I said, my sex throbbing at the idea.

'In fact,' Kit said lightly, 'why don't I take a few photos?' I looked at Jane, not sure if she realised what he meant, but it seemed she understood him perfectly.

'Be my guest,' she said, and they swapped places as if they were merely changing seats at a dinner party. We looked oddly right, together on the bed, Jane in her suit and me in my wedding dress. Kit took his place in the chair Jane had been sitting in, the shutter release in his hand.

I felt suddenly shy with Kit watching us. It was one thing, messing around with Jane in private, but I had never done it for an audience. She seemed to sense my nervousness and took the lead, kissing me full on the mouth, her hand on my chin to lift my face to hers. I closed my eyes and let myself relax into the sensation, the unfamiliar softness of her kiss and the lightness of her tongue as it played over mine. Instinctively, my hand reached inside her jacket and felt the curve of her breasts through the cotton shirt. I opened my eyes to undo her buttons and saw Kit's face, fascinated and aroused, watching me. As I undid Jane's tie and threw it aside, and opened her shirt button by button, I made sure that Kit – and the camera – could see every detail. The idea of performing for the camera made me feel dirty, hot, like a porn star. Pulling Jane's shirt wide open, I buried my face between her breasts and heard her moan with pleasure as I ran my tongue over their lush curves.

I was still encased in my lacy bodice, but I was pulling off Jane's clothes as quickly as I could, tugging her trousers down and pulling her free of the jacket and shirt. She lay back in her underwear and it was my turn to take the lead, my mouth roaming over her breasts, into her smooth, soft armpits, and down across her flat belly. I undid her bra with an expertise few men ever attain and released her breasts to fall softly apart, the nipples dark and erect. I had never before explored another woman's body so thoroughly, marvelling in its uniqueness and its familiarity. With each touch of my tongue or fingertip, my imagination told me what Jane would be feeling. I rubbed my breasts over hers, knowing that the hardness of the pearls would grate deliciously across her tender skin.

The musky scent of her pussy rose to meet my nostrils and my fingers found their way inside her G-string, plunging smoothly into her slippery cleft. As I ground my thumb against her clit, my tongue matched its rhythm on her nipple, making her cry aloud with pleasure. I made sure we were sideways on to the camera, so Kit could see every detail of what I was doing to Jane. I could see from the swelling in his trousers that he was enjoying it a great deal, but he said nothing, merely clicking the shutter every few seconds. I wanted to arouse him to the point where he could not help himself, where he would throw himself upon me like an animal, and I wanted too for Jane to find under my hand and tongue the climax she had given me in the fitting room. I pulled her panties off and buried my face in her pussy, lifting her right knee so she was angled for the camera. My hands lifting her pelvis to my mouth like a ripe fruit, my thumbs opening her lips wide to receive me, I plunged my tongue inside her and felt her buck against me in ecstasy. My lips pulled on her clit, sucking it like another nipple, and I sank a single finger deep into her, flicking against the most sensitive point inside her, making her writhe with arousal.

She was wriggling around on the bed, turning herself so that her face was between my legs, disappearing under the silk skirt. As I worked my tongue over her quivering sex, I felt hers seek mine, and a moment later the sweetest mirroring of my own actions. The excitement was almost unbearable; each flick of my tongue or finger was answered in my own pussy, not just in imagination but in reality. We were driving each other on, the growing urgency of our desires pulling us towards our shared climax. I thought nothing when I felt Kit pulling my skirt out of the way, exposing my rear, except that he wanted a better view for the camera. As the first wave of my climax broke, though, I felt his cock bury itself in my shivering cunt, filling me with his hot flesh even as Jane's lapping tongue on my clit brought me over the edge.

I had brought him to this point of irresistible desire, but I no longer cared; all I knew were the intense feelings ricocheting through my body. Jane, too, was racked by a deep orgasm, her body trembling beneath me. Kit's fingers dug into my hips as he pulled me back against his thrusts, but he seemed to be resisting his own climax. As he felt mine subside, he slowed his movements, but he did not pull out of me as Jane rolled away and lay on the bed watching us.

He reached out a hand, apparently to steady himself on the bedpost, but I heard a bell ring as he did so, and saw that he had pulled a little handle hanging there. 'Room service,' he said, 'I thought we could do with a drink.' I made to move, or at least to pull away from him and cover my exposed rear, but he gripped me firmly. 'Don't move,' he ordered me.

'But . . .' I made to protest that someone would be coming in, and felt a stinging slap across my flank.

'Do you think they've never seen a newlywed couple before?' Kit said. Jane lay naked on the bed, apparently carefree at the idea of being found in this state by a member of staff. I heard the door open and dropped my head in shame at being found like this, impaled on my husband's shaft.

'Your champagne, sir,' said a voice that was somehow familiar.

'Thank you,' said Kit. 'Could you pour it for us, please? As you can see, we are a little busy.' I heard the cork pop and the sound of pouring, but still Kit held me motionless. 'Thank you,' I heard him say again. 'Would you care to join us?' Who was it that Kit was inviting to stay so nonchalantly? I craned my head around, but still couldn't see.

'That would be most pleasant,' said the familiar voice again, and Alex sat on the edge of the bed to remove his shoes and socks.

Jane was only too happy to help Alex off with his

clothes, running a little pink tongue over his smooth, chocolate-brown chest as he pulled off his shirt. As we watched him lie back on the white coverlet and Jane run her mouth and fingers over his slim body, I felt another twitch of arousal, my cunt clutching at Kit's cock. He did not resume his thrusting though, instead pulling out of me and undoing the back of my dress. My body was finally freed from the constriction of the boning, as Kit pulled the dress off over my head. Kit swiftly removed his own clothes as well, and we were all naked.

Jane was taking Alex's long, smooth prick into her mouth, her red lips moving up and down it, leaving it shiny with her spit. Her blonde hair was draped across his stomach and her scarlet nails were scratching his chest. He was swelling in her mouth, but making no movements of his own, merely lying back and watching her as his length disappeared between her lips. 'Get your arse round here,' he told her, and Jane spun round so her pussy was hovering over Alex's mouth. I watched as Alex's tongue delved into Jane's intimate folds, knowing exactly what he would be tasting and feeling. As he moved his expert mouth over her pussy, she began to moan and grind herself against his face.

Kit was standing behind me, his hands caressing me freely as we watched the couple on the bed and sipped our champagne. He reached behind him into the ice-bucket and took a cube of ice, rubbing it over my bare breasts while he held me tightly to him. I gasped as the cold burnt into my skin, making my nipples stand aloft. The ice wandered across my belly and pressed against my clit, the sensation almost too intense to bear. Kit popped the cube into his mouth and joined Alex and Jane on the bed, nudging Jane's head out of the way and sliding his own mouth over Alex's stiff pole. I could see from the twitch in Alex's hips that the cold of the ice was as strong a feeling on his prick as it had been on my cunt.

Jane sat up and stretched out her arms to me, her damp pussy still pressed into Alex's soft mouth. I embraced her, kissing her deeply and caressing her breasts, pinching her nipples till she moaned aloud. She touched my own nipples and then ran her fingers down to my sex, stroking it softly. When I felt Kit's hands pulling at my hips I resisted, trying to stay in contact with Jane's sensuous lips and light fingers, but he was too strong for me and I slid backwards on the bed. His hands lifted my hips and placed me astride Alex, the younger man's cock nudging at the entrance to my hole.

I needed no encouragement: all this watching had made me wet with excitement and I was aching to be filled by a thick shaft. I took him deep inside me, sliding myself over his full length and then rocking on my heels so he was working in and out of me. Jane leant forward on her hands and resumed her kissing, her soft mouth a delicious counterpoint to Alex's hard member. I rubbed myself up and down Alex so his cock hit my deepest parts and my clit was banging against his body. Both Alex and Jane had their hands on my breasts now, the stronger hands and the softer, kneading and squeezing me, sending sharp darts of pleasure that shot through my body. Alex placed a finger against my clit and I thrust myself against it, moaning softly. As I arched my back, lifting my breasts forward, Jane took my nipple in her mouth and sucked it hard, nipping it with her little teeth.

Kit was behind me now, kissing the back of my neck, his erection pressing against my rear. I raised my arms to let him run his hands down my body, over my breasts and belly and round my waist. I had three people making love to me and I was almost too aroused to reach a climax, raised to such a heightened

240

state of sensuality that I was only aware of the sensations of that instant. Kit leaned heavily against my back, pushing me down against Alex's chest, and at the same time he took hold of my wrists and put them into Alex's hands, where they were held fast. Against my rear I felt Kit's cock rubbing itself, sliding across the wetness where Alex's shaft was penetrating me. It seemed to be seeking the slippery juices, coating itself with my stickiness. Then I felt it place itself against the puckered mouth of my hind hole, and I tensed as I realised what Kit was intending.

He paused. 'Do you want it?' he whispered in my ear, and I nodded. I wanted it, more than anything, this double possession, this impalement on two cocks at once, so only the most delicate wall of my flesh would separate Kit's thrusts from Alex's. I braced myself on my straddled knees as Kit pushed against the resistance of my tight opening. Without artificial lubrication, he had to force his way in, a sharp flash of pain burning through me as he breached my defences. Helpless, my wrists pinioned and my legs held firm by Kit's weight, I could only try to relax the ring of muscle as he pushed his length into me, I felt stretched, filled to bursting point by these two men. As their pricks rubbed together inside me, I felt the most intense orgasm of my life erupt deep within me and shake my whole body. All the distinctions between inside and outside my body, between pleasure and pain, seemed to have melted, consumed in the furnace of sensation.

As Kit and Alex, excited by my own abandon as well as by the feeling of the other man's prick sliding against theirs, increased their thrusts, my orgasm seemed to carry on and on, receding a little and then hitting a new peak. Jane, whether from Alex's licking or from the sight of me sandwiched between the two men, was giving herself up to a climax of her own.

Only seconds apart, I felt both men shoot their spunk into me, quivering with release.

I don't know at what point Jane and Alex slipped away, but I do know that I awoke in Kit's arms in our bridal bed with no guests. They'd even removed the camera and the champagne. As usual, Kit was still asleep, and I lay listening to the sound of the water against the ship and the seagulls above, imagining that we were moored somewhere in the South Seas. Our voyage of discovery was just about to begin. Soon, I knew, Kit would stir, and then we could get up and ride away on our new bikes, off to spend our honeymoon on the steeply curving roads of mountainous Europe. With the peak of each pass, a new vista would spread out before us, full of promise and unknown delights. There were no limits to what we could do together. I looked at his sleeping face, the full lips slightly parted and the calm brow curtained by his silky fringe, and I smiled as I said to myself, 'That's my husband.'

Visit the Black Lace website at
www.blacklace.com

BLACK LACE – THE LEADING IMPRINT OF
WOMEN'S SEXY FICTION

TAKING YOUR EROTIC READING PLEASURE
TO NEW HORIZONS

Black Lace Booklist

Information is correct at time of printing. To avoid disappointment, check availability before ordering. Go to www.blacklace.com.
All books are priced £7.99 unless another price is given.

❑ PHANTASMAGORIA Madelynne Ellis   ISBN 978 0 352 34168 6
❑ THE PRIDE Edie Bingham   ISBN 978 0 352 33997 3
❑ THE SILVER CAGE Mathilde Madden   ISBN 978 0 352 34164 8
❑ THE SILVER COLLAR Mathilde Madden   ISBN 978 0 352 34141 9
❑ THE SILVER CROWN Mathilde Madden   ISBN 978 0 352 34157 0
❑ SOUTHERN SPIRITS Edie Bingham   ISBN 978 0 352 34180 8
❑ THE TEN VISIONS Olivia Knight   ISBN 978 0 352 34119 8
❑ WILD KINGDOM Deana Ashford   ISBN 978 0 352 34152 5
❑ WILDWOOD Janine Ashbless   ISBN 978 0 352 34194 5

BLACK LACE ANTHOLOGIES

❑ BLACK LACE QUICKIES 1 Various   ISBN 978 0 352 34126 6 £2.99
❑ BLACK LACE QUICKIES 2 Various   ISBN 978 0 352 34127 3 £2.99
❑ BLACK LACE QUICKIES 3 Various   ISBN 978 0 352 34128 0 £2.99
❑ BLACK LACE QUICKIES 4 Various   ISBN 978 0 352 34129 7 £2.99
❑ BLACK LACE QUICKIES 5 Various   ISBN 978 0 352 34130 3 £2.99
❑ BLACK LACE QUICKIES 6 Various   ISBN 978 0 352 34133 4 £2.99
❑ BLACK LACE QUICKIES 7 Various   ISBN 978 0 352 34146 4 £2.99
❑ BLACK LACE QUICKIES 8 Various   ISBN 978 0 352 34147 1 £2.99
❑ BLACK LACE QUICKIES 9 Various   ISBN 978 0 352 34155 6 £2.99
❑ BLACK LACE QUICKIES 10 Various   ISBN 978 0 352 34156 3 £2.99
❑ SEDUCTION Various   ISBN 978 0 352 34510 3
❑ LIAISONS Various   ISBN 978 0 352 34516 5
❑ MISBEHAVIOUR Various   ISBN 978 0 352 34518 9
❑ MORE WICKED WORDS Various   ISBN 978 0 352 33487 9 £6.99
❑ SEXY LITTLE NUMBERS Various   ISBN 978 0 352 34538 1
❑ WICKED WORDS 3 Various   ISBN 978 0 352 33522 7 £6.99
❑ WICKED WORDS 4 Various   ISBN 978 0 352 33603 3 £6.99
❑ WICKED WORDS 5 Various   ISBN 978 0 352 33642 2 £6.99
❑ WICKED WORDS 6 Various   ISBN 978 0 352 33690 3 £6.99
❑ WICKED WORDS 7 Various   ISBN 978 0 352 33743 6 £6.99
❑ WICKED WORDS 8 Various   ISBN 978 0 352 33787 0 £6.99
❑ WICKED WORDS 9 Various   ISBN 978 0 352 33860 0
❑ WICKED WORDS 10 Various   ISBN 978 0 352 33893 8
❑ THE BEST OF BLACK LACE 2 Various   ISBN 978 0 352 33718 4
❑ WICKED WORDS: SEX IN THE OFFICE Various ISBN 978 0 352 33944 7